MIDNIGHT SKY

JAN RUTH

*To Pam
All the very best!
Jan Ruth
x*

MIDNIGHT SKY
Copyright Jan Ruth

THIRD EDITION 2013
(original edition 2011)

Published by Celtic Connections.

This publication is written in British English. Spellings and grammatical conventions are conversant with the UK.

All rights reserved; no part of this publication may be reproduced, stored in a retrieval system, or transmitted by any means, electronic, mechanical, photocopying or otherwise, without the prior written permission of the publisher.

This is a work of fiction. While the locations in this book are a mixture of real and imagined, the characters are totally fictitious. Any resemblance to persons living or dead, is coincidental.

Acknowledgements:
My son; for his patience with all matters technical.
John Hudspith Editing Services;
for super sharp crossing and dotting.
JD Smith Design; for beautiful insides and outs.

FOR ALL THE HORSES

Contents

Chapter One - Laura	1
Chapter Two - Laura	19
Chapter Three - Maggie	37
Chapter Four - Laura	57
Chapter Five - Laura	75
Chapter Six - Maggie	93
Chapter Seven - Laura	111
Chapter Eight - Laura	129
Chapter Nine - Laura	145
Chapter Ten - Maggie	163
Chapter Eleven - Laura	181
Chapter Twelve - Laura	199
Chapter Thirteen - Laura	215
Chapter Fourteen - Maggie	229
Chapter Fifteen - Laura	251
Chapter Sixteen - Laura	271
Chapter Seventeen - Laura	289
Other Titles by Jan Ruth	298

CHAPTER ONE

Laura

Her biological clock had started it. Before it sounded its alarm, Laura had been perfectly content. Maybe she should have taken the battery out a bit sooner, but it was more likely it ran on hormones, and they could be tricky.

She drove much too fast along the M56, recklessly even.

The mobile phone on the passenger seat took message after message from Simon. She glanced at it from time to time, then finally switched it off and threw it on to the back seat, where it lay silenced, buried under sample swatches of wallpaper and fabric.

She was already running late because of their argument.

It hadn't started as an argument; it had started as a *discussion*. Before she knew it, Laura was fighting her corner again. The discussion was all about family, to start with. It was different for Simon; he had loads of relatives, while Laura only had her sister. It was unfair of him to moan about her spending so much time with Maggie, when the demands of his ex-wife and kids were at times off the Richter Scale.

The forty-minute drive from Chester into North Wales led her off the dual carriageway and through the tiny village of Rowen. She sped past The Farmers' Arms, its smoky dimly lit windows just visible in the January dusk. She turned left at the crooked chapel, where her mother lay beneath the dark stars and the shadow of Cefn Bach. Laura shivered but not with the chill of the evening. Although brought up a farmer's daughter, Laura could never decide if it was habit or a desire to understand her dislike of it, which brought her back to her rural birthplace. It certainly wasn't sentiment, and yet this time she felt an unexplained stirring of hope.

She was forced to slow down and concentrate; the turning for Hafod House was easily missed on the narrow twisting lane. Seconds later, she was pulling up outside the Victorian property, where her elder sister Maggie lived with Pete and their daughters. Before she announced her arrival, Laura opened the car window and lit a cigarette, but Maggie had heard the car and trotted across the forecourt, wearing a typical combination of tracksuit and a plastic apron with love spoons on the front.

'Happy birthday!' Laura said, but Maggie ignored this and peered sideways through the top of the window. 'Where's Simon? Is he coming on later?'

'No. Sorry he's got to work, bit of an emergency,' Laura lied, grounding out the cigarette and avoiding her sister's knowing eye.

'Oh, that's a shame,' she said, pulling a face. 'Eleven is an odd number. I wanted him to meet the Morgan-Jones'. Could be loads of work in it for you. The brother took a *lot* of persuading to come at all.'

'Well, they'll just have to meet me instead,' Laura said and even managed to turn a bright smile in Maggie's direction.

Once in her room, Laura scanned through the messages from Simon, then deleted them all and cried in the noisy privacy of the shower. Why was he so stubborn? He was the same in his business affairs, but that was different, attractive even. Sometimes he only saw it from his side of the fence, but that was why they made such a good team. Laura always put the client's feelings forward, and Simon saw the black and white business plan. Somehow they all came together in the middle, and everyone got a deal.

Dragon Designs was their joint venture. Five years ago, they had purchased a rundown riverside apartment in Chester, and with the help of Simon's father, had transformed it and sold it for twice as much as its original worth. Encouraged by the property boom, they went on to purchase two more apartments in the same block, with the same success. Simon, more or less gave up his job as a surveyor to work alongside his father's building yard, buying run down houses in the right area and getting them up to scratch.

Laura was the creative head of the team. It was her job to dress the finished shell, to use all her skills as a designer to give the property a new identity. Dragon Designs was born, and financially, they'd never looked back.

Peering at her reflection in the gloomy mirror, Laura dried her shoulder-length hair. An almost natural dark blonde, helped along a little with subtle highlights every now and again, Laura was blessed with a classic face and a generally well-behaved complexion. Although it was slightly spoilt now with puffy brown eyes, she concealed the worst of it with carefully applied, mostly neutral make-up. Pleased with her appearance, but feeling unsettled and miserable inside, Laura knew she'd have to work hard to hide her angst from Maggie, *and* keep herself together enough to talk shop.

Simon was good at mixing business with pleasure, gently filtering in the right information, so subtle, the recipient didn't feel pressured or monopolised. Laura had no such skill. She found her way into the impressive dining room, and the buzz of pride it gave her lifted her spirits. Designing and helping to furnish the dining room had been Laura's gift for her sister's thirty-ninth birthday last year. Laura had ripped out the sixties era attempt at modernisation, and restored it back to its original style, with cream walls, ornate cornicing and a rich mahogany floor. To complement all the dark furniture they'd found in local junk and antique shops, Laura had handmade the soft furnishings in a combination of powder blue, cream and white. The effect was quite dazzling, especially when there were logs roaring in the massive fireplace and the chandeliers lit up the silverware on the huge table.

Pete passed her a glass of wine. They exchanged the usual pleasantries, but Laura struggled to make conversation with Maggie's husband. He had fairly set opinions about most things, and the only time he became animated was when the subject included football or council business. Dinner was late because Maggie was hopelessly disorganised with everything and Pete never offered to help. Well not properly, he always pretended he'd been thrown out of the kitchen and shambled in with a hangdog expression and another six-pack. Eventually though, Maggie materialised with the starters, and everyone took their place.

'This is my sister everyone!' Maggie said, loading Laura's plate with prawn and olive salad. 'I know she doesn't look related to me because I'm fat and forty, and she is so obviously *not*.'

Everyone made polite laughter, and Laura made the usual token protest. Her sister was always running herself down, but Maggie wouldn't be shushed, 'She's an interior designer so if you want one of those make-over jobs she's your woman.'

After a few moments, the woman seated opposite Laura said, 'I believe you did this room for Maggie; it's just *so* beautiful. Really complements the house.'

'Oh, thanks,' Laura said, and pushed some food around her plate.

'I'm Liz by the way, Morgan-Jones.'

'Laura Brown. My sister said you had some cottages you wanted to renovate,' Laura said, trying her best to be professional and not let the opportunity pass.

'Well, I think so. Nothing this grand though,' she said, glancing at the swag and tail curtains, then leant in more discreetly across the table. 'I'm afraid my brother doesn't agree with my plans, and he has the majority share in the business.' She inclined her eyes to the left, and Laura looked across the table at the exact second Mr Morgan-Jones did. He looked to have been in conversation with Pete, but met Laura's curiosity with a blank stare. Liz said something about her brother being unsociable, and the elderly male guest sat at Laura's right butted in, 'James is a genius, he's allowed to be unsociable, if that's how he feels.'

'Yes, but not *all* the time, surely?'

Laura took in Liz's outdoor complexion and the strong-looking hands, no nails and the no-nonsense outfit. From what she could ascertain, without staring, the unsociable majority shareholder was wearing a barely ironed shirt, with the sleeves pushed up; and favoured the same dark weathered look. Farming, or horses she thought. Great. Just about the most uninspiring combination she could possibly think of. She missed Simon's clever banter. He would know what to say.

The downside of that skill was his ability to make her feel crushed; he could defeat her with his logic as if she were a business problem and it could all be subtracted away with a calculator. Well, this one wasn't going to be solved with hard fact. Sometimes life happened without prior warning or planning, and that was when Simon struggled to cope.

Suddenly, aware of staring at her plate, Laura speared a prawn and looked back at Liz.

'What is it you do?'

'Horses. Private liveries and teaching is the main bread and butter, and that's mostly *what I do*,' she said, glaring at the old gent, and began to butter her bread roll briskly. 'Anyway, I'm getting too old to be working outside. A menopausal woman shouldn't be expected to stand shouting in driving rain.'

'And, your brother, what does he do?'

'James? Oh, a multitude of side-lines,' she said with a tired smile. 'No, to be fair he looks after about forty acres of land. His real time is taken up with training and specialist teaching. Only he prefers the more dangerous stuff,' she went on, 'you know, horses destined to be shot because they're loopy, or half dead. He loves nothing better than resurrecting a lost cause. All very commendable, but have you any idea how long these projects take? And you can't get rid of them because of their history.'

The man next to Laura vacated his seat and a woman with overpowering perfume slid into his place. 'Excuse me, but are you talking about Indiana Morgan-Jones?' she said smoothly, wine glass tilting.

'Why do you call him that?' Laura said, unsure whether to laugh.

'Because he has a big leather whip for one.'

Laura did laugh then, but Liz said, 'Oh, leave it out, Carla! Laura, this is Carla. She's had about three hundred riding lessons with my brother, with the sole intention of seducing him.'

'It's true! He's one of about, oh, let me see, *two*, eligible men of this parish. I've even bought a bloody horse off him,' she said. 'I've got thighs like steel and I can mount without stirrups.'

Liz rolled her eyes in Laura's direction. 'Carla is the queen of double entendre on the yard.'

The roast minted lamb arrived with jugs of red wine jus, and Laura was a bit disappointed when Carla went back to her seat and the old man returned.

'Help yourself everyone,' Maggie said, plonking down huge silver platters of roasted vegetables between the candelabra.

'For goodness sake sit down and start enjoying yourself!' Laura said, but Maggie just wiped her brow with her napkin and flapped it vaguely at Laura's glass. 'I am, I am! Why is your glass empty? And have you met Liz? I'm taking Ellie up there for a riding lesson tomorrow, why don't you come?' she said loudly.

'Could you?' Liz said, unfazed by Maggie's total lack of discretion.

'I could take a look,' Laura said slowly. 'To be honest all the initial estimating is my partner's territory.'

'Oh, I only want ideas at this stage,' Liz said, 'you know, something to entice James round to my way of thinking.'

'Did someone say entice James?' Carla said.

*

After dinner, they congregated in the sitting room for coffee and brandy, and homemade truffles. From the safety of the sagging sofa, Laura had a better look at Mr Morgan-Jones. He was younger than Liz; borderline scruffy. Shirt half in half out of old Levi's. He looked quite bored, leaning on the mantlepiece and trapped by Carla and the old man, who was very animated and talkative. It appeared to be a conversation about horses jumping hedges, because the old man was making arching gesticulations with his hands and trotting backwards and forwards, presumably to illustrate taking off and landing. He even bent his knees and might have swished his tail, had he owned one. When the old man went to get another drink, James sidled away. In fact he tried to leave the party more than once, but his sister herded him back in again.

'You can't go straight after being fed, it's just *rude*.'

'I've left the dogs outside.'

'So what? They're dogs!'

Eventually, he was presented to Laura.

'This is Laura Brown of Dragon Designs,' Liz said firmly, 'Laura, this is my brother, James.'

Laura scrambled to her feet. 'Hi,' she said, offering her hand. It seemed an age before he accepted. It was a reassuringly firm grip, but he couldn't have cared less who she was or what she had to say. He had very dark, green eyes, like seaweed or olives. They were sad eyes, she remembered thinking later.

'I've asked Laura to come and take a look at the cottages tomorrow,' Liz said, throwing James a warning look.

He sighed, 'Not tomorrow. I'm busy.'

'She can still look!'

'I'd rather it wasn't tomorrow, that's all.'

'We need to get something moving,' Liz hissed at him, 'In case you've forgotten about the overdraft, we need to realise some capital instead of arguing about it. The cottages won't go through another winter, and while we're on the subject, another winter feed bill for those brood mares will cripple us. It's a *ridiculous* situation!'

'I'd rather not discuss this in public.'

Laura moistened her lips, 'Let's discuss it in private, tomorrow.'

'With you?' James said to her. 'I don't need help to match up curtains and cushions.'

'Is that what you think I do? Play house?'

Liz pursed her lips. 'James, Laura runs a property developing company. Stop being so bloody patronising!'

'Sorry,' he said to Laura. 'Now if you'll *both* excuse me, I'm going *home*.'

They watched as he retreated across the room. He found Maggie, kissed her goodnight, and gave her a rare smile when she reciprocated. When all the other guests had more or less done the same, Laura sat staring into the struggling fire whilst Pete snored in an armchair. She could hear

Maggie waving off the last of the stragglers at the front door. When her sister materialised, still wearing her plastic apron, she waved a bottle of something at Laura. 'There you are! Nightcap?'

She didn't wait for a response and began to pour vintage cognac into mugs because she'd run out of glasses. 'All right, out with it Laura Brown,' Maggie said. 'Don't try and fob me off, I know there's something wrong, so out with it. You've had a row, haven't you?'

'I'm pregnant.'

At first her sister's eyes lit up, until she took in Laura's expression, and then her face fell. Several beats passed before she spoke, 'And…?'

Laura shrugged, 'I don't know. Simon is, well he's already a daddy twice over, isn't he?'

'But not with you,' Maggie said.

The previous day, when Laura had plucked up the courage to tell him, he'd been slightly incredulous. When he'd understood the mixed emotions on her face, he'd become steadily more frustrated, mostly by her lack of instant decision.

'We agreed about the kids thing, when we first got together. You know the problems I already have in that department,' he'd said, obviously panicked by the thought she'd turn into Alice, who used their children to great effect when she required something of him.

'Yes, yes I know, but this is different,' Laura had said. 'This is *ours*.'

He'd paced about, anxiously. 'So, you've already made your mind up?'

'No… I just want us to talk about it.'

They hadn't really talked about it; emotions were running too high.

Maggie said, 'But what about you? How do you feel?'

'Honestly? I don't know.'

Laura saw the instant disappointment in her sister's face and felt torn again, pushed one way by Simon, pulled back again by her sister. Maggie did her best to be impartial and supportive, but really she'd had too much to drink, and after all, it was her birthday; so Laura felt mean drawing her into a deep discussion. It surprised her really, how much she valued her sister's opinion these days.

It was only since Laura had entered her thirties that they had begun to tolerate each other's point of view and really communicate, even though they were almost opposite in every way.

*

In the morning, Laura moved the heavy curtains back to see the long, hopelessly messy garden, the bottom of which resembled a landfill site. Maggie spent hours digging in it and trying to keep the hens from scratching out the vegetables, then complained about her bad back and the soil under her nails.

Downstairs in the kitchen, Maggie's seventeen-year old daughter was making dandelion tea. Laura studied the sprayed on denim, the midriff tattoo and the wild black hair from a different perspective. Beneath the gothic styling, the lithesome blue-eyed Jessica was quite stunning, her behaviour somewhat challenging. Maggie's youngest was sweet-faced ten-year-old Ellie, a different prospect altogether. She had a mild form of autism. What if Laura had a child with more pronounced special needs? Could she cope? What would happen to her life?

Maggie had a hangover and slumped into one of the kitchen chairs with a glass of fizzy water. 'Oh Lord I'm too old for partying.'

'Dead right,' Jess muttered under her breath.

*

After a very late breakfast, it was time for Ellie's riding lesson. Only ten minutes out of the village and Maggie turned the Toyota into a farm track bordered by tall hawthorn hedges and preceded by a white wrought-iron sign, J & E Morgan-Jones, Equestrian Centre. They bounced over a cattle grid and Ellie shrieked, holding on to her hat. Maggie pointed out some cottages and a barn over to Laura's left, where the undulating fields gave way to the rearing mountains behind.

'I think those must be the properties Liz wants you to see.'

Laura contemplated the windswept stretch of land. The buildings were too far away to see any detail but it was good grazing, she knew that much, and the rugged up horses strung out across the wind flattened grass looked like thoroughbreds. She noted the miles of neat hedging, post and rail fencing and proper water butts, rather than saggy barbed wire and an old bath to catch rainwater.

Presently, they came to the yard, and Maggie parked alongside several smart cars. The January wind was biting, and Laura shrank into her astrakhan coat but looked with interest at the immaculate rows of looseboxes. It wasn't what she was expecting at all. There was real money here. If she could secure any kind of future project for Dragon Designs, especially a barn conversion, Simon would be over the moon. Not only were they short of work, but it might also buy her some thinking time as regards their personal problems. It would certainly earn her a lot of brownie points.

There was a small farmhouse and a jumble of outbuildings housing tractors, hay and equipment, and an outdoor menage, busy with horses and riders. They walked across to the house, heads down against the weather. Liz was in the little front room, which looked to be used as an office. On the desk there was an untidy jumble of computers, printers and phones, and the walls were decorated with notices and photographs, and some rosettes.

Liz compared hangover symptoms with Maggie, until Ellie dragged her mother away to watch her riding lesson with James.

'You look frozen. Coffee?' Liz said to Laura.

'Please, thanks.' Laura found a chair. She felt suddenly wobbly, and the smell of bacon sandwiches from somewhere wasn't helping her queasiness. Liz passed her a mug with images of Welsh Mountain ponies cantering around the rim, in a never ending circle.

'I apologise for my brother last night,' she went on, adding a number of unopened letters to an already towering pile. She sorted through the mess of paperwork propped against the keyboard with mounting exasperation. 'Look at this! It's like trying to run a business with Doctor Dolittle or some… I dunno, gypsy horse whisperer!'

'I can see how that might be difficult,' Laura said, but Liz laughed. 'Oh, I don't want to keep running him down, you'll give up before we've started, and I need all the help I can get,' she said, and looked over Laura's head, through the window. 'He's actually an amazingly patient teacher. Far more patient than me, more instinctive.'

'Horses, or people?'

'Oh, both,' she added seriously, 'most definitely both.'

Liz took her to preview the cottages whilst James was busy with Ellie.

There was a single-track lane behind the house. It swept around in a giant horseshoe and continued over a pretty stone bridge. Liz pulled up outside a small terrace of three cottages, and an impressive barn. After a struggle with the keys, they shoved open the worn door of Mefysen Cottage. Inside, it was pokey and rundown with plaster falling off in places and a lot of rotten wood. Someone had ripped off the original picture rails and cornices, but the fireplace was still there, full of old newspapers. Laura glanced through the dirty windows. To the rear of the cottages there was a tumble of wild garden falling away to a steep bank and a foaming white stream. Beyond the stream reared the foothills of Minas Bach, partially obscured by cloud.

Next door, the two smaller cottages had been knocked into one. 'Wow, this is big!' Laura said, surprised. 'Actually, it's fabulous!'

'Dad knocked them through years ago.'

Most of the fifties' style fixtures had been ripped out and there was half a brand new kitchen, but not much else. It looked like a promising job had been abandoned.

'Who's done this?' Laura said, running her hand across the worktop. It was solid oak and well made, and there was a Belfast sink and an Aga.

'James. He lost interest, lost heart, I suppose.'

Dragon Designs had lost count of the work they'd managed to procure because someone had run out of time or money, or expertise. 'That's a shame,' Laura prompted, then because Liz failed to make further comment, studied the old sepia prints on the newly plastered walls, mostly old men proudly holding horses. She loved to get the feeling of a place, carry it forwards if she could.

'So, who lived here? What's the history?'

Liz brightened at this. 'Oh, we grew up here, James and I. It's been in the family for generations. Dad eventually bought out the neighbouring farm and land, and that's the bit you see now,' she said, indicating the yard. 'James lives in the original farmhouse and I live in the village with my partner. It works well enough. We need someone on the premises full time. And James prefers old buildings, you know, something to fix all the time. That said, he's no good with neighbours, I reckon he'd just shoot most of them in time.'

Laura laughed, moved to look through the little windows.

The cottage overlooked the fields of horses she'd seen from the drive. They were alert and restless in the high wind, their movements so fast and fluid they looked to be dancing above the ground.

'What kind of horses are those?' she said, moved by their joie de vivre, their spirit almost tangible, even to her untrained eye.

'Beautiful aren't they? They're all Arab mares, pure bred. Three generations I think.'

'Are they all yours?'

Liz gave her a wearisome smile. 'My brother's. They're worth an absolute *fortune,* and he won't do anything with them. And they eat like horses, if you'll pardon the pun.'

Laura dragged her eyes away and focused on the business in hand. 'I'd love to handle this project. What do you want to achieve with these buildings?'

'The main goal is to release capital; the running costs of the yard are far too high. We have too many assets, which don't actually earn us anything. These cottages, the barn, and the mares.'

'And James, what does he really think?'

'Let's go back to base and discuss it shall we? It's freezing here.'

Back on the yard it was just as cold. Liz was drawn into some problem with the staff as soon as she climbed out of the Range Rover, so Laura wandered over to the menage, where Maggie was leaning on the fence watching James and Ellie. Laura wrapped her cashmere scarf over her head to try and stop her teeth from chattering.

Her niece was astride a huge horse, her hands buried in a mass of chestnut mane as it described a perfect, measured circle with the smoothest, most controlled gait. When she realised the horse had no saddle or bridle, Laura looked at her sister with sudden surprise, but Maggie was completely focused on the intimacy of the scene.

James was stood in the centre with a long schooling whip. His commands were mostly to the horse and he spoke so softly Laura couldn't distinguish many words above the wind. Sometimes he simply raised his hand and the horse stood still. When he turned away, the animal followed, nudging his pockets, and Ellie laughed out loud. It was nothing like the riding lessons Laura had endured as a child, which mostly consisted of Maggie yelling at her and eventually giving up because Laura just wanted to stop.

'Can you believe that's Ellie?' her sister said.

Laura knew the painstaking time it had taken her sister to persuade the little girl to even sit on a pony. Maggie spent hours on the Internet researching animals and autism. Laura knew of the therapy and how it could be a channel for communication, but it didn't always work for every case and Laura had been concerned that Maggie would push too hard. But James was nothing like Maggie.

Laura was impressed with the evidence, Liz rather less so. She joined the sisters at the paddock rail and watched with a mostly set face as her brother brought the horse to a halt. When it bowed rather majestically like Champion the Wonder horse and bared its big yellow teeth in a sort of horsey smile, Laura thought Liz might expire. Her mouth dropped open with disbelief, then clamped shut.

James lifted Ellie down before she slid off.

'Is he magic?' Ellie said.

'No, but you are.'

'What's his name?'

'Mr Ed.'

Thrilled with it all, Maggie and Ellie disappeared down the yard together, Mr Ed following like a huge dog. When they were out of earshot, Liz ducked under the rail.

'Are you *completely* mad?'

James looked at her for all of two seconds, then began to rake over the surface sand and throw horse droppings

Midnight Sky

into a bucket. Liz followed him. 'Health and Safety would have a total meltdown if they knew you were playing circus tricks with the clients. If there was an accident we could be sued, since you refuse to follow any guidelines! And there's the small issue of our British Horse Society membership, remember that? Are you listening to anything I'm saying?' She folded her arms. 'Where did that horse come from anyway?'

'A circus.'

Liz looked up at the sky, counted to about five. When he made to go, she snatched at his arm. 'Don't just walk off, we need to talk.'

'Like I said, I'm *busy*.'

'No, you're not. I've checked your diary.'

'I don't put everything in it.'

'Yes, well that's another problem!'

'Look, I don't want to do this today.'

'Tough. I do, and Laura's waiting.'

He rubbed the bridge of his nose and shot them both a dark look. Laura thought she'd die of the cold, and yet he only wore denims and a dirty wax jacket, hanging open and soaked with sleet. Liz marched into the office, motioning Laura to follow.

More drinks made, Laura opened her briefcase and found a notebook, and blew on her fingers. James closed the door behind him and took the chair next to her. His prickly presence made her nervous. If he began talking figures she'd be sunk.

'I'll make a few notes today and send you some details in the post. If you like what you see, Simon will come and carry out a proper valuation and draw up estimates.'

'That would be great,' Liz said.

'From what I've seen, the simplest and fastest way to raise capital is for Dragon Designs to buy the cottages and the barn as they stand and...'

'No,' James said. 'I want complete control over who lives on my land.'

'Okay... fair comment,' Laura said. 'The next option is to have us develop the properties in order for you to sell or rent.'

'How much?'

'I can't give you a formal estimate without a proper valuation, and that's not really my area.'

'Can you not give me an informal one?'

'James,' Liz cut in, 'you heard what she said.'

Laura smiled briefly at Liz. 'Of course if you want to sell on, it would involve you making an initial investment to make the properties more marketable, if you want the best return.'

'And that's where you come in, is it?' James said, tapping a pencil on his teeth.

'It's where Dragon Designs come in. We can oversee the whole project, work to your budget and we have top quality builders and suppliers to hand.'

'And we can sell to whomever we see fit?' Liz said.

'Technically, yes,' Laura said carefully. 'You can't afford to be too choosy though. Sales are tough at the minute.'

'What if we were to rent them?' Liz asked.

'You would be in complete control with tenants, and rentals are very lucrative at the moment,' Laura said, warming to her theme. She chatted about the rental market, looking at James to ascertain his reaction, but he was staring moodily into the middle distance. 'If you didn't like the tenants walking on the grass, you could always give them a six-month contract with a two-month notice to quit,' she went on, then almost bit her tongue. Sarcasm wouldn't work. She reminded herself how big this contract might be, and turned a smile in Liz's direction.

'The downside of that is you would realise no capital, but you would get a steady income. You might want to consider holiday lets, maybe cash in on the riding as well.'

'Oh, I hadn't thought of *that*,' Liz said, deeply impressed.

Encouraged, Laura added, 'You could always raise capital another way. Sell some land say... or horses.'

There was an uncomfortable silence, broken only by the telephone ringing.

'Oh, excuse me, Laura,' Liz said, and picked up the call.

James lit a cigarette and stared at the floor. Laura did her best to ignore his mutinous face, but his attitude was beginning to get on her nerves. He might be the majority shareholder, but it was glaringly obvious he didn't want her there. Neither did she wish to sit in his smoke.

Laura hunted in her bag for a business card and slid it on to the desk. 'Give me a call?' she mouthed to Liz, who gave her the thumbs up sign by way of a reply.

James followed her out of the office.

Laura put her case into Maggie's vehicle, aware that he was right behind her.

'You can stop the designer speak now,' he said.

'I was asked my opinion, and I gave it to the best of my ability.'

'*What*? All that bloody *waffle* was your advice?'

'Look, why don't you just go ahead and do it all yourself?' Laura said, slamming the car door shut. 'You didn't get very far last time.'

'It's a deal.'

Laura opened her mouth to backtrack but she wasn't quick enough. She was left with his back view, ambling across the yard calling up his dogs, a huge grey Lurcher and a funny little white Terrier covered in mud. But Laura didn't really take in the scene. All she could see was her dream job falling apart brick by brick. And she'd demolished it all by herself.

CHAPTER TWO

Laura

Laura stood for several minutes, wondering how she could make such a big blundering hash of something so simple. She became aware that Liz was banging on the office window. She'd obviously witnessed their conversation, if you could call it that.

Laura put her professional hat firmly back on, and went back inside.

'What's he said? He charged out of here like a raging bull!'

'Nothing really, well, I think we both said the wrong thing at the wrong time.'

Liz seemed undecided, distracted for a moment. Suddenly, she took the phone off the hook and dropped the catch on the door. 'Look, there's something you should know. He won't like me telling you, but I can't see us getting very far like this, and despite what he says, he knows something has to be done.'

Intrigued, Laura sat back down. 'Go on.'

'James lost his wife two years ago. She died very suddenly.'

'Oh...' Laura said, 'when I mentioned the horses...'

'The Arabian mares? They were hers, she bred them. And the double-fronted cottage, they were going to live there, him and Carys. Hence, the half-finished job. Hence, everything grinding to a halt.'

The information seeped in and Laura suddenly felt a bit thrown, well quite a lot thrown. And although she knew it was selfish, she couldn't help wondering how on earth they would approach the job with James so hung up on memories. She knew how powerful memories could be.

'You weren't to know,' Liz said, watching her face. 'It's my fault really, I should have said. He normally handles it a lot better, but I've just realised it was two years ago *today*. Talk about bad timing.'

*

Back at Hafod House, Maggie made lunch and Laura sat at the kitchen table trying to make notes, but her concentration was all over the place. Pete was reading the paper and listening to loud, live football commentary.

'How did the meeting go?' Maggie said to Laura, busily buttering bread. 'Pete, turn that racket down will you? You should have seen Ellie today. James had her on a horse he'd bought from a retired acrobat. What do you think of that?'

'It sounds expensive, that's what I think of that.'

Laura said, 'Why didn't you tell me his wife was dead?'

'Dead? Who are you talking about?'

'James. His wife died two years ago.'

Maggie said, 'I didn't even know he'd been married! He's a dark horse.'

'He sure is,' Jess said, making an entrance with her friend, whom she introduced as Lucy. 'Lucy works on the yard. You are talking about Jamie, from the stables?'

Laura looked up from her notes, 'Yes, do you know him?'

'I *wish*. He's *mega fit*,' Jess said, pinching shreds of

cucumber from the chopping board and exchanging wanton looks with Lucy. 'I want him to roll me over and over in his hay. O.M.G. he's got *the* most *amazing* body.'

Maggie looked askance at Laura, then back at Jess, unsure how to react.

'Don't tell me you haven't noticed?' Jess said, hands on hips. 'Are you *blind?*'

'Stop being so rude!' Maggie snapped, and went back to chopping. 'Apart from which he's old enough to be your father!'

'Actually, he's way *older* than my dad,' said Lucy.

'Experience is so not a negative,' Jess said, and waggled a long stick of limp celery in front of her mother's face, until it slowly drooped over and she bit the end off.

'Pete, are you not going to say anything?' Maggie said, horrified.

'Huh? What about?' he said, turning up the radio again.

'Did you know his wife?' Laura said to Lucy.

'Nah, it was ages ago. I've seen her photograph though.'

'How did she die, was she ill?'

'Dunno. He doesn't talk about it.'

'Is he always so angry?'

'Angry? No, not ever. Jamie's a total sweetie. It's his sister I can't stand. She's proper bossy, real sergeant-major stuff.'

'Yeah, she's even got the moustache to go with it,' Jess said, and pursed her lips, balancing a carrot baton under her nose.

Laura gave up, not really daring to ask any more questions in case Lucy thought she was being interrogated, and it would likely go around the tack room at the yard during break time and no doubt find its way back to Mr Morgan-Jones. This was potentially another professional little touch.

As soon as lunch was cleared away, Laura escaped to her room to lie down. She felt extraordinarily tired and nauseous, and she needed to think. She'd told Maggie more about the meeting after Jess and Lucy had gone out.

'I haven't made much of an impression. Simon would be furious if he knew.'

'Rubbish.'

'Do you think I should apologise to James?'

'No. I think you should forget all about work, get Simon to follow it up and start looking after yourself, you look really peaky,' Maggie had said. 'Laura, you know I'm here for you, whatever you decide to do about the baby.'

That should be Simon's line, shouldn't it?

Before she'd discovered her unplanned pregnancy, Laura had always happily perceived she was a typical career girl; independence and a comfortable lifestyle within a modern relationship. A lot of her friends were envious and told her so, and so did Maggie, usually when she was having a tough time with the kids or Pete was driving her mad. Yet, when Maggie had been watching Ellie today the connection between them made Laura question herself a little more thoroughly. The motherhood thing was something she had never experienced.

Maggie had a son as well, away at university and doing well in politics. Her sister was so good at family life. She seemed to sail through everything with or without her husband's help. And although she sometimes wondered what Maggie saw in Pete, Laura was aware of a tiny prick of envy. Where had that come from?

It was dark by the time Laura had repacked her overnight bag, said goodbye to everyone and nosed her silver Mercedes back down the drive. She got as far as the little roundabout on to the dual carriageway, then went full circle and headed back the way she'd come.

In less than ten minutes, she was pulling up in the Morgan-Jones' yard.

It was busy with evening stables. There was a radio playing somewhere and two teenage girls larking about with an overfull wheelbarrow. Laura walked across to the farmhouse and the treacle-like smell of fresh meadow hay filled the air, reminding her of one of the nicer aspects of her childhood. Once on the doorstep, she stood for a full minute staring at her boots, working out what to say, ready to eat humble pie no matter how rude he was. She needed to remember what Lucy had impressed about him being a total sweetie, although that took a lot of imagination.

She knocked tentatively on the door and an age seemed to pass before he answered.

'You again?' he said flatly.

'Can I come in, just for a minute?'

He held the door open for her. Laura followed him down the hall, past the little office and into a large, messy kitchen. There was a ferocious open fire, a huge farmhouse table strewn with small items of tack, and a mountain of unwashed dishes. He was in the middle of cooking dinner, something with pasta and garlic, and there was an opened bottle of Shiraz, one glass.

'I'm starving so don't expect me to stop and listen.'

'No that's okay.'

Because the room was so warm, the richness of the cooking smells made her feel queasy. Laura dragged out a kitchen chair and perched on the edge, resisting the urge to put her head between her legs. She pinched the top of her nose and took several deep breaths. Oh, God, please not now, she thought. Morning sickness couldn't last all day, could it?

The huge grey dog under the table got up to look in her bag, and she struggled to retrieve it, keys and loose change spilling out. James seemed oblivious and carried on stirring something on the hob so she mostly stared at his back. The Lurcher, bored with her bag, stuffed its long nose in the direction of her crotch.

'I wanted to apologise, for earlier today. I think we got off on the wrong foot and...'

'You've been talking to Liz?'

'Well yes, she did tell me about... about your wife,' she began, pausing to push the dog away as hard as she dared. 'I didn't mean to be insensitive.'

There was a long moment of silence before he said, 'Okay, is that it?'

'More or less. Actually, do you think I could have a glass of water?' she said, feeling the familiar watery mouth and clammy forehead. She was about to ask him where the bathroom was when he turned to look at her, saw her begin to retch, and guided her towards the Belfast sink. Gratefully it didn't amount to anything too disgusting, which she was immensely thankful for, because during the long seconds she was staring at the plug he remained in close proximity, one hand on her back.

When she felt it was safe, Laura sat back down. 'Must have been something I ate,' she said, too embarrassed to look at him, but he didn't seem fazed, more mildly concerned, 'Are you saying your sister's poisoned you?'

'No,' she said, horrified he should think that. The only plausible solution Laura could think of to redress the farce, which was taking over the entire weekend, was the truth.

'Okay it's not something I ate. It's morning sickness, but at night.'

James nodded sagely and his face softened ever so slightly, not quite a smile.

'I think I might have something for that.'

'You've got something for morning sickness?' she said warily, watching him going through the kitchen cupboards, all kinds of paraphernalia falling out.

He made ginger tea.

Laura didn't know what to make of him, or the strange infusion.

The telephone ringing saved her, and James disappeared

into the office. He was quickly engrossed in a conversation, something about a delivery of linseed and two tubs of molasses. Laura, quickly splashed some cold water on her face, then because she couldn't find anything else more suitable, scrubbed at the sink with what looked like a dandy brush.

Although rustic to the extreme, it was a remarkably well-stocked kitchen for a man living on his own. He even had a bag of split lentils *in date.* She looked sideways at the spines of all the cookery books piled on top of a box of wine. The titles were extremely diverse and the wine was top-class, definitely not just for cooking. There was an iron rack suspended from the ceiling, full of well-used pans, two bridles, a set of red leg bandages and a string of onions.

Nothing was decorative; everything had a use.

But the rural imagery of it all was flawed. He was, without question a total slob. As well as the unwashed dishes, there was a heap of filthy wet clothes on the floor and a huge raw marrowbone covered in fluff, on top of the ironing board. A lot of the stuff, like the nuts and bolts and buckets, looked as if they should maybe be outside.

When James came back into the kitchen, Laura was using a pan lid as a mirror. She put her lipstick away and got to her feet.

'Better?' he said, putting the lid back on his sauce.

'Yes, much, I must get some of that magic potion.'

'You may as well have this,' he said, giving her the box. 'Don't think I'll be needing it.'

Laura made her awkward escape, clutching the teabags. Both conversations now with Mr Morgan-Jones were the most unorthodox business meetings she'd ever had, if that's what she could call them. She just hoped she'd done enough to smooth the way. At least he hadn't slammed the door behind her. In fact, Laura had the distinct feeling he was watching her reverse her car.

Laura drove home slowly, not knowing what to expect. The unplanned baby was like an unexploded bomb between herself and Simon. She pulled into her parking space at their apartment in Chester, relieved to see his blue BMW. All she wanted to do was sink into a bath and sink into Simon's arms, and somehow, sort out the mess they seemed to have got themselves into.

When she arrived outside number six, she could hear excitable children's voices and Alice making a screeching snorting noise, the kind of laugh a hyena might make after a bottle of Chardonnay. Laura opened the door tentatively and saw two pairs of trainers on the polished oak floor. The occupants were surprised to see her, but only Simon jumped to his feet.

'Oh, hi, Laura,' Alice said, and gave her a girly wave. She was flicking through Laura's magazines, a large glass of wine in her hand. The children, who'd been arguing over the Wii Olympic Games, simply stared at Laura, as if she were an impostor.

Simon came into the hall and quietly closed the lounge door behind him.

'Laura, I've been worried about you, I've just spoken to Maggie and she said you left ages ago.'

'Oh, I drove really slowly and my phone's out of battery. Sorry.'

'You look a bit white, love, come here,' he said. 'I'm so sorry about spoiling Maggie's birthday.'

Laura almost collapsed against him with tiredness. 'Simon, why are Alice and the children here? I didn't see the car downstairs,' she said, dropping her bag to the floor so that the ginger tea spilled out of its grubby box. 'I've had a horrible day, I feel ill, and I just want to talk to you.'

'I intend to put all that right,' he said emphatically, '*and I will*. Just as soon as I've run Alice and the children home.'

'Run them home? But where's Alice's car?'

'I'll tell you all about that when I get back.'

'Simon, all about *what*?'

He looked at her full on, his hazel eyes ablaze with exasperation before taking hold of Laura's arm and manoeuvring her into the kitchen. 'She's only gone and lost her license through drink driving. *Disqualified!* She's *sold* the car to pay her Christmas credit card bill,' he said, and began counting off items on his fingers, 'The children's swimming lessons, some overdue gas bill, a *Harrods* account, can you believe? Six months of French manicures and her *bloody wine merchant!*' He paused, to run a hand through his dark blonde hair. It was already thinning, something he blamed on Alice. 'The damn woman is a nightmare!'

Twelve-year-old Tara knocked on the kitchen door, then sidled up to her father and cuddled him, all doe eyes and pulled down mouth. 'Daddy, we were having fun, and now that Laura's here you're all serious and grumpy.'

'Oh, I'm sorry darling. Is it my turn again?' Simon said, and raised his brows at Laura, 'We're playing downhill ski run and Mummy's winning. Can't have that can we?'

Laura went straight to their bedroom, locked the door and ran herself a deep bath, brooding on it all. Tara, who was not only a cunning spy, was now also developing impressive father-daughter wheedling skills, and in case she missed anything, six-year-old Cameron repeated everything she and Simon discussed with scary accuracy.

Sometimes it all got her down, but love was very powerful glue.

Five years ago she'd had an affair with a married man.

Contrary to everything her sister and her friends told her, Simon did actually leave his wife and children for her, but Laura sometimes felt that Alice still had the majority share. The financial mess of the divorce went on and on, a continuation of the demolition job Alice had started on the marriage in the first place, with drink and debt.

Midnight Sky

Alice continued to charge full price for Simon, like he was on never-ending loan.

Laura put a hand across her still flat stomach. Would another child make the situation much worse, or would it shift Simon's focus onto a new family unit and force Alice to move on? But that felt manipulative, the wrong kind of glue. The cheap, tacky kind which eventually dried out and lost its cohesion.

When Laura padded back into her immaculate stainless steel kitchen, it was to find everyone had gone and she had the apartment to herself. Simon had bought her favourite cream cheese and smoked salmon, and there were fresh bagels, but she couldn't face any of it. She made more ginger tea and went into the lounge to wait.

The white marble coffee table was littered with pizza boxes, cola cans, and an empty wine bottle, one glass with vivid red lipstick smeared around the rim. There were DVD cases and games all over the floor, and her dark brown suede curtains were sticky and dishevelled, as if the children had been playing in them. Laura hated mess, it didn't suit the clean lines of her furniture, but she didn't have the energy to be cross, or to clear anything away. It was a whole lot easier to simply stare through the huge picture window overlooking the roman town with its city walls and the river Dee. A pretty view in daytime, now just a vast blackness, streaming with rain and car headlights travelling along the dual carriageway.

Considering Alice only lived two miles away, it was another hour before Simon came home. He took one look at Laura's face and began to tidy up, slinging rubbish into a bin liner. 'Sorry love, this won't take a minute. I had to put the kids to bed, Cam wanted a story, and then Alice and I had a blazing row. You know how it is?'

'I know how it is,' Laura said quietly. If he heard her weary sarcasm he chose not to comment on it. 'I hope she's not going to rely on you for lifts everywhere. Is that what the row was about?'

'Oh, no, there's more! Can you believe she's talking about going out to *Australia* for six months?' he said, slotting games and films back into the wrong sleeves, before throwing them under the television unit with more force than required. 'I told her, *no way*.'

Laura sat up. 'Australia? What's that about?'

'Oh, well it's initially for her sister's wedding,' Simon said, finally pouring himself a very large scotch. 'She's getting married to Crocodile Dundee, remember that big twit in the hat she met last year? She thinks it will be a good experience for Tara and Cameron. I mean, what about their education, and what about *me*?' He threw himself down into the leather chair opposite, tugged his shoes off and rubbed his eyes. 'I told her I'd fight it all the way.'

Laura didn't really trust herself to comment on Australia, it sounded too good to be true.

*

In the morning, Laura lifted her head slowly off the pillow and was relieved to feel normal, but Simon was moody and hung-over, and they were both late for work.

Dragon Designs had a first floor office suite above two shops on a side street in the centre of town. It was small but better than trying to work from home, and it looked more professional for meetings. There were three desks, because they managed to employ Barbara, a part-time assistant.

'We haven't got much on,' Simon said, scanning through his e-mail. 'There's an auction at Tower Bridge this afternoon, I think I'll see if I can pick up that semi. Did you make me an appointment for that job Maggie's always going on about?'

'I need to talk to you about that.'

Laura tentatively outlined the condition of the cottages and the barn. He wasn't pleased that she'd already seen the place, but the lucrative aspects outweighed the fact that Laura had tried to do his job.

'I'll give them a call today,' Simon said, reading her notes.

'I think we should wait a bit before we do a follow-up.'

'Why? We can't afford to, and they might approach someone else. Who's the owner?'

Laura explained the set up. 'You need to tread carefully. He's not sold on the idea, and I think if you pressure him there'll be no going back,' she went on. 'I think you should also know he lost his wife.'

'Oh?' he said, not really listening. 'Recently?'

'Two years ago.'

He half laughed. '*Two years?* For goodness sake, he either wants the job doing or not.'

'I'm just warning you, your brisk approach won't work with him.'

'Bollocks. Trouble with you is you get personally involved. It doesn't pay in the long run, people think you're a soft touch.'

'Knowing what makes people tick gives you an insight.'

'Oh, stop all that arty talk.'

It was an argument they'd had before, but Laura couldn't reply because she had to run to the tiny bathroom. Simon followed her and found her bent over the toilet. When she came out, he folded her in his arms. 'Laura, I'm sorry, I'm in a horrible mood. Can I get you anything?'

She shook her head and buried her face in his shirt, inhaled his familiar citrus aftershave. 'We need to talk, Simon.'

'I know. Let's do dinner tomorrow, you choose.'

'Why not tonight?'

'I'm taking Tara to the cinema. I thought you were

going out?'

It was true, she was meeting 'the girls' for drinks, but Laura would happily have cancelled if it meant they could have talked. She knew a day didn't make much difference, but just this once Laura had rather hoped that arrangements with the children would take second place. 'I could come with you,' she said, 'we could talk afterwards.'

'What! Miss all the gossip to sit through Disney Darlings?'

Laura hated the latest wave of cult cartoons. When she gave him a wan smile back, Simon kissed the top of her head, in much the same way he did to Tara on the rare occasion she didn't get her own way.

*

Later in the afternoon, Simon went to the auction, and Laura worked on the kitchen plan for a terraced house they'd purchased two weeks previously. It was in a first-time-buyer district, so Laura was designing a contemporary style featuring faux black granite worktops, glossy white units and stainless steel accessories.

Simon's father, Bill was busy plastering and they'd already had a conversation about getting the electrician in. Laura needed to work out the number and location of sockets, the positioning of lighting and where all the appliances were going to fit, in line with the floor plan.

Alice rang the office. She had a breathy, excited way of speaking. Maggie said she sounded like she was having a permanent orgasm. 'Oh, Laura! Are you really busy?'

'Well, I am rather.'

'Oh, poor you... just wondered if I could pop up for a little chat?'

'What... now?'

'I'm just outside on the pavement,' she said in a little voice.

Cursing, but admittedly curious, Laura pushed her paperwork to one side, went down the stairs and opened the outer door. Alice followed her back up, laden with bags of shopping and looking unusually well-groomed but of course, she had little else to fill her time with. She was tall and skinny with big boobs and striking blonde hair, always in a different style. The same age as Simon, but she didn't look thirty-nine, whereas Simon looked considerably older.

Alice made herself at home on the leather sofa reserved for client meetings and flapped her hands about, blowing on her nails.

'Coffee?' Laura said sweetly.

'Lovely,' Alice said sweetly back. 'I'd offer to make it, but I've just had my extensions done.'

'No problem.'

'I want to apologise for sending Simon home in a foul mood last night,' Alice said and pulled a silly, perturbed face. 'We had a little disagreement.'

'I know,' Laura said carefully, handing Alice a mug.

'Laura, I've had a little idea.'

'Have you?'

'I know Simon is upset about the children and I going to Australia, but then it came to me. Why don't I leave Tara and Cameron with you?'

'With… us?'

'Yes,' she said, her face full of shining benevolence, as if she'd found a cure for cancer or world peace. She put her hand up. 'No, don't give me an answer now. Have a chat with Si.'

She drank her coffee then, her innocent baby blue eyes watching Laura over the rim. When Laura went to wash up the coffee mugs, she heard Alice call a taxi, using the phone on Simon's desk and no doubt charging it to him. Everything Alice did was provocative. With that in mind,

Laura refused to mull over her 'little idea'. She had bigger things to think about.

Nevertheless, she struggled to concentrate after Alice had gone. Not only was she bored with the job on her desk, she was itching to get started on the cottages and the barn. On a whim, she rang the Morgan-Jones' yard, hoping to get Liz, but it was a breathless Lucy who picked up the call.

'Liz isn't here, and Jamie's got private clients from R.D.A.'

'Sorry, what?'

'Riding for the disabled. One's a soldier and the other's got Down's syndrome, I think.'

'Oh, I see. Oh, well, don't disturb him.'

Disappointed, Laura replaced the handset and looked out of the window at the busy street below. The school bus went past exactly on time. If she had a child, she'd be dashing off to pick them up and going home, her working day done, and her role as a mum just beginning, making tea and organising homework, bath and bedtime. After that, it would be dinner and Simon coming home with a bottle of wine. She wondered if that was a realistic image or wishful thinking. It wasn't like that for the harassed looking young women in the supermarket with their cheap prams, shopping piled on the handles.

Neither had it been quite like that for her sister, or rather more importantly, for Alice.

*

On Tuesday evening, Laura waited for Simon in her favourite bistro. It was French and expensive but quiet and unpretentious.

Simon was late, but on the point of calling him, she spotted him in the entrance and Laura looked at him critically for a moment in his dark grey Armani. He knew how to dress well without being stuffy. The suit was formal, but his Hugo Boss shirt was casual. He wasn't a classically good-looking man, his nose was slightly aquiline in profile and he had a tendency to gain a bit of weight round the middle if he lapsed with the gym. His attractiveness lay more in the confidant way he carried himself, his energetic charisma. Simon loved a challenge, both in business and in his personal life, but he had to win. He was a typical Leo, actually, so was Alice.

He leant across the table to kiss Laura's upturned face. 'Sorry I'm a bit late. Called in last minute to see Graham Gallagher,' he said, grabbing a menu. Graham was their solicitor. They passed quite a bit of conveyancing his way and probably kept him in holidays to the south of France with the on-going cost of Simon's divorce and related topics.

Simon looked at her and smiled, 'How are you feeling?'

'Fine actually, quite hungry for a change.'

They ordered food, and Simon chose a bottle of Burgundy. 'Any progress on the Morgan-Jones job?'

'No,' Laura said. 'But I want you to promise to let me handle this, just to start with.'

Simon grinned, his hazel eyes dancing, 'Okay *partner*, just don't lose it. It's all we got on the horizon.'

'What about the auction?'

'Oh, the semi? Went for too much. But I did get *something*,' he said, fishing in his pocket. He slid an old battered box across the table.

Inside, on an antique silk cushion, was a silver bracelet with a tiny dragon inscribed on the clasp. Simon was good at this: impromptu presents and messages of love. Laura fastened it over her wrist and admired the way it shone on her tanned skin. 'I love it, thank you.'

He smiled and covered her hand with his. 'Laura, I'm sorry about the argument and all this mess with Alice over the weekend. I sent Maggie some flowers, apologised for missing her dinner.'

'She came to see me at the office,' Laura said, and unfolded her napkin, 'Alice did.'

He took a measured sip of Burgundy and moistened his lips. 'What did she say?'

Laura filled him in on the gist of the conversation, over their lamb and garlic potatoes. 'Simon, I don't want to look after Tara and Cameron while Alice goes on an extended holiday, which we will likely end up paying for.'

'No, quite, I quite agree.'

'You agree?'

'Well, it just wouldn't work, we're both trying to run a business here.'

'Okay... so what did Graham say?'

Simon pushed his plate to one side, refilled his wine glass and threw his napkin down. It was the same story she'd heard before. If they opposed Alice the cost could run into thousands with no guarantee of success. Alice held the trump cards with custody of the children. The slow process of the British legal system struggled to keep pace with the complications of modern family disputes.

'Alice needs to stay *here, with* the children,' he said.

'I think you should call her bluff.'

'What?'

'Tell her you would be happy for them all to go,' Laura said, flicking her eyes onto his astonished face.

'Oh, I don't know. I need to think about it.'

'Anyway, enough of Alice. We need to discuss something more important.'

'Yes I know,' he said, staring into his coffee. 'And I have given it a lot of thought.'

He ran his hands through his hair, and looked at her square on, his eyes steady on hers.

'I'm really sorry, Laura, but I just don't think I want another child.'

Laura filled her wine glass at last, and swirled the rich Burgundy around to catch the light. Their conversation was beginning to sound like some kind of deal.

CHAPTER THREE

Maggie

Maggie replaced the telephone receiver and went to find Pete. He was in the sitting room, reading the Sunday papers, but he looked up when Maggie sat down heavily in one of the old armchairs. She felt much older than forty years and a week.

'Who was on the phone, love? You've been over an hour.'

'Laura,' she said. 'Oh, Pete, she's going to have a termination. I can't believe it. I really thought she'd warmed to the idea.'

'Huh. That'll be him, that will.'

'Simon?'

'Arrogant twat.'

'Joint decision Laura said. Neither of them wants a family, some people are like that, aren't they?' she said, flicking through the supplement. 'Anyway, freedom of choice and all that.'

'Cut it out, Maggie, you're gutted.'

It was true; she was both upset and puzzled by her sister's decision. Somehow she'd felt sure that Laura would have gone ahead with the pregnancy. Her sister would never play God or endorse any kind of intentional threat to a life; it just wasn't in her. She never even stood on ants as a child as a matter of principal. And yet, Laura had already had the consultation at The Willows in Chester.

'I'm going with her, to the clinic on Wednesday,' Maggie said.

Pete frowned, 'Shouldn't that be Simple Simon's job?'

*

They arrived at the stables too early, but Ellie liked to look at the horses first. Jess had decided to come and watch, not because she was interested in her sister's riding lesson but because James was teaching. She was wearing a strange outfit of black leggings, a tiny little summer skirt and a fur jacket. Big boots, backcombed hair and hoop earrings completed the look.

'How come the family dimwit gets Jamie to herself?' Jess said, tapping away on her phone.

'You know why. And stop calling her a dimwit,' Maggie said, reminding herself that Jess went through this wind-up routine purely to get a reaction. 'We could maybe get her a little pony, if she keeps improving, what do you think?'

'Dad said no way when I asked for a horse.'

'Jess, you're getting a car for your eighteenth next month. I seem to remember you lost interest in ponies when you discovered boys.'

'*What*? I've *never* been interested in boys or ponies,' Jess said, as if the very words were poison, then looked across the yard to James, 'They're called *men,* and horses,' she said, just loud enough for her mother to hear. Maggie played along.

In contrast to the previous weekend, it was a gorgeous winter day with ice blue skies. The crystal clear relief of the mountains was broken only by the shadows of scudding clouds. James lifted Ellie onto a little golden pony with a mane and tail the colour of flax.

'Is it a girl or a boy? I don't want a boy one,' Ellie said, one hand on the front of the saddle, one hand still holding on to James. 'And has it got a nice name?'

'She's called Peaches,' James said, slotting her feet into the stirrups. 'Nice?'

'Uh huh. Nice.'

James had the pony on a long lunge line so that he was in complete control, leaving Ellie to concentrate on her balance. After about twenty minutes, he led the pony out of the menage, and they walked down the lane behind the house. Ellie was perfectly at ease and holding the reins normally. They began to climb the sheep track on to Minas Bach, weaving through a sea of cinnamon bracken until they were lost to sight behind the ancient fir trees.

Disappointed, Jess went to find Lucy, and Maggie tapped on the office door.

Liz said, 'Oh, Maggie, my excuse for a break. How's Ellie getting on?'

'Amazingly well. They've gone up the mountain.'

'Well, I hope you don't mind waiting,' she said, spooning coffee into mugs. 'My brother's idea of the end of a session is when Ellie gets tired, or he runs out of fags.'

'It's fine, really.'

'I've spoken to Laura, and she's sent me some sample designs,' Liz said, throwing invoices into a box. 'She's clever, that sister of yours.'

'Oh, I know. Laura scooped the lot in the looks and brains department,' Maggie said, with no bitterness whatsoever. 'No one believes Laura and I are even related.'

'I know exactly how you feel.'

*

On Wednesday, Maggie had arranged to collect Laura, drive her to the clinic and drive her home again, if she got the all clear.

'It's only a local anaesthetic, it won't be as bad as the last time,' Laura had said.

She'd been referring to the operation she had in her twenties.

Since she was about twelve, Laura had had endless gynaecological problems, resulting in the removal of an infected ovary. Due to lots of complications at the time, the consultant said there was only ever going to be a slim chance of Laura conceiving naturally. Maggie had been upset at the time, but Laura was well into her career and was just relieved she felt better. The fact that her fertility was low was a bonus and meant she could take a low hormone pill. Then she'd met Simon with a ready-made family, and it had never been an issue.

'Are you certain you don't want Simon with you?' Maggie had reiterated.

'No, I want you, it's a woman thing.'

Maggie thought it was a strange response, but set off for Chester in good time. She was a bit late because the traffic was so heavy, and Laura must have been watching for her because she came down to the car park straight away. She looked pale but composed, barely any make-up and with her hair tied back in a brown velvet ribbon. She put a small leather holdall onto the back seat.

'Just in case they don't let me out,' she said, and Maggie's heart turned over. All the things she wanted to say caught in her throat, but Laura didn't seem to want any conversation and stared out of the passenger window all the way.

The clinic was more like a small private hotel. Maggie felt ridiculous in her old jeans, which were too tight, a pair of gardening shoes and Pete's old fleece. They were shown into a waiting room with complimentary coffee and lots of glossy magazines.

'Blimey, you can tell this isn't the NHS,' Maggie whispered, sinking into a huge comfy chair and bouncing up and down appreciatively. Laura gave her a miserable smile.

A full minute of silence passed.

'Liz was impressed with your artist's impressions,' Maggie said.

'Simon's there today.'

'Oh, good, that's good,' she said brightly. 'Ellie is impressed with James. He showed her how to make bran mash for Peaches' dinner. In a bucket. And stir it well, with a stick.'

A wistful smile at this, then Laura wandered over to the window. Maggie could have kicked herself, but not talking about the kids was difficult. Someone called her away soon after that, and Maggie just had time to squeeze her hands. 'Come on love, it'll be all right.'

Maggie had barely got herself a drink and found a magazine before she was aware that someone had entered the room. She straightened up from crouching in front of the vending machine and almost dropped a full cup of cappuccino. Laura was there, tears streaming silently down her face.

'I can't do it Maggie, I just can't.'

Maggie caught hold of her and they clung together, sobbing and elated at the same time.

Less than thirty minutes later they were ordering coffee in the city centre, glad for once of the noisy, crowded surroundings. It took Laura a good ten minutes before she could speak because she was so emotional, and Maggie just passed tissues to her, then Starbuck's napkins.

'I'm glad you didn't go through with it.'

'Could be my only chance,' Laura managed to say, wiping at the mascara under her red eyes.

'Well, yes you're ancient at thirty-three.'

'You know that's not what I mean,' she mumbled, blowing her nose.

'I know that's not what you mean.'

'I don't know what I'm going to say to Simon.'

'He'll understand. Won't he?'

'But Maggie, he was adamant he didn't want another child. We even talked about him having a vasectomy, so we're never faced with this dilemma again.'

Maggie was a bit shocked. 'Oh. That's all a bit final.'

'Yes, well, he made his decision five years ago and it hasn't changed. It's me who's had the massive about-turn. The biological clock bites back.'

'Sounds like a film.'

Laura drank some cold latte. She started to tell Maggie about Alice and some notion about a trip to the other side of the world. Really, Simon's ex filled up a lot of Laura's thinking time, but Malice, as Maggie preferred to call her, did seem to have an extraordinary knack of keeping a tourniquet of control over their time and money. She could understand why her sister would welcome the opportunity to be shot of Malice for a while, but Laura rather implied that the price for Simon's passivity over the latest development was two appointments at the clinic.

'Laura, he has to put you first,' Maggie said.

'He *does*. He will.'

Laura rallied a bit and repaired her lipstick. Maggie glanced at her watch and realised with a small panic there was no way she'd get back in time to collect Ellie from school. Pete would have to nip out from work. She found her mobile at the bottom of her bag, brushed the crumbs off it and called his office, praying he wouldn't be in a meeting. All they seemed to do was have meetings.

A girl Maggie didn't recognise answered in a very bored voice, 'Housing benefit.'

'It's Maggie. Pete's wife.' Silence. 'Can I *speak* to him, please?'

'Er... who?'

'Pete Thomas. He's the manager.'

'Is he? Hang on.'

Maggie hung on for an age before the assistant manager cleared his throat.

'Pete's not here, is that Maggie?'

'Yes! Well, where is he?'

An awkward silence. 'Have you tried his mobile?'

Mildly annoyed, Maggie tried his mobile but that went to voicemail. Unable to think of anything else, she rang one of the other mums instead. 'School runs! You've got all this to come,' she said to Laura, whilst she waited for an answer. 'Honestly, that bloody council. He's worked there thirty years.'

But her sister wasn't really interested in Conwy council; in her head she was miles away. Maggie dropped her back home. 'Don't worry about Simon, he'll come round.'

She took a last glance through her mirror as Laura waved her off and Maggie couldn't help thinking how forlorn her sister looked with her little leather holdall. Like poor, lonely Paddington Bear... please look after this bear.

*

At home, the kitchen was in its usual permanent state of disarray. Breakfast pots were piled in the sink because the dishwasher was full of clean dishes waiting to be emptied, but no one could ever be bothered to do it. Pete claimed he didn't know where half the stuff was kept, Jess hardly ever set foot in the kitchen, and Ellie bless her, although willing, took about three weeks to complete a task.

It was cold, because Pete had altered the central heating clock on his mission to save money, and he'd still not fixed the wobbly plug to the tumble drier, probably another cunning ploy. She'd just filled the kettle when Maggie heard the front door slam and Pete shuffled in with his briefcase.

'There you are!'

'Here I am.'

'Pete, where have you been?'

'You know where I've been, Maggie.'

'When I rang the office, no one knew where you were.'

He was exasperated and tetchy, told her that there were new staff, all the offices had been moved round and the internal phone system was mixed up. 'Well, what did you want?'

'I've sorted it now.'

'So what's all the bloody fuss about?'

She rolled her eyes at him, puzzled by his touchiness; he was normally so easy going. Maybe at fifty-one he was having a male menopause. He looked unusually tired as well, so she didn't mention the heating or the plug and concentrated on hunting through the fridge and the cupboards but nothing resembling a balanced meal leapt out.

'What's for dinner?' Pete said, going through the post and throwing bills into an unopened heap, one of which was from Quayside Travel. Hopefully it was the confirmation for their holiday to Florida in February half-term.

'Where's my slippers, Maggie?'

'I'm going to the supermarket,' she said, snatching up her car keys. 'Keep an eye on Ellie and her friend, they're upstairs. I've no idea where Jess is. And yes thank you for asking but my sister is fine.'

Twenty minutes later Maggie trudged through the store, deflating further when she caught sight of her reflection on a metallic promotional poster for a holiday. For a moment, Maggie Thomas was superimposed on a Maldives beach, still wearing a baggy old fleece and slippers, and pushing a wire trolley through the sand. It had a ballooning effect like one of those mirrors from the fun house. The only passable aspect was her hair, still a rich conker brown in a glossy curtain to her jaw line, enhanced by quite a lot of conker brown hair colorant, but still.

It would be nice just for once, to have Laura's reflection, or even just Laura's weekly shop, which amounted to a selection of expensive goodies. Simon and Laura ate out a lot, and Simon thought nothing of shopping for food and throwing a meal together. As far as Pete was concerned the man went to work, and the woman did everything else. It didn't normally bother her, Maggie was more than happy to be a full-time mother; she just didn't want to be Pete's mother.

Carla found her by the freezers. 'Love the slippers.'

'Well, actually, I think they make a bold statement.'

Maggie looked pointedly at Carla's basket of organic salads. She'd obviously been riding but still managed to look as if she'd come from a photo shoot for Vogue, in white jodhpurs, long, black leather boots and an expensive-looking padded jacket. Her blonde hair was twisted up into a complicated bun with attractive tendrils escaping around her face. She wore rather too much make-up, but she didn't look forty-five.

Maybe it was her nicely balanced life. Carla worked for a yacht company, had a smart house on the marina and a variety of men friends she could call on. They were graded according to specific use, such as an intellectual companion for theatre and trips to London, a rich catamaran owner for Mediterranean holidays, and so on. Maggie had asked her once if she was serious about James.

'Serious? Good God, no, I don't want to wash his bloody socks. I only want sex and the odd dinner. I think he'd fill my rustic slot very nicely.'

Maggie's life with Pete had somehow evolved to be the opposite of that.

'I've just been talking to your daughter, the dark Welsh beauty, Jess, isn't it?' Carla said, choosing a tiny tub of honey ice cream.

'Oh, where?'

'On the yard. Got herself a weekend job.'

'Has she now. Who gave her that? James?'

'I think so. Although I heard Liz say she had to get rid of the false nails, all the jewellery and wear a better bra. *Honestly.*'

'I've been trying to do that for years,' Maggie said cheerily, secretly seething. Jess was a little madam. She'd had unsuitable crushes before, and an element of jealousy had crept in where Ellie was concerned. Maggie would be furious if she spoilt her sister's little world.

'Actually, James is over there, by the organic meat. You can ask him to fill you in.'

Maggie pushed Carla's arm and laughed, a tad hysterically. She wondered if James would think she was demented if she pre-warned him of her daughter's fascination with the older man, but then she reasoned that Carla was a very attractive woman, and she'd been chasing James for years with no strings, but with no progress whatsoever.

He was by the cereals. Maggie tried to weigh him up from a different perspective. He was rustic certainly, a bit dark and sinuous, in his usual ensemble of muddy jeans with frayed hems trailing on the floor, a sweater with a lot of holes in it and the sleeves pushed up. He had a massive horse-sized bite on his forearm, which was turning purple.

'That looks nasty,' Maggie said.

'What? Oh yeah. My fault,' he said, and gave her a rare smile.

Okay, he was quite attractive. But he needed a bit of spit and polish.

Like Pete needed a bit of dark and sinuous. What the hell was the matter with Pete? James was only eight years younger, Pete shouldn't look that dilapidated surely? He used to look after himself, play a bit of squash. She pushed the trolley onwards, only to be faced with the tedious prospect of talking to her next-door neighbour, Linda. Maggie quickly ducked down behind the freezers.

Why was Linda always so glamorous? Was it normal to weed the garden in kitten heels and full make-up? She seemed to revel in catching Maggie at her very worst and she was a terrible show-off, to the point where her conversation was exhausting because it was so competitive. She spotted Ellie in her riding outfit once and fell over herself to tell Maggie that her daughter had a first in dressage. Well bully for her.

When Linda went to the cheese counter, Maggie followed James to the checkout and had a good look in his trolley. There were a lot of vegetables, none of the ready-prepared variety, six bottles of Italian red wine, some stilton and a huge tub of gravy-coated dog biscuits. He listened politely when the assistant asked if he wanted help with his packing, did he have a store loyalty card and did he want the vouchers for school computers? James said no to the first two, gave Maggie the vouchers and paid with a roll of dirty notes. She was heartened to see he still wore a wedding ring.

Maggie was in the middle of piling her shopping onto the belt when Linda shouted, 'I thought it was you! I said to Carla, isn't that Maggie Thomas hiding behind the frozen turkeys?'

'Dropped my purse! How are you?'

'Only two weeks to New York now! I've been picking up a few outfits in Chester, you know a bit of bling for the evening, and I saw Pete. Did I tell you we're going to New York?'

'Yes, Linda, you did.' Maggie stuffed toilet rolls, window cleaner and Pete's foot spray into bags with the super-value mince and twenty crazy cool yoghurt pots with feet and faces. Why did her shopping look so cheap and nasty, and yet it managed to cost more than the average mortgage?

'So, er… where did you see Pete? Was he shopping for

bling as well?'

'Oh, no, he was having a boozy lunch at Ronaldinho's with that woman who used to work in accounting,' she said, glancing down at Maggie's slippers.

'Oh, council business,' Maggie said, quickly pushing a big box of tampons and a bumper pack of baked beans back into the trolley. She paid for it all on her credit card, and made her escape.

In the car park, Carla was chatting to James as he leant against his filthy Land Rover, his arms folded with negative body language. By the time Maggie had loaded all her bags into the car and returned the trolley, Carla was getting into her sporty BMW. James gave Carla a lazy, enigmatic sort of smile, before heading into the petrol station. There was a big grey dog hanging out of the back of the Land Rover, wearing a striped jumper.

At home, Pete had fallen asleep, and Jess was doing something complicated to her hair with dye and strips of foil. 'I'm starving!' she said, shouting from half way down the stairs, 'Did you get any tofu?'

'No,' Maggie said, and dumped assorted bags of McDonald's on the kitchen table. There was no way she was cooking three different meals, especially since Pete had secretly eaten out, Ellie had school dinners and Jess, well Jess was old enough to get her own fads ready.

'What's this I hear about you working on the Morgan-Jones' yard?' she said to Jess.

'Dad said I couldn't have a car for my birthday until I had a job,' she said, 'So I got a job, what's the problem *now*?'

'Dinner everyone!' Maggie yelled. She felt like yelling all kinds of things but restrained herself. Ellie and her friend were devastated that Maggie had forgotten the little pots of sauce. Jess pulled a face, 'You do know that the chicken is like, boiled brains or something, then they reform it and bleach it to make it look nice?'

'Like you're doing to your hair?'

'There you are!' Pete said.

'Yes, here I am,' Maggie replied, busily stacking tins into the cupboard, chilled stuff into the fridge. Pete stood in her way, looking hopefully in the cold oven.

'I thought you said dinner was out?'

'It is,' she said, carefully watching his face, 'It's in that bag.'

*

Sunday turned out to be not the run-of-the-mill day it usually was. Laura and Simon came over early because Simon wanted to look at the cottages again, and Laura wanted to take some measurements in Maggie's hall and show her some floor tiles and wallpaper. The makeover on the hall was her birthday present. It was originally going to be the kitchen, but when Pete had seen the estimates for all the maple wood units and the Italian tiles, he'd put his foot down.

Sunday lunch already in the oven, Maggie was on her hands and knees looking for the big coffee pot. Pete, still in his dressing gown, was talking football with Simon in the sitting room and Laura was trying to find the matching cups. Her sister looked very stylish in her Victoria Beckham denims, and a gorgeous, chunky pink sweater with a matching hat

'I told you he'd be all right about it,' Maggie said, her head in the cupboard.

When Laura made no reply, Maggie had a sudden horrible sixth sense and twisted round to look up at her. 'Oh, my God! *You haven't told him have you?*'

'Er... no.'

'*Laura!*'

'I know, I know.'

'But hasn't he noticed you're still sick and pregnant?'

'Not really. He's been busy.'

'The longer you leave it the less he's going to understand,' Maggie hissed.

'I'll tell him tonight. Pete won't say anything, will he?'

'Huh, only if he's awake long enough to remember who you are.'

'Oh, problem?'

'Not as big as yours.'

Maggie drove everyone over to the stables, except Pete who didn't want to stand around in the cold. It was a bleak day at the end of January and there was a thick mist suspended over the pools of water, which had formed in the fields. When Laura was little, Maggie would tell her the haze was dragon's breath and Laura used to shiver at the thought for years after.

She was about to remind her but when Maggie saw her sister's downcast face, thought better of it. Simon was especially attentive, obviously imagining Laura had been through an unpleasant ordeal the previous Wednesday, and kept his arm firmly around her. Once at the stables though, he was bored in about five minutes and looked around for Liz.

'I'm not talking to that brother of hers if I can help it,' he said, rubbing his hands and stamping his feet. 'He kept me waiting over an hour the last time.'

Laura and Maggie followed Ellie to look at the horses and see if they could find Jess. At the rear of the main stable block there was a section of looseboxes with No Entry signs and grills across all the doors. Ellie said they were all the unhappy horses. In a small grass paddock two men were watching James struggle to hold on to a black thoroughbred mare. It looked highly-strung, pulling James across the ground at every opportunity, and when he went to touch its head it half reared, showing the white of its eye. Carefully, he unbuckled the purple monogrammed rug and slid it from the mare as it skittered around. When he removed the head-collar, its muscular body was charged with fear, and it galloped and cavorted around the small space, until its flanks heaved with exertion and ran with sweat.

The two men ran for cover, skewering over the fence, but James stood watching the mare, shielding his eyes against a flash of winter sun.

After a moment Laura said, 'Why is it so scared?'

'I don't know. It could be something really tiny. Sometimes the most frightening things are irrational in truth, aren't they? Remember the dragon's breath?'

James caught sight of them and shouted across, 'I'm late, am I?'

'Not really. Is it a racehorse?' Maggie said.

'Steeplechaser.'

'What's the matter with it?'

'Don't know yet. Have I got time for breakfast?'

'Sure.'

They found Jess and Lucy in the tack room, where it transpired there was some kind of drama. A crowd of mostly teenage girls, some younger, were listening with their heads close to the wall, claiming they could hear cheeping and scratching from behind the old boarded up chimney.

'What in heaven's name is going on?' Liz said in a loud voice, hands on hips. 'Why is half the pony club and all the staff in here?'

'There's a bird trapped in there,' some of the small ones wailed.

'I'll get James, he'll know what to do,' said Lucy.

Liz put her hand up, 'James has got Ellie now; he's already running late because of Lord Brixton-Smith. If the bird flew in, it will fly out again.'

The pony club was up in arms. 'It might be injured. You can't just leave it in there to *die!*'

'I'm sorry about this, Maggie, nothing seems to happen

on time.'

'Oh, it's alright. I've got pot roast today.'

Jess cast a snigger at Lucy, 'How freaking sad is my mother?'

James materialised with a bacon sandwich, dragged along by four children in various states of distress, one of them bringing up the rear with a huge toolbox. The problem was explained in a noisy, excited rush. James listened to the garbled explanation for a moment, then lay on the floor and tried to reach through a slight gap in the boards.

Jess was meant to be directing the torchlight for him, but found more amusement in running the beam across sections of his horizontal torso, until Lucy was convulsed with laughter, snorting and holding her nose. Maggie snatched the torch, and shoved it down the opening. Failing to reach the bird anyway, James began to rip off the front of the chimney with a claw hammer. Liz was fuming. 'How long is *this* going to take?'

'Not long.'

It took quite a while. The bird was a whinchat, according to James. Once they'd all had a good look at it, Liz clapped her hands. '*Right*, drama over. Lucy, you are in charge of the pony club, and Jess you can get Peaches ready. James you're running *very late*.'

His response was to take hold of Ellie's hand, the tiny bird in the other. 'Come on, we'll wash off the soot in the kitchen sink and put him by the Aga, see if he cheers up.'

Liz rolled her eyes at Maggie and threw her hands up, but Maggie wasn't worried. It was immensely gratifying to see her little girl so absorbed, the subject was irrelevant. Simon looked round the door and tried to persuade Laura to accompany him and Liz over to the cottages but she wouldn't budge. 'I'm too cold, you go.'

Once Peaches made an appearance in the menage, Maggie linked arms with her sister, and they watched Ellie for a while. Laura seemed morose, introspective.

'Man of few words, isn't he?' Maggie said, trying to draw her out.

Laura shrugged, 'Sometimes you don't need very many.'

When Ellie began to tire with instruction, James shouted across to Jess to tack up O'Malley. She brought out a big restless, chestnut hunter with the martingale fitted inside out. Jess made James show her exactly what was wrong but with no real interest, just a lascivious expression.

'Look at her! Flirty madam,' Maggie said.

James eventually mounted O'Malley, with Peaches alongside on a lead rope. They both went slowly up the lane, Ellie's little pony jogging to keep up with the long swinging walk of the horse. Maggie watched until they lost sight of Peaches' white tail, and until the sounds of their iron-shod feet were lost to the mountain. There was weak sunlight filtering through the mist, setting alight the damp woods, and Maggie knew how magical it would be. Out of the blue, she felt a sudden rush of nostalgia for her youth, when it would have been herself on that horse.

She told Laura, and was taken aback by her enthusiasm.

'So, why don't you ride again?'

'Pete would have a coronary, that's why, especially with this holiday coming up and Jess's eighteenth. Anyway, I'm too old and fat.'

'Same old excuses.'

Back at home, Maggie rushed round checking the pot roast, pulling the dessert out of the fridge and opening some wine, becoming steadily more annoyed that Pete was reading the papers, as if nothing was happening. At least he'd got dressed, although she was dismayed to see that he'd pulled on a pair of tracksuit bottoms and a baggy top. He'd not bothered to shave and he was wearing a pair of Homer Simpson novelty socks. On a fifty-one-year old man carrying too much weight, the whole thing was faintly repulsive.

Maybe Carla was right, Maggie thought gloomily and put the plates in to warm.

'I only want to wash his socks,' she said to herself, in a fake Carla voice, and poured herself a big glass of wine. 'I don't want sex, or the odd dinner.'

'Want a hand, Maggie?' Simon said, 'Does Laura seem alright to you? I'm thinking of taking her on holiday, somewhere warm.'

Maggie shoved the condiment set at him. 'A holiday, lovely!'

At the table, Simon talked non-stop about the Morgan-Jones' job, about how he was pushing for the barn conversion. After a short while, even Laura was beginning to look bored with it all and was more interested in Ellie when she began to talk about Peaches, and the ride through the woods. Slowly, Ellie got to the story about the whinchat and how it had been flying around the farmhouse kitchen on their return, and eventually out through the window and up into the sky. She made all the movements with her arms and hands, wanting to share it all. Maggie beamed at her little girl, and glanced at Pete. When he made a small acknowledgement back, something sentimental caught in her throat.

James had tapped into something which made sense in Ellie's world. Ellie had found something, which Maggie couldn't process for her in quite the same way. It was all about patience, detail and feeling. All criteria, which Maggie knew she was very good at trampling over in her effort to see an end result. James had said to her it wasn't so much the destination, it was the journey, which was important. Laura used to try and tell her as much but Maggie always perceived any kind of sensitivity as a weakness. Lately though, the more she learnt about Ellie, the more she changed her mind.

She looked at her sister across the table and felt a stab of regret now for all the years they'd wasted being at odds with each other. Laura had hardly touched her lunch, and neither had Pete, which was highly unusual. When she looked more closely, he was pale and sweaty and his breathing looked tight.

'Pete, what's the matter?' she said quietly.

'Nothing. Indigestion,' he said, thumping his chest, but his face was suddenly contorted with pain. Laura went to get him a glass of water, but Simon looked concerned and pulled Maggie out of earshot of Ellie.

'I think you should maybe call an ambulance,' he said.

Maggie felt her legs go to jelly, 'Why?' she said, knowing the answer.

CHAPTER FOUR

Laura

They were both subdued on the journey home. Simon was lost in thought, but Laura knew he was thinking about work, and not about Pete and Maggie.

'It was a shock. Pete's heart attack.'

'Not really,' Simon said smoothly. 'He has the most appalling diet, he's pretty overweight and takes no exercise.' He overtook several cars, then after a moment, sighed and picked up her hand. 'I'm sorry, that sounded churlish. I'm sure he'll be fine. He was almost recovered by the time he was sat in the ambulance. But he will have to take it as a serious warning.'

The remainder of the journey passed in silence.

At home, the apartment was littered with the plans Simon had been working on for the Morgan-Jones' job. Although it certainly wasn't in the bag, it seemed likely they were going to get the go ahead in two stages, with the barn as a secondary consideration later in the year. Next week, she would need to research her designs for the cottage interiors. Simon busied himself with making tea and running her a bath. He'd been such a sweetheart since last Wednesday, and Laura had been feeling the burden of guilt and doubt lie heavier with each day.

Until today. When James had been lying on the cold

stones with his arm down the back of the fireplace, all the time he was struggling to locate the tiny trapped bird, Laura had felt over-full with emotion, willing him to find it. When he was ripping off the wood, she must have been holding her breath because when the bird finally lay still in his hands, she suddenly exhaled and wanted to kneel on the floor with him and all the overjoyed children.

For a few seconds, just before she turned away to wipe her eyes, Laura knew that James was watching her. If she'd had any doubts about her pregnancy, they'd welled up into a cloud of vapour and vanished. Somehow, her feelings had crystallised there, caught up in the whinchat's fragile fight between life and death.

Laura knew she'd made the right decision for herself. All she had to do now was convince Simon. After her bath, she wrapped herself in her white robe and perched on the sofa. Simon was listening to the messages left on the landline telephone. There was a short speech from Maggie saying that everything was alright and not to worry, a reminder from Pam about a birthday dinner, a fortnight Friday.

There followed a much longer message from Alice, something about Simon having the children the following weekend because she was going to Barcelona. The children had prepared a list of what they wanted to do; the usual shopping, cinema, McDonald's. The recording ended with a ridiculous cacophony of kissing noises and shouts of 'love yous' from all three of them.

'Damn the woman!' Simon exploded, almost breaking the machine in his haste to delete it all. 'Has she *no* comprehension of what separated, pending divorce *means*? She's promised the children before she's even spoken to me! If I say *no* guess who's the baddie here?'

Laura said, 'Simon, I need to speak to you.' She knew it wasn't the best timing, but if she didn't get it out, she'd keep putting it off until he guessed, or she was buying school uniform.

'I need to speak to you too,' he said, re-setting the machine. He sat next to her, suddenly contrite. 'I think I should go ahead with the vasectomy. I don't want you; well, I don't want us, going through this again. I should have done it years ago.'

'But we haven't talked it through!'

A beat passed. 'I thought we had?' He held her at arms' length, puzzled by her downcast expression. 'Laura…?'

'I'm… still pregnant.'

'What?' Simon searched her eyes and an eternity seemed to pass, 'What do you mean?'

'I mean I didn't have the abortion.'

He jumped to his feet, then crossed to the window and chewed on a nail. After a moment, he turned to face her. 'So… you let me believe for five days that you had gone through with a termination? But we agreed!'

'I know. Simon, please sit down.' She waited till he was seated again, but he wouldn't look her in the eye, and he fidgeted with his legs and drummed his fingers.

Laura said, 'I'm sorry, I should have told you.'

'That's a bit of an understatement.'

'I… I changed my mind.'

'Am I allowed to know why?'

Laura wasn't sure how to explain it all, she wasn't even sure she had a concise answer ready. It was all mixed up with her biological clockwork, the children at the yard and the trapped bird, Jess and Ellie. She wanted to know what it felt like, to have that extra layer of love in her life. She just wanted to be a mother, no other long-worded explanations necessary, surely?

'I just want to be a mum,' she said, 'I let my heart make the decision.'

To her immense relief when she leant in towards him, Simon caught hold of her and they sat for a long while just staring through the window.

Later, Laura spent an equal measure of time getting ready for bed, choosing the coffee-coloured silk slip Simon had bought for her birthday the previous year. She teamed it with pale silk stockings, an obvious prelude to sex. On one level, it seemed like a cheap trick, but she longed for intimacy, longed for his reassurance. She watched Simon undress and shower, then slide into bed next to her. He was quiet, and although it was tender, their lovemaking was reserved. Something had changed, and it scared her a little, but Simon said it was because of her delicate condition, and his choice of words made her laugh, because it sounded quaint and Victorian.

'We can make this work, can't we?' she said, lying in his arms afterwards.

'If it's what you really want,' he said, first kissing her forehead, then holding her face in his hands. 'But it might take me a little while to get used to the idea again. Is that alright?'

It was more than alright. It made her feel warm and fuzzy inside, although it was less romantic when a couple of days later, she made her way to the local surgery and dutifully produced her urine sample in a clean peanut butter jar.

'From what you've already told me, I probably don't need to do this,' Doctor Wilson said, and carried out the same sort of test Laura had done with the kit from the chemist.

The doctor read her extensive medical history concerning all things female.

'Goodness, you've had a tough time.'

'Yes, long time ago.'

Doctor Wilson was female, young and sympathetic, and just what Laura needed. She took her blood pressure, palpated her stomach gently, listened to her moans about morning sickness and asked a lot of questions concerning the dates of her erratic menstrual cycle, the bane of Laura's life.

There was an anxious wait while Doctor Wilson checked the little tubes of chemicals she'd mixed with the urine sample, followed by a smile.

'Yep, you're definitely pregnant, congratulations.'

'Thank you,' Laura said, expecting to feel elated but instead she felt slightly cheated because Simon wasn't sharing the experience with her. The doctor tapped a pen against her teeth.

'Can I ask, was the baby planned?'

'No,' she said, 'but it's okay I'm pleased about it.'

'And the father?'

'It's fine, really.'

Doctor Wilson typed away at her keyboard, no doubt adding substantially to her medical notes, after which she handed Laura a selection of leaflets about early pregnancy, and worked out her due date from a little calendar wheel.

'Well, if we're right in thinking you're five or six weeks now, that makes you due around the last week of September. We can be more precise when you've had a scan.'

The last week of September was close to her own birthday.

She told Simon about her due date over a dinner of pan-fried trout, new potatoes and watercress salad. He listened patiently to everything she had to say about calendar wheels and scans and although he smiled benevolently at her, Laura knew he wasn't especially interested. But she couldn't expect him to be. He'd already experienced the whole package twice before, with Alice.

*

On Thursday evening, Alice rang with various timings and instructions regarding the impending weekend and to warn Simon that Cameron had a mild bout of German measles.

Laura saw Simon pale slightly, but Alice was resolute and had no intention of altering her plans, primarily because Cameron would likely be over it by the weekend, and anyway, she had lost *count* of the number of times she had sat up all night with the children, and it was her turn for a holiday without them. 'Come on Simon, it's a *measly* two days,' she said, and honked with laughter.

Laura, listening with her head next to the phone, was panicked. 'Simon, you can't bring him here, I *can't* get German measles,' she hissed, 'it's dangerous.'

He pinched the bridge of his nose, and closed his eyes for a moment. 'No, no, course not. What do you suggest?'

'You'll have to stay at Cherry Grove,' she said, unable to think of a better solution.

The ex-marital home, the home Simon paid for, but no longer lived in. Alice was over the moon with the idea and pounced on an opportunity to utilise Simon's DIY skills. Laura left him irritably scribbling down a list of jobs.

'*Yes,* I've got the central heating clock, and the radiators need bleeding. And you want an aerial extension in Tara's room... what else? Spot of decorating? Alice... *I was joking!*'

Simon ended the call with a scowl and ran a hand through his hair, 'Well, that's all turned into a bloody shambles, hasn't it? Will you be alright?'

'Fine. I'll probably just work, there's plenty to do.'

'I think I'd rather work as well,' he said, but then he caught hold of her. 'Don't do too much, you need to rest as well, you know.'

She basked in his concern, but Simon grew steadily more morose as the weekend approached. On Friday, he was absent from the office most of the day, and on the occasions she'd needed to speak with him, he'd been pensive.

His father, Bill called in, looking for Simon and a cup of tea.

'He's not in? So why is he not picking up his calls? I need

to have a look at those cottages in Rowen.'

Laura concentrated on the online bookstore. She ordered two books about pregnancy and one about soft furnishing for the nursery.

'He could be at Tools R Us, or the chemist,'

But the joke was lost on Bill, plus he was slightly deaf, and responded with 'Come to think of it, he was offhand with me last night. Have you had a barney, is that it?'

'No, he's just a bit fed up.'

Laura made him a cup of tea, and Bill sat on one of the expensive leather chairs, something he wasn't normally allowed to do in his overalls. Laura told him about the baby.

'Well, I'm pleased for you, love,' he said, mildly surprised and grasped her hand. Bill got to his feet then, groaning and rubbing his back. 'I'm ashamed of his bloody behaviour though, all moody like. He was like this with his second.'

Laura frowned, 'With Cameron?'

He stood up straight and grimaced, 'Hammering? No, plastering, that's what it is.'

When he'd gone, Laura rang the yard to arrange another inspection, and to meet Liz for lunch.

Liz said, 'Just get the keys from James, will you?'

'Is James okay with everything? I mean I don't want to press on with it if he's not prepared to sign a contract of works.'

'Don't worry about James. We had a proper talk at last,' she said, and sighed. 'He hasn't been sleeping, that's the latest problem. Yesterday, he was discovered comatose in the car park at KFC for three hours. The staff thought he was dead.'

'But... he was just asleep?'

'The police were called because his head was hanging out the window, he had the humane shotgun on the passenger seat and the dogs were howling, classic FM on the radio. Not quite Midsomer Murders, but you get the picture.'

'I'm not sure if that's funny or not, but I can't help laughing.'

'Oh, I know, the police saw the funny side, *eventually*. Made a big fuss about checking his firearms certificate to save face.'

'James has got a gun licence?'

'Mostly for slaughter,' she said dismissively, 'so if he's asleep on Saturday, throw a bucket of cold water over him, with love from me.'

*

Simon got up in the early hours of Saturday morning, as instructed, to get to Cherry Grove, leaving Laura to wake up slowly with her ginger tea and croissants. She set off for Rowen with the windscreen wipers on full. James wouldn't need a bucket of cold water. It was cold and wet, teeming with rain, and the sky didn't get properly light till after ten.

There was no one around at the stables, well no one she knew. When Laura knocked on the farmhouse door, the only response was from two dogs. After a few minutes of peering through the grubby windows, Laura wandered across the yard and found herself at the back paddock.

He was there, with the black mare. But something made her hang back and watch. James had the horse, side on against the fence, and for an age he just ran his hands over its body. It looked as though it was barely tolerating his touch in the way it tossed its head high out of his reach and flattened its ears.

The mare had a padded leather strap around its girth, but nothing else. Presently James took hold of this and pulled himself up, leaning his weight across the mare's back. At first it lunged forwards with frightening speed and everything about its body language said it looked ready to bolt, but after a few seconds, the mare slowed and for a moment it was as if it recognised something safe. The instant the horse relaxed and dropped its head, James slid back to the ground, and the mare trotted away as if surprised, then stopped dead and turned to look at him.

The scene was absorbing, even to Laura's untrained eye, and she was loathe to call out and break the spell. But James knew she was there, and presently, he walked across to her.

'I'm impressed,' Laura said.

'Why? It's been ridden before.'

'It looked so wild last week.'

'Not wild, just scared.'

'What of?'

'Life, I guess,' he said, and turned to look at the mare cantering around the perimeter of her enclosure minus her expensive, monogrammed rug and plastered in mud. 'At the moment, she doesn't know whether to run, or to hide.'

'I can empathise with that. So, how long before she's confident again?'

'Could be six days, could be six months. Unfortunately for Lord Brixton-Smith, it's probably the latter,' he said, and climbed over the fence. They walked back to the house, Laura struggling to hold on to her little checked umbrella. James hunted through the drawers in the office and slid some keys across the desk.

'You may as well keep a set,' he said, rubbing his wet hair with a towel.

At the cottages, Bill was waiting for her in his truck with Simon's notes. Mefysen was the more dilapidated but Laura opened the door with a rise of anticipation. Bill was only interested in assessing the building work and that was extensive enough with a huge amount of plastering, a full roof retile and some brick re-pointing. Laura was looking forward to dreaming up an interior to reflect its Welsh roots. She concentrated on the major modifications, mostly concerning the bathroom and kitchen.

'Would it be okay to take this wall out?' They were in the old pantry and she wanted to create more space in the kitchen.

'No, it shouldn't fall out,' Bill said, 'Look love, this business with Alice and the kids.'

'What business is that?'

'Australia. It's bloody daft.'

'That's what I said.'

'All I've said is, I would be willing to say in court that I'd be unhappy about my grandchildren being taken to Australia, for anything more than a holiday.'

Laura dropped her end of the tape measure. 'That's understandable,' she said carefully. 'Simon's discussed this with you?'

'Only to suss me out if he chose to oppose her.'

'I see,' Laura said.

'And I'll tell him he should be more supportive of you, now you're starting a family. It's no good him being in a bloody mood.'

'No.'

Bill drove home after an hour, but Laura stayed. In the larger cottage, she had intended to make a few sketches of how the finished look would be, but it was so cold and damp that she lost the enthusiasm. She kept thinking about Bill's words. Laura had started the day full of love and hope, and now Alice had disturbed the foundations again, niggling away at her peace of mind.

Crossing to the window, Laura tried to think about blinds and curtains and bring herself back to the job in hand, but found herself staring at the Arab horses and drawing them instead. They were standing quite still under a belt of skeletal-looking trees with their rumps to the wind.

When James appeared she was startled because she hadn't seen or heard any vehicle.

'Still here?' he said, prowling around the cottage, looking at the pencil marks Bill had made on the wall, and kicking at the loose plaster on the floor.

'I've finished for now,' Laura said, and collected her papers together, anxious to go in case he picked a fight over something. There was something menacing about him, and yet she knew he must have bucket loads of compassion and endless patience to do the job he did with the broken horses. Pity he never showed any beyond the schooling menage.

'Is this what I'm paying you for?' he said, finding her sketch of the Arab mares.

'No, there's no charge for the art.'

To her surprise, he rolled it up neatly and kept hold of it, then tapped it against his hand. 'I owe you an apology. I'm sorry, I haven't talked to you about the renovations.'

'Oh. It's only early days,' she said, but looked pointedly at the partly finished kitchen. 'Actually, now that you are here...' she started, 'how would you feel if I was to go with your original plan? I mean, I think I can match it and it would be a waste to rip it out.'

'No, go ahead. I'm not *that* disturbed.'

She smiled, added to her notes.

He said, 'How's the morning sickness at night?'

Laura snapped her eyes back on to his. She'd completely forgotten he knew about her pregnancy. 'Oh, it comes and goes. The ginger tea is remarkably good though,' she added. 'Liz said you were having trouble sleeping, at night.'

'I think the whole of North Wales knows that now. I'm on YouTube, apparently.'

Laura wasn't sure whether to take him seriously. 'YouTube...! Really?'

'Yeah. It's called... man asleep in car park.'

'I can recommend chamomile tea.'

'Chamomile?' James narrowed his eyes. 'That's the one that smells like dog's feet, or damp grass in high summer.

Somehow, I don't think a herbal infusion is much of an antidote for the black hole of depression. It swallows everything whole. Chamomile flowers would have no chance.'

'No, I'm sure you're right,' she said, gathering up her belongings.

James looked through her with that penetrating stare of his, as if by being there and drawing the horses, she was intruding on his innermost privacy. His pain seemed tangible, she could feel it emanate from him in that room.

Laura left soon after, unable to concentrate. The image of him sitting on the floor with his back against the crumbling wall, just staring at the ceiling, haunted her short journey to Hafod House, and she kept going over his sad, funny exchange of words. Laura even had to stop the car to wipe her eyes, not knowing where the sudden tears had come from, or whom they were for.

Maggie's house was a direct contrast in that it was noisy and chaotic, something Laura was grateful for. She dropped her overnight bag in the hall and hugged her sister.

Pete had been discharged a couple of days previously. The hospital had confirmed he had dangerously high cholesterol. He was on a strict diet with no saturated fat, a prescription of statins and instructions to both relax and take mild exercise.

'I nearly killed him with happy meals, didn't I?' Maggie said.

'No, don't be silly,' Laura said, and followed her sister through to the kitchen, where she began to feverishly chop salad. 'He's got to have this with tuna fish. He won't like it.'

'Think how slim he'll get.'

In the sitting room, Pete was lying across the sofa wearing an airline eye mask and listening to Sounds of the Sea, featuring the Mammals of the Pacific. The room was filled with those strange squeaky noises dolphins make when they communicate with each other, with lapping water and gulls in the background. The effect wasn't quite there, drowned by the heavy metal emanating from his daughter's bedroom.

Jess materialised when Laura was unpacking her bag in the guest room. She looked different, the heavy black eyeliner and the purple lipstick had gone. Minus the gothic mantle, Jess was naturally striking with very dark hair and brilliant blue eyes, like her grandmother.

'Can I come in?' she said.

'Course. All ready for your party?'

'Almost,' Jess said, inspecting Laura's La Perla underwear. 'You are coming, aren't you?'

'So long as I'm not going to cramp your style.'

'Oh, there won't be any style, it's only in The Farmer's Arms,' she said, then crossed to the dressing table, and began fluffing up her hair and trying Laura's lipstick. 'I fancy a change of image, more sophisticated,' she said, pulling a pout.

'Tell you what, how about a shopping spree, my treat. Not every day you hit eighteen.'

Jess spun round and her eyes lit up. 'In Chester?'

'If you like, come up on the train. We can come back over in time for your party.'

'*Awesome.* Any chance you can like, do my hair and make-up?'

'Are you trying to impress someone?'

'Not really,' she shrugged, not giving anything away, her face boldly impassive. 'Can I borrow that lace bra? We're the same size.'

*

After dinner of steamed fish and vegetables, Laura mentioned the conversation to Maggie, and there was a mixed response.

'I can't say I'm sorry to see the end of the Goth phase, but I know Jess, she's up to something.'

'Maybe she'll let something slip to me next week,' Laura said, drying the dishes. 'I'll let you know if it's anything to worry about.'

'Oh, don't you worry, it will be.'

Later, Laura rang the landline phone at Cherry Grove, and had the shock of her life when Alice answered. 'Oh, hi Laura! Do you want to speak to Si?'

'Well yes,' she said, stunned.

There was a muffled moment as the phone exchanged hands, and the sound of a door clunking shut. Simon said, 'Laura? I've had the day from hell,' he said quietly. 'Her damn flight has been delayed, can you believe?'

'No, not really.'

'What's that supposed to mean?'

Laura sighed, 'Nothing. How's Cameron?'

'Whinging, mostly.'

'I know how he feels. Simon, why have you discussed Alice with Bill? I thought we were calling her bluff over this Australia idea?'

A beat passed. 'All right. Laura, don't take this the wrong way but you know you said you were following your heart over the baby? Well, I'm following my heart over the children.'

'I see. The cost of a court case is not something we want to get into though, surely?'

'It's not about the cost, it's about losing my kids!'

'I know, I know, I'm sorry.'

He made an exasperated noise. 'Let's keep calm, otherwise she's got one over on us again.'

'I'm just tired of double guessing,' she said, knowing he was right.

They talked about the cottages, Pete and Jess, the weather...

Eventually, Simon said, 'Laura, I love you, remember

you'll *never* have to double guess that.'

*

Overnight, it turned incredibly mild for the start of February. The fields were muddy and misty, and the mountains looked lifeless beneath a low sky, shot through with slashes of dull, yellow light. Over in the menage, Jess was leaping a course of complicated jumps. James was perched on the five-bar gate, cringing at her riding technique. 'Half halt!' he yelled at her, seconds before she sent a coloured pole flying to the ground.

'I don't know what you mean!' she shouted, flying past, red Wonderbra clearly visible.

'She's showing off,' Maggie said, and marched into the office with Ellie, but Laura stayed to watch with Lucy, enjoying the spring air.

'Shall I go again?' Jess shouted across to James.

'All right but you need to go much slower, more control.'

She cantered in a circle, but the horse still had the upper hand, and they set off at more or less the same speed with the horse fighting for its head at every turn. Despite James shouting instruction, Jess landed in the middle of the first fence, and because the strides were out, skewered at least a foot too high over the second. The horse put in a massive buck on landing by way of protest, and Jess flew about six feet over its head and landed on her back. She lay like stone, her shirt gaping open. Lucy's hand flew to her mouth.

'Jess? Stop fucking about and get up,' James shouted. Nothing. He jumped down off the gate, and they watched anxiously as he loosened the strap on Jess's hat and it fell off, all her hair tumbling out. She opened her eyes and sat up slowly.

'I feel really woozy,' she managed to gasp, and collapsed

against him like a rag doll, her arms firmly around his neck, her shirt gaping open. 'Help me, I can't stand up.'

He helped Jess to her feet, but she still managed to loll all over him, then started to giggle and stuck her thumbs up at Lucy behind his back. James wasn't amused and removed her arms from their stranglehold, 'You're some actress.'

He shoved her hat back at her and caught up the loose horse, which was still trotting about with the saddle lopsided and the reins trailing. 'You know you'll have to jump it again, I don't want my horse thinking he can get away with that,' he said, throwing the reins at her. Jess threw them back with equal force.

'No way. I need a breather. My bra's bust. You do it and I'll watch,' she said, and looked up at him under her false eyelashes, 'Why don't you show me... *slow* and *controlled*?'

'Behave.'

He lengthened the stirrup leathers and mounted the horse, whilst Jess and Lucy rebuilt the course, weak with laughter as they lifted all the heavy poles up to their maximum height.

'What the fuck are you doing?' James shouted, cantering a tight circle. 'It's not the fucking Olympics you know!'

They all heard Liz banging on the window. Everyone on the yard looked round except James, to see her gesticulating towards her open mouth and pointing at her brother. She was incredibly angry, on the point of actually bursting into flames, Lucy said. Laura hid her grin and walked over to the office. The first thing she saw was her sketch of the Arab horses, pinned to the notice board.

'I apologise *profusely* for the swearing,' Liz said, still puce. 'And his timekeeping again, Maggie. He should be with Ellie now,' she said, briskly flicking through the diary. 'In fact he's running so late he's double-booked with Annalise. How's he going to co-ordinate that?'

They all heard loud whooping and clapping from outside

as James cleared the fences.

Maggie hovered, wanting to go home and check on Pete, but was cross with Jess for messing up the afternoon, so Laura volunteered to stay with Ellie.

James hadn't double-booked; he wanted Ellie to share a session with Annalise. She was an ex-catwalk model, an absolutely stunning young woman in every way, until Laura realised with a shock, that she had half her right leg missing from just below the knee.

James and Ellie pushed her wheelchair to the privacy of the back paddock. Ellie quickly become engrossed in how Annalise would use a side-saddle, and communicate the same signals she used on Peaches, substituting a long whip alongside her withered right leg. And Annalise was interested in Ellie, drawing her in, telling her about the physical problems of a prosthetic limb she hadn't yet mastered.

Laura asked James if she could stay and watch. He asked his client first, then nodded in the affirmative. By the time Lucy had got Ellie onto Peaches, James had his hands full. Laura watched, as he had to practically manhandle Annalise onto the horse, and patiently went through the reins and whip routine whilst holding on to Ellie's pony, the reins looped over his arm.

Annalise looked like an eighteenth century heroine born into the wrong century. Within minutes though her beautiful face was contorted with pain. James lifted her back down and sat her back in the chair, listened to what she had to say and they removed the artificial limb, then he lifted her back on to the horse carefully, painstakingly re-positioning the leg stump.

'Can I help?' Laura said, ducking under the paddock rail.

'Yeah,' James said, and passed her the artificial leg.

By the time Laura was on the road home, she'd changed her opinion of Mr Morgan-Jones considerably. Her first impressions at Maggie's party had been all wrong. The sadness behind the eyes was the only part she'd got correct.

The rest of him was quite unexpected.

CHAPTER FIVE

Laura

Alice didn't come home till midnight on Wednesday. Simon said she was hammered, woke up the whole house by slamming the taxi door, falling over Simon's briefcase in the hall and singing some stupid Spanish pop song in the bathroom. Rather predictably, in the morning she refused to be roused from her slumber.

He was livid; three days of meetings had been cancelled because Cameron wasn't well enough for school and none of his friend's parents wanted him farmed out with them, for obvious reasons. Tara played up the situation by claiming her school had three teacher-training days.

'You're going to have to wise up Daddy Simon,' Laura said, '*Three* teacher-training days!'

'You don't know what it's like. It was easier to let it go in the end,' he said, going through the post on Thursday morning. 'Sick children and lack of sleep does something to your brain.'

'Well, you can play *Uncle* Simon instead on Saturday.'

Laura explained about the arrangements with Jess, and he groaned, caught her round the waist. 'Can we not have one weekend where it's just you and me? We should book a holiday, you choose, I don't mind.'

'Can we afford one?'

'The answer to that is has Morgan-Jones signed yet?'

'Well, I've e-mailed him the estimates, I've got a spare set of keys and I'm meeting Liz for lunch here in town for a chat about interiors, so it still looks good.'

'Right,' he said, and twisted his lip, 'try and get it tied up, will you? Could do with knowing that's in the bag.'

'What's the urgency?'

He began to tell her about some project Steve, their architect, wanted to joint finance in Spain. A complex of holiday flats in San Pedro, on the outskirts of Marbella. The majority of the money from the Morgan-Jones job could potentially be their half of the investment.

'Looks like a real money spinner,' Simon said, pulling out a brochure to show her.

Laura pulled a face, 'I dunno, buying abroad is a minefield.'

'You know me, I like a risk,' he said, grinning. 'I was thinking of going out there with Steve for a look, end of February.'

'Why don't I come? We can make a holiday of it as well?'

'A holiday? Looking at rundown flats and trying to communicate with Spanish plumbers?' he said, and kissed her firmly. 'Get Morgan-Jones to sign up and we can do a lot better than that.'

*

Alice was waiting for Laura on the office doorstep, wearing a belted raincoat and a frightening face. 'Where is he?' she demanded. 'I've tried his mobile and I've tried your home number. I know he's playing games.'

'Good morning, Alice,' Laura said, unlocking the bottom door. Alice followed her up the stairs, filling the air with her heady perfume. 'So, where is he?'

Laura opened the door to their suite, feeling distinctly queasy. All her own fault since she'd not eaten very much dinner the previous evening and couldn't force anything down for breakfast other than the ginger tea. Alice's, 'Obsession' did little to help.

'He's out. Trying to catch up with appointments.'

'Well, he's already been to see Graham Gallagher,' Alice said, brandishing a letter.

Laura switched on her computer and scanned the e-mails quickly. There was news from the estate agents saying that Clarence Road, a previous project, had completed, but they'd had to reduce down from the full asking price. It was a sign of the times.

Alice leant across the desk. 'Have you any idea what this could cost you?'

'I'm sorry, I don't know what you're prattling on about, Alice.'

'Australia! He's fully opposed to me removing the children from UK jurisdiction.'

'Yes, well, they are his children as well.'

'What?' she said scornfully. 'Simon's a fair-weather father. A fucking waste-of-space father.'

'He's always been there for the children, and for your short-notice, alcoholic trips.'

'Short notice? He knew about Barcelona for weeks!' she said, and pushed her face closer to Laura. 'I *have* to go away to get him to do his share!'

'Look, if he didn't care, he wouldn't be opposing you.'

Alice turned away at this, wrapped her arms round herself and stared at the ceiling. Suddenly, she whipped round, her eyes blazing, 'It isn't the children he's trying to stop, it's *me!*'

Laura narrowed her eyes, 'What are you saying?'

Alice leant across the desk, 'He wants me back.'

'More the other way about, judging from the amount of times you fabricate reasons to involve him in your life.'

Alice smiled pitifully, 'Is that what he tells you? Sounds like he's on a repeat.'

'Oh, just go away, Alice, I've things to do,' Laura said, then clamped a hand over her mouth and made a dash for the bathroom. It only lasted a couple of minutes. Laura rested her forehead on the cold glass of the mirror. She could hear Alice pacing about, no doubt having a good look at all the paperwork on her desk.

When she emerged, Alice grinned. 'Hangover? No, course it isn't,' she said, holding Laura's pregnancy book and the leaflets from the doctors. 'You're pregnant, aren't you?'

'So, what if I am?' Laura said, pulling her chair out. She kept her eyes on the screen and began to respond to the e-mails and enquiries. 'We're both pleased about it.'

Alice laughed but there was no mirth in it. 'It all makes sense now,' she said, one manicured finger on her lips. 'Let me guess, he's gone all tentative in the bedroom.'

'Alice, just *get out!* I'm busy.'

Barbara, their part-time assistant materialised, shot Alice a look of utter disdain, and went to fill the kettle. Subdued by the older woman's disapproving presence, Alice slid off the desk and made to go, but stopped at the door to mouth at Laura, 'You poor, poor cow.'

Laura waited till the bottom door slammed, before she snatched up her trilling phone.

Liz said breathlessly, 'I'm really sorry, Laura, I've got to cancel on you,' she said. 'Had a bit of a crisis here.'

'Oh… serious?'

'Possibly. James has had an accident. According to the girls, that black mare went up in the air, reared over backwards and crashed through the paddock fence. Just panicked, I think. The girls didn't know what to do with it, it galloped and bucked like a bronco, then leapt the five-bar gate.'

'James?'

'Blood everywhere. We had to *force* him to go to hospital... can I call you back?'

'Of course... I hope he's okay,' Laura said quietly, and stared at the phone for so long that Barbara had to ask her twice if she was alright, but there was another call waiting. It was Simon, not happy that she'd told his father about the baby, and to say he'd be late home because he was taking the children to their Tai Chi lessons, followed by a party.

Thereafter the remainder of the day was basically non-productive. Before she was pregnant, nothing distracted her from the job in hand but her head was all over the place. After she'd digested the conversation with Alice, all she could think about was the horror of being trapped under a panicking horse, its flailing hooves and crushing weight.

Later, Simon was crushed by the news.

'Blast. Think it'll hold everything up?' he said, putting naan bread to warm in the oven. 'Bloody dangerous, what he does, I hate to think what he pays for insurance,' he went on, glancing at Laura. 'Are you sure you don't want any of this Madras?'

'I couldn't eat a thing.'

'Shall I make you something different?'

'No, no thanks.'

'Have you already eaten?'

'Simon, I've had a really horrible day.'

He turned to look at her and a frown crossed his face, 'Is this because I was a bit off with you on the phone? I just thought it was a bit soon to start telling people, that's all.'

'Alice came to the office.'

Simon took a few seconds to take in her expression. '*Again?*'

He slid the foil trays of food into the oven and sat opposite her at the little kitchen table while Laura went over the conversation, and Simon grew steadily angrier.

'The woman is completely delusional. I'm not having

her upset you like this,' he said, and took hold of her hands, 'Please tell me you don't believe her, do you?'

'Simon, you've told me the truth about your marriage over and over.'

'I know, but she's so convincing!'

When he learnt that Alice had guessed about her pregnancy as well, he jumped to his feet and ran a hand through his hair. 'Oh, great, that's just great, Laura.'

'I kept the books at work so the children wouldn't find them.'

His shoulders dropped then, and he pulled her gently to her feet, and caught her up in his arms. 'I'm sorry, love. It's just I wanted to tell the children in my own time. Knowing Alice, she'll use the information against me somehow.'

Laura nodded into his chest, her eyes welling.

*

Friday night was Pam's birthday celebration with the girls. The group consisted of two friends from when Laura was studying her arts and crafts degree at university. Pam Tanner, Steve the architect's partner, made up the four. Laura had deliberated whether to go, but she had cancelled on them the previous time because of the unplanned, undecided pregnancy. This time she would have to explain why she wasn't drinking, but as Simon pointed out Alice was still on speaking terms with Pam and the news would already be global.

Simon had been quiet all evening. He was up and out early, to drop the children at school because Alice had strained her back and couldn't get out of bed. Simon joked she'd probably tried to lift a crate of Chardonnay, and they'd both laughed. The news of Alice's incapacity was delivered by a dawn telephone call from a tearful Tara, who was in the school play and was desperate not to miss rehearsals.

On Simon's orders, Laura also spent the morning in bed and felt in a much more rested and optimistic state of mind by the evening, and pulled in to Gino's looking forward to catching up with the gossip, apart from one niggle at the pit of her stomach.

In the car park at the restaurant, Laura scrolled down the contact list in her mobile and stared at Liz's number for a full two minutes before she called.

'Oh, Laura!' Liz said, 'So sorry I didn't call back. Shall we rearrange that lunch?'

'Is... is James all right?'

'Oh goodness, yes. They kept him in overnight. He's got two fractured ribs, loads of bruising and a smashed wrist *again*. All strapped up, he walks like the tin man. Oh, and a bad mood, but what's new there? I asked him 'does it hurt?', and he said only when he laughs, so he won't even feel any pain.'

'Is... is that all?'

'I know! I swear he's not normal. And what's the first thing he does? Catches the mare to bathe its cuts and pull splinters out of its legs.'

'He's not riding it again, surely?'

'Not this week. He spent the rest of the day lying down, swallowing painkillers.'

They rearranged the aforementioned lunch and Laura made her way to the restaurant, desperately wishing she could have some alcohol in any shape or form. The girls were waiting for her, having already finished two bottles of wine. Laura ordered a mineral water and detected Pam's knowing smile instantly.

'Happy birthday, Pam,' Laura said, handing over her gift of a spa day. 'What have I missed?'

Pam stood up to hug Laura awkwardly across the table. 'I hear you've got more news than us,' she whispered playfully.

'Right, okay. I was going to tell you all, just not so soon.'

Trisha and Chrissie listened avidly to Laura's news, and they all reacted quite differently, eager to offer advice depending on their own experiences and very different personalities.

'So,' Pam said, after they'd all offered a mix of congratulations and raised eyebrows, 'is Simon getting used to the idea of becoming a daddy again?'

'I think so. Anyway he's got another seven months before he has to get up in the night.'

'Huh. The only thing men get up in the night is their todgers,' Trisha said.

They all laughed at her deadpan face. Trisha was the most cynical of the group, but having gone through three marriages with as many children she had a wealth of blended family relationship knowledge, and tended to be right a lot of the time. Although on this occasion, Chrissie looked at her with pursed lips, 'Give the guy a chance, can't you? I saw Simon this morning dropping Tara off at school and carrying her costume for Don Quixote. You know he even offered to play Sancho Panza's donkey?'

'I'd pay to see that,' Laura said, trying to lighten the mood but only Pam laughed.

'Simon's a lovely man, away from that hard faced ex-wife of his. Alice is always on his back,' Chrissie said, determined to make her point.

'Why shouldn't she be on his back?' Trisha went on. 'She's trying to bring up two kids while he went off and had an affair with a younger woman if you recall. Sorry, Laura but that's how Alice sees it.'

'Oh, I know, there's a price to pay for everything, and Alice doesn't do discount.'

Pam said, 'Even if Simon was hung like a donkey and Alice had to sit on him, she would still complain about his backbone.'

Chrissie ignored this and raised her glass. 'To Laura, a happy and healthy pregnancy.'

The other two women joined in, but the only one with any real conviction was bubbly, soft-hearted Chrissie.

'So, what made you change your mind about babies?' Pam said, tearing apart the garlic bread and handing it around the table. 'I thought you were a bit like me, no kids to worry about and enjoying the good life. And I thought you were going places with this business of yours?'

'She can still do her job,' Trisha said indignantly. 'She's still got a brain you know. Anyway, the support is there if she wants to do both, look how many times I've done it. Plus most of the time without a bloody man!'

'We *are* going big places with the business,' Laura said. 'I understand Steve and Simon are talking overseas?'

Pam gave her a wearisome look, 'Spain? Yes, I believe so.'

'Oh, I loved being at home with my babies,' Chrissie said, taking a big mouthful of pasta. 'I think being a working mother is *so* overrated.'

'Well, I didn't have a choice.' Trisha muttered, and the usual argument went full circle again. They were good company, but their sharp opinion was often abrasive, difficult to swallow when mineral water was the only buffer. Laura excused herself quite early, both her reasons being perfectly legitimate. She was not able to do justice to the food and drink, and in less than ten hours she had to be ready for the start of Jess's shopping and hairdressing extravaganza, followed by another birthday party.

*

On Saturday, Jess duly arrived on the early train, full of brassy bounce, and fully wired to the rest of the world with her i-Pads and i-Pods. They hit the hairdresser's first.

'I want it layering with blunt edges and then big sections, like, low lighting?' she said, to Laura's confused stylist. After that, it was the party outfit. Jess had her mother's directness in a more fun package, and she was fully aware of her sexuality, a somewhat volatile combination. Her personality manifested itself via a tight black bodice, a floating, wraparound silk skirt the same sapphire blue as her eyes, with stockings and suspenders, and stiletto ankle boots. Basically it was femme fatale meets burlesque maiden.

Over lunch, she asked Jess, who was going to the party. 'Anyone I know?'

'Not really,' she said, wrinkling her nose and eating slivers of veggie burger.

'No one special?'

She glanced at her bleeping phone, 'Oh, yeah, a couple of hotties.'

'Someone from college?'

She laughed at this, flicked her hair over her shoulder, 'No way! They're all kids. I don't think he even went to school, but we're the same star sign, how cool is that? And the other one is, like, a lecturer?'

Not much further on with Maggie's enquiries, other than one was uneducated and the other possibly in with a chance of being struck off the teacher's register, Laura decided to keep the information to herself and watched as Jess happily photographed the new-look hair, and mailed the image to all her friends. Exhausting as she was with her urban chatter, loud excited telephone conversations, all abbreviated so Laura didn't really get it, and the frantic texting, Laura was kept both amused and busy all day.

Later, at home, Laura put the finishing touches to Jess's makeup, outlining her full lips with crimson crush. She had of course made an impressive cleavage out of the corset top and fastened the skirt so that it fell open to her stockinged thigh when she sat down.

'Right, Uncle Simon,' Jess said, and twirled round slowly, 'tell me what you *think*.'

Simon wasn't quite speechless, but it took him a lot longer to reply than normal. 'Crikey,' he said lamely, and firmly held her arms down while he gave her a long distance peck on the cheek. 'Happy birthday, love!'

Jess was dismayed, 'Come *on*... you're a bloke, is it *hot?*'

For a moment, Simon looked like a rabbit caught in the headlights. 'Jess, you'll knock 'em dead!' he said, then scuttled into the kitchen to escape, giving Laura the eye to follow him.

He closed the kitchen door with an air of conspiracy, 'I hope you know what you're doing there?' he whispered.

'Jess? I know, she looks completely different.'

'Well yes! Last week she was just a kid in a baggy sack.'

'She's grown up, that's all,' Laura said, and ignored Simon when he laughed incredulously. 'Look,' she went on, 'they don't wear sweet and demure these days.'

'Jess, has never been sweet, or demure.'

'No, okay, fair point,' Laura said with a grin, and headed for the door, but Simon caught her hand, 'Laura, do you mind if I don't tag along tonight? If I go and take the kids bowling now, it means we can have all day tomorrow on our own.'

'Oh. Well, I guess so.'

*

The Farmers' Arms in Rowen, was packed full of the usual locals as well as Jess's party guests. It was a basic sort of pub with slate floors, knocked about chairs and tables, and massive open fires. There was a Happy Birthday banner above the bar and a pulsing beat competed with the noisy hum of a dozen different conversations, arguments and laughter.

There was a loud cheer when they walked in, and Jess was whisked away to some dark corner by Lucy. Laura saw Maggie waving furiously from a table near the bar, and squeezed her way towards it.

'Pete's playing darts in the back room and Ellie's at her friend's,' Maggie said, pushing a solitary orange juice across the table, 'so I hope you're going to keep me company. No Simon?'

'No,' Laura said, almost downing her drink. 'White wine?'

'Yes, please. Where's Jess? She's not even said hello.'

'Oh, she's with Lucy,' Laura said, wishing for the second night in a row she could have a glass of wine as well. To her surprise, James was leaning awkwardly on the bar with an almost finished pint of beer, his right wrist in a dirty plaster cast and a grubby bandage. He looked distinctly subdued, with a fresh-looking cut to his cheekbone, but he gave her a nod of recognition and a barely-there smile.

'Oh, James...' she said slowly. 'I gather you had an accident.'

'Don't tell me that's on YouTube as well?'

She half laughed, fumbled for her purse, 'No, Liz told me. How are you?'

'Sore, and bored with lying flat.'

'Can I get you a drink?'

The whiskery old farmer stood next to James said, 'Never refuse a drink from a lady.'

'You don't have to do that,' James said, but Laura ordered the beer anyway and one for his companion to keep him quiet. 'Did you get the final estimates and the plans?'

'Yeah.'

'And...?'

'You're expensive.'

'So are you. Maggie sometimes struggles to pay you,' Laura said, then looked at the yellow ceiling and counted to five. 'Sorry, can we start again?'

'You first.'

'I've wanted to say for ages, that you've totally transformed Ellie. And I'd very much like to transform your cottages.'

He thought about that for a moment and nodded with appreciation, 'Good to know. And none of that comes cheap does it?'

'Okay, so have we got a deal?' Laura said, hoping she was reading him correctly.

He was about to respond when Jess came and tapped him on the shoulder.

'Where's my birthday kiss?' she said, her heels making her almost the same height as James, giving him the full benefit of her cleavage. The old farmer looked her up and down with a long, appreciative wolf whistle then rubbed his hands together, 'You'd be too much for him, love, he's injured. I'd be willing though.'

Jess looked down her nose with icy contempt. 'Are you like, *serious*?' she said, and ordered a dozen different drinks with tequila slammers. The farmer was amused by her snooty reaction and nudged James again. 'All the ladies after you tonight, Jamie, both beauties.'

'How *disgusting* is that old man?' Jess said to Laura under her breath, and tottered away with a tray full of brightly coloured bottles of alcohol, shot glasses, lemon and salt. When Laura looked back at him, James was deep in conversation with the vet. Her opportunity lost for the moment, she made her way back to their table. Maggie had caught sight of Jess and was slightly open-mouthed.

'You are okay with the new image, aren't you?' Laura said.

'Well, she looks *fab*. I just hope she behaves herself. Did you find anything out?'

'No, not really,' Laura said, gulping down more orange juice.

'I know she's in love again, and it's always someone too old.'

'Well, she does have an upper age limit,' Laura said, and told her about the old farmer. Maggie laughed, but Laura thought it was a little forced. Shortly after, she went walkabout on the pretext of checking that Pete wasn't eating pork scratchings behind her back. James slid a glass of white wine onto the table for Maggie, and a tall glass of sparkling tropical fruit juices for Laura, topped with slices of fruit and what looked to be a Christmas themed cocktail umbrella and a glass stirrer, exotic for The Farmers' Arms.

'No cherry?'

'Funny.' He turned to go and Laura caught his arm. 'James, what we were discussing before, are you happy with the estimates, seriously?'

'Yeah, okay. Just don't go overboard on all the fancy stuff.'

Laura looked at her drink, grinned, and twirled the umbrella. 'Fancy stuff? Overboard?'

'Funny,' he said again, 'all right, send me the bit I have to sign. Lucky for you I'm left-handed.'

Laura smiled and accepted his left hand by way of an agreement. They were interrupted by Carla carrying a large gin and tonic, 'Oh you *poor lamb*. Next time you get on that mare, James, use some protection,' she said, at the sight of his cuts and bruises, then turned to Laura, 'Mind if I join you?'

'Please do, I don't know where Maggie's got to.'

'She's telling Jess she's had far too much to drink already and warning Pete about the fat content of pork pie.'

'That sounds like my sister.'

Platters of sandwiches made their way round the tables and Maggie reappeared, hot and flustered, 'I've sent Pete home, he looked a bit grey,' she managed to say, just before the landlord rang the bell and killed the music. He brought out a huge old-fashioned microphone from under the bar, and for a moment there was a loud muffle through the crackling speakers, followed by some hesitant testing.

'All right can I have your attention please ladies and gentlemen?' he said in bingo-caller style. 'Today is the sixth of February. That's number six Tom Mix. And that means it's a certain young lady's birthday today. Please put your hands together and raise your glasses for Jessica Thomas, eighteen today,' he said, then dropped his voice to a suggestive growl, 'and looking *fully legal I must say! Eyes down and look in, lads.*'

There was a tremendous whooping and banging of tables at this. They did the happy birthday song and dimmed the lights whilst Jess blew out the candles on a red heart-shaped cake, after which everyone demanded a speech.

Jess got shakily to her feet amidst a lot of giggles and smirks. 'Right,' she said, putting her champagne flute down. 'Thanks for all your pressies and everything, but there's something I've got to do now. Mum don't watch.'

Maggie watched like a hawk. The whole pub watched like hawks, the expectant atmosphere broken only by the odd whistle, or word of encouragement from the younger crowd, who were all suspiciously poised with party poppers. Jess made her way unsteadily across the pub to where the vet was sharing a table with James. He had to sit with his legs more or less straight out in front of him because of his strapped up ribcage, but Jess used this to her advantage, and straddled his lap. The vet looked at her with a slack mouth, but quickly removed the pint glass from James' hand. 'Be gentle with him love, he's already got injuries.'

Jess looked a lot more sluttish than Laura remembered; with her hair coming loose from its tousled topknot and her skirt just about covering its job description.

'I've come to collect what I'm due,' she said huskily, 'you haven't paid me this week.'

'You want me to pay for all that lousy horsemanship?'

'Maybe I ride men better than horses,' she said, hands on hips. She had a spectacular figure, and her provocative stance attracted a few whistles.

James frowned. 'What... what are you doing?'

Satisfied she had his full attention, Jess leant forwards, placed her hands on the arms of his chair and placed her mouth on his. Trapped by his inflexible torso, and the way she was sprawled across him, James was rendered fully incapacitated and automatically put his arms around her to try and balance the chair. It was only when Jess slid her hands under his shirt that they both suddenly went over backwards and hit the floor, Jess somehow still in his embrace.

'Right, *that's it!*' Maggie snarled.

Before anyone could stop her, she'd marched to the bar and grabbed the ice bucket, flinging the entire contents over James and Jess, then threw the bucket as well for good measure. It fell a long way short of its target and hit Maggie's next door neighbour on the shin. Jess staggered to her feet, hysterical with laughter, trying to tug her corset back into place, with Lucy recording it all on her phone. 'Oh, my God, this is like, *so* happening!'

The landlord didn't seem concerned, and even played the soundtrack from some spaghetti western, pretending to sling whisky shots down the bar. To Laura it seemed more like a Carry On film, but the music from any of those wouldn't have had the same effect.

James slowly managed to get onto all fours, obviously in some pain and might have remained in that position forever or just crawled away, had the vet not come to his aid.

'Christ almighty it's like trying to manhandle an arthritic bullock,' he said, finally managing to get James upright, both of them sliding on the wet floor. When Jess saw James hanging on to the back of a chair, his face buried in his arm, she dramatically pushed Lucy out of the way and scuttled to his aid, shoes in her hand.

'*Oh baby I'm so, so sorry,*' she whimpered, stroking his back. 'Take deep breaths.'

'Really... bad idea.'

Mortified by his discomfort, she put an arm across his shoulders and inclined her head next to his, so that the remainder of their conversation was private. Laura could only guess the gist of it, which seemed to be mostly placatory on James' part, and although Jess continued to look at him in a dream of adoration, there were tears in her beautiful bleary eyes and there was a quiet reservation about her.

In direct contrast, Maggie was busy righting chairs and sweeping up glass in a raging temper. Eventually, James was recovered enough to stand upright, a distinct impression of crimson crush branded across his jaw. He went woodenly across the room to pick up his jacket, then turned to his dog, who was frantically chasing ice cubes around the floor.

'Washboy, car time. Night, Maggie.'

This was starchily ignored, but everything settled down once James had gone, except Maggie, who turned on Jess, 'Showing me up, behaving like a strumpet!'

'A *what?*'

Lucy said, 'I think it's like, a medieval musical instrument, or something?'

They both collapsed with laughter, holding on to each other until Maggie intervened.

'Jess, home time. *Now!*'

Gradually, the music filtered back and the bingo was announced as if nothing had happened.

CHAPTER SIX

Maggie

Maggie replaced the phone in its charger after speaking with her sister, mostly apologising for disappearing in a huff, but Laura was more concerned that Simon wasn't home. It was midnight and the bowling alley had closed hours ago. Honestly what a fuss, he was probably in the pub. She said as much then had to apologise again.

In fact Maggie had spent most of the evening apologising; to Linda for bruising her shin, to a complete stranger for spilt drinks, and somewhat begrudgingly to the landlord for the broken ice bucket and ensuing mess, adding that she thought some of his leery remarks were inappropriate.

Jess bounced down the stairs, 'Who was on the phone?'

'Not *him.*'

'No matter, I'll see him tomorrow.'

'You will not! I've told you what is happening tomorrow. Grandma and Granddad are coming for tea and you are going to help me.'

'Are you having a laugh? So not going to happen. I'm working with Jamie all day,' she said defiantly, thumped back up the stairs and slammed the door. Pete appeared on the landing with a weary face. 'Give it a rest, Maggie,' he said, and shuffled back into the bedroom, his feet not in his slippers properly.

In the morning, Maggie had a pounding headache, more from tossing and turning all night and going over several humiliating scenarios she'd rather forget. She fully expected Jess to have a monstrous hangover, and was both amazed and dismayed to find her bed empty, her riding gear gone and her new car missing from the drive. So, it must be lust, Maggie thought, or just plain bloody-minded defiance.

She had half a mind to go marching up to the yard and tell James what she thought of him, letting Jess loll all over him like that with her underwear on show, lipstick all over his face. And she saw them huddled together while she rubbed his back and whispered sweet nothings. All intimate and touchy feely they were. What was he, forty-three?

Maggie slammed the kettle on, and stared out of the window, ignoring the washing still in the machine and Ellie's schoolbag still unpacked since Friday. Why did Jess put her through this? She'd always been selfish and wilful, a beautiful wild child who always got her own way. Her son, Nathan, was blessed with common sense and had never been any trouble with the opposite sex. Even Ellie was easier, despite all the attention she needed.

But as the cold light of day took hold, Maggie had to admit, if only to herself, she was just as much embarrassed as angry, and with Jess already in situ at the yard, it kind of watered down anything she might have to say. After all, Jess was eighteen not fifteen.

Ellie came home from her friend's house, and Maggie had to explain that James was busy. The look on her little girl's face was the last straw. Because of her big sister's attention seeking antics, everything was sullied and spoilt for Ellie. Still in her dressing gown, Maggie went down to the bottom of the garden, let the hens out and cried in the shed. No doubt Linda was watching every move from her back-bedroom window.

*

Halfway through the afternoon, Maggie answered a knock at the door and was taken off guard when she saw it was Mr Morgan-Jones.

'Can I talk to you?'

Maggie let him in and stood with her arms folded. He filled her hallway with his dark brooding presence, and seemed out of place indoors, sort of caged.

'Why didn't you bring Ellie this morning?'

Now that she had her chance, Maggie could give him both barrels. Instead, the best she could muster was a harrumphing sound.

'Look, I'm not having any kind of relationship with Jess, nor do I intend to,' he said, reading her easily, as if it was all written like a script on her forehead, but because her face remained passive other than a slight frown, he added, 'They all lark about, the girls at the yard. If I took any of them seriously my life would be hell. If it's any consolation, I was in agony after Jess fell on me.'

'Well, that's your own fault, you did nothing to stop her!'

He went on to explain why he was moving so slowly and carefully, something about the black mare and accident and emergency.

'Oh…!' Maggie said, slowly taking in his cut face and the padding beneath his dirty sweater. His breathing was shallow as well, now she came to think about it. 'I didn't know that.'

'So, now that's all cleared up, will you bring Ellie over?' he said, but clearly sensed her hedging. 'Maggie, I can help her!'

'I know, I know,' Maggie said, feeling a big lump in her throat. It was those two words in the same sentence: help and Ellie.

James inclined his head to one side, 'Do you want me to sack Jess?'

'No, she's got a car to run.'

He looked exasperated then, and he was losing interest. Maggie felt exasperated. Damn Jess, she got away with appalling behaviour and still got her own way. On the other hand, denying Ellie because of Jess was quite possibly the worst reason for not taking her.

'Maggie, she was just drunk, that's all,' James said. 'What do you want me to do?'

'Don't flirt with her, *stand* up to her!'

'I meant Ellie.'

'All right, I'll bring her,' she said, feeling back in control now that a clearer picture had been formed. 'But you're not off the hook yet. How about some riding for me? By way of a full apology.'

'So, it's a truce. Can you ride?'

Maggie dashed a stray tear off her cheek, 'Can I ride?' she said indignantly. 'I'll have you know I won the cross country cup in 1982 for Rowen and District Ladies club.'

'Yeah? So you'll come up to the yard later? You and Ellie?'

Maggie nodded and watched him go down the drive. He struggled to get back into his vehicle, like her father did with his severe arthritis. Even though she felt a tiny bit sorry for him, she had to have the last say.

'I'll be watching you though, Mr Morgan-Jones!' she shouted. 'Lace thongs or not!'

James closed the door of his Land Rover with a definitive clunk. She wasn't certain, but Maggie had the feeling that Linda was listening through the hedge as she hoed under the rhododendrons.

The more pressing problem was what to wear. 1982 was a long time ago. There was nothing remotely suitable in her wardrobe other than a very old pair of canary yellow Capri pants. She couldn't remember wearing them the first time but was overjoyed when they actually fastened up. They were tight; they were very tight.

Gingerly, Maggie tested them out on the Queen Anne bedroom chair, going through a routine of mounting and dismounting, finishing with a brisk rising trot. After a while, she became aware that Pete was watching her. 'I won't ask what you're doing,' he said with a deadpan face, 'because I'm not sure I'll even understand the answer.'

'I'll make it easy for you. I'm going riding, me and Ellie.'

Deciding the pants were hideous but trustworthy, and there was much to be said for that, Maggie dismounted the chair with a dignified flourish.

'Right, groom, fetch me my hat and boots,' she said to Pete, indicating the top of the wardrobe. He dutifully reached them down and brushed the dust off.

'Maggie, just be careful, will you?'

She tutted at his concerned face, but by the time she'd pulled in to the yard, Maggie was already beginning to regret telling James about the cross-country championships. It had been a long time ago, the other competitors had been rubbish, and she felt fat and rusty.

Lucy took Ellie to find Jess while she waited nervously in the paddock. Carla wandered across with a saddle over her arm. 'Interesting outfit today, Maggie.'

'Yes, well, I never did subscribe to that old adage, 'all the gear but no idea".'

'If you want to know where Jess is, she's boiling up the barley and linseed. It's an awful job with a hangover. Ellie's enjoying it though.'

'Good.'

James brought out a huge chestnut horse. Close up, it was at least sixteen hands and had much bigger pecs than the bedroom chair. Carla raised her brows, 'You're honoured. *No one* gets to ride O'Malley.'

Somehow, with the help of a box, Maggie managed to mount, and James shortened the stirrups to short-fat-leg length, while Maggie fretted about the way the horse jostled and pawed the ground.

'Give me a couple of circuits,' James said, ' and if we're both happy you can clear off.'

Her limbs went to jelly as soon as the horse stepped out, but it was beautifully responsive, to the degree where she only had to think about changing pace or direction, and O'Malley obliged. He was easy to bring to a halt, respectful of her, and she liked that.

'He's a dream,' Maggie said.

James opened the gate for her, and Maggie was deeply touched that he should trust her to disappear over the hills with his horse. She'd expected to get a riding school hack.

'Are you sure?'

'Positive. Not sure about the bright yellow pants, but at least you'll be easy to find now that the gorse isn't in flower,' he said, then squinted up at her. 'Have you got a phone on you?'

'Good idea,' she said, feeling her pockets. 'No, it's in the car and the keys are in the office,' she said, and half laughed. 'Last time I rode, they weren't even invented.'

James gave her his and she secured it in her jacket, 'Tell Jess to look after Ellie will you?'

'Maggie, I'll look after Ellie, just get going before it gets dark.'

O'Malley echoed his words and sprang into an eager trot along the lane, until they came to the steep mountain track and had to walk. Maggie patted O'Malley's warm neck and felt something she hadn't felt for years. Freedom.

Freedom was difficult to achieve when you had lots of ties. And it wasn't that Maggie wished to be free of her family, it was more to do with being free in her head for a while, free to be just Maggie and not someone's mother, older sister, younger wife or eldest daughter. At the moment, other than Nathan, she felt suffocated with all their demands, whether they were justified or not.

Even Maggie's father was fed up because he was old and couldn't do the same chores. He badgered her all the time to get the family over to Ireland to visit. Fat chance. The compromise was that she spent hours talking to him on the phone, telling him what everyone was doing because no one would do it for themselves, not even Laura. She'd fallen out with him years ago over her affair with Simon.

Maggie turned the horse along a well-worn path, a steady climb with an old stone wall running along one side and a sharp rise of mountain ash and fir on the other. For a while, there were just the cries of red kites and the rhythmic exertion of the horse as he toiled up the incline, his nostrils wide, ears pricked forwards. Gradually, the ground levelled and gave way to an old Roman road across the top of the hills, striking out across miles of coarse springy grass studded with alpine flowers. The peaks of the Snowdonia mountains reared in a jagged outline to her left, and fell away in a soft blur of heather-covered hills, where they eventually joined the Irish sea.

Close up, the ground wasn't level but O'Malley tossed his head expectantly, the high breeze snatching at his mane and tail. Maggie felt the old adrenaline of her youth, just in loving the vastness of this beautiful land, and knowing that perhaps the horse felt it too. She let the reins slip through her fingers, praying that she could trust his instinct to get them both safely over the buried rocks, rabbit warrens and ditches. At first, the sheer power of the gallop took her breath away, but the big horse expertly judged the cadence of the ground, his four metal-shod hooves beating out four distinct beats. Maggie squeezed the reins back, testing the brakes, and O'Malley responded, dropping back into a perfectly balanced canter. Mr Morgan-Jones knew his job all right. Confident then, Maggie gave O'Malley his head again, and enjoyed the best freedom she knew.

A long time later, when the sun had dropped low and left the late chill of a winter afternoon, Maggie turned the horse for home and the phone in her pocket began trilling and vibrating. It made her smile when O'Malley, chestnut ears twitching, automatically stood still, as if the call might be for him, while Maggie fumbled to get the reins in one hand. She hesitated which button to press, then held it to her ear. A small tearful voice said, 'Jamie? I really need to see you, where are you?'

'Jess, it's Mum.'

'*Mum!* What are you doing with Jamie's phone? Are you *with* him?'

'No. I'm out riding and he lent it to me,' she said patiently, but the line was already dead. Maggie sighed with frustration. They could even get to her in the middle of nowhere. She nudged O'Malley on, and he quickened his pace, sensing her irritation.

Almost back in the yard, Maggie could see Ellie and Lucy absorbed in the task of adding carrots and apples to buckets, although the rest of the staff were shrieking around a hosepipe and flicking dung at each other. Liz was struggling to be heard above Radio One.

'James!' she shouted, hands on hips, 'You need to keep on top of these girls!'

'Ooh, me first,' Carla said smoothly, and they all shrieked with laughter. James sauntered across the yard and held on to O'Malley's bridle whilst Maggie dismounted. She felt like a ton of King Edwards trussed up in a sack, being pushed backwards off a huge wall. James held her elbow till she rebalanced upright, and inquired how the horse had ridden.

'He was the perfect gentleman,' Maggie said, vigorously shrugging down her custard yellow trousers, which had ridden up considerably. 'And they are in short supply.'

'I've a feeling that's directed at me.'

'Not really, just couldn't resist the parallel,' she said, running up the stirrups, 'Seriously, thanks for this afternoon; it's the best therapy there is. He's a fantastic horse.'

James gave her a satisfied nod, and Maggie walked across to the office, feeling the shock of her unfit muscles kick in all over her body. Her legs felt like they'd had a general anaesthetic, and everything else felt as if it had been bent the wrong way. Even her ankles felt unnatural.

'James said *not* to ask you for any money,' Liz said with a wry smile, 'so I presume he's upset you? Must be serious. Even I'm not offered O'Malley to ride, and James and I have more fallouts than Chernobyl.'

'No, it was more Jess.'

'I've heard about last night,' Liz said, making coffee. 'She's gone home unwell, didn't finish her shift.'

'Jess is not ill, she's hung over and heartsick,' Maggie said, sitting down heavily on the chair, 'She's got a crush on your brother.'

Liz shot her a slightly pitiful, humorous expression, 'So I gather. Actually I'm a bit worried about James. He's in pain with those injuries, but he won't give in, and it's nothing to do with being macho. He's depressed to the point of not really caring about himself.'

'He doesn't look as athletic as usual.'

'His way of dealing with it is to do as much physical work as possible, so he's exhausted enough to sleep. I mean, is it normal to chop logs till one in the morning? Why can't he take pills instead?' she went on, passing coffee to Maggie, 'Sorry, I'm prattling on. How's Pete?'

'Pete? Well, I think he might be depressed as well.'

Driving home, Maggie was annoyed with herself that she hadn't seen it as depression. Maybe she'd get him an axe and some logs. At least he'd be fitter. They needed to talk, but as usual there was always something more pressing, usually Jess. Her car was parked erratically across the drive, which didn't bode well. And there was another vehicle with a Disabled Driver notice on the windscreen and a Wheelchair Access Required sticker on the back. Maggie groaned, she'd forgotten all about Ted and Beryl. Inside the front door, she fell over the recycling waiting to go in the respective bins outside, and a mountain of footwear waiting to go in the cupboard in the hall, mostly belonging to Pete and Ellie.

Why couldn't Pete work anything out for himself? He had a responsible job, he had to problem solve and make decisions, and yet as soon as he was inside his own front door his brain went to mush. It irritated the hell out of her.

Ted and Beryl were in the kitchen, Beryl going through all the cupboards, muttering something about her blood sugar level and not being able to eat after five. Ted thought she'd said something about being dead or alive, and they had one of their stupid protracted conversations based on misinterpretations. The wheelchair seemed enormously threatening in the small space, preventing Maggie from doing a thorough search of the freezer or more importantly, getting to the wine rack. They were difficult visitors at the best of times, hard of hearing and demanding. It was Maggie's fault that Pete had been in hospital, and why was Jessica so rude? Never said a word to them; just went straight to her room.

'I bought her a lovely locket,' Beryl shouted, showing Maggie the box.

'Oh, it is, it's in my pocket,' Ted said, and pulled his hearing aid out, 'Who put that there?'

'That's nice,' Maggie shouted at Beryl, knowing it would never get worn.

'Rice?' Ted said, 'Can't eat rice love... it gets under my teeth.'

'Who's for fish and chips?' Maggie said cheerfully, ignoring Beryl's face. 'Not for us, we can't digest batter.'

Ted looked Maggie up and down with a frown, 'I think she is, she is fatter.'

*

Hours later, with Ted and Beryl departed and Ellie asleep, Maggie knocked on Jess's bedroom door for about the third time. 'Jess, I've got you a brandy. A large one.'

The door opened and Jess appeared, still in her grubby stable attire.

'Why were you riding O'Malley?' she said accusingly.

'May I come in?' Maggie said politely, knowing she'd have to think on her feet, although she was beginning to feel simply dead on them.

Permission was granted, and Maggie stepped in to the hormonal hornet's nest, which was her daughter's bedroom, and sank on to the unmade bed. The space was an overflowing mess of clothes, make-up, boxes of oils and potions for her aromatherapy and holistic course, and a whole range of gadgets charging up and draining the electric, epilators, phones, laptops, iPods, and a scary massage thing. Even her choice of career was intensely personal and hands on. There was an arty photograph of Mr Morgan-Jones, looking especially moody against a dark sky.

'I'm not stupid, I can work it out,' Jess said, making no move to reduce the volume of the music she was listening to: powerful rock ballads, all about angst-ridden love, and Maggie almost drank the brandy herself.

'You've been discussing me, and you made James make an apology with O'Malley.'

'I happened to mention in the pub that I wouldn't mind riding again, and James offered, that's all,' she said airily.

'You're such a *liar!* You *control* freak of a mother. You've had a go at him. And you only want to ride again so you can spy on me!' she said, her eyes full of angry resentment. 'So, how come you only decided today? After you were angry last night?'

'I was at the stables because of Ellie.'

'Oh, it's always about Ellie! Ellie and Nathan,' Jess shouted, and Maggie stared at her, astonished. Pete thumped on the wall, his voice all muffled. 'Give it a bloody rest!'

'I can't work there now,' Jess howled miserably. 'You've made me look such an idiot.'

'No, Jess, you've done that all by yourself,' Maggie said, seeing an opportunity to take strong parental control. 'You've got to learn to take responsibility for your actions. If you go around throwing yourself at men, you'll eventually suffer the consequences.'

'But, Mum,' she said, tears rolling down her face, 'I really love him.'

'You don't *know* him,' Maggie said, 'It's not all about sex, you know.'

Jess made a noise like a wild animal with a dart in its neck. '*I know that!*'

Pete banged on the wall again, this time with the heel of a shoe.

It was after midnight when Maggie finally ran her bath. Poor Jess. Unrequited love was the worst kind. Love had the power of life and death when you were eighteen. She looked at Pete fast asleep, oblivious to the emotional trauma of the day, and it was difficult to feel any compassion, to have anything left for him. Jess might be young and looking for love, but her mother was desperately trying to hold on to it.

In the night, Maggie was woken three times, once by Pete complaining that his stomach was rumbling, and then by James' mobile, trilling away in her jacket pocket on the bedroom chair. Two voicemail messages came through, an interesting one from someone with a horse that wouldn't load into a trailer, and a less complicated one from Jess.

*

The following day, Maggie was relieved to find that Jess had gone to college. She discovered a letter in Ellie's schoolbag from her form teacher to say that reading practice must be *every* night. Her school uniform was still in the washing machine, in a dried-out creased ball and Maggie had to make jam sandwiches to put in her My Little Pony lunchbox because there was nothing else. She did the school run on autopilot, remembering to collect two more children on the way, although Maggie had a horrible sinking feeling that one of them didn't actually go to Ellie's school.

On her return journey, Maggie called in at the yard and found James bandaging the front legs of a hunter. She passed him his phone. 'Sorry, took it home by mistake,' she said, 'I think there might be a message from Jess.'

Actually, there had been twenty-two texts, but Maggie had deleted all the more graphic ones and the incomprehensible babble, leaving the last one, which said she was handing in her notice. It was quite rude as it implied James had only given O'Malley to Maggie because they were either in collusion, or it was the fact that he was the only horse on the yard that could carry her enormous tits up the mountain.

Maggie waited while he went through his message system, impressed by how little his face gave away. 'Tell her I can give her next weekend off, but I need her to come back after that.'

'No! I mean good idea, but can you tell her? Can you text her, or something? Otherwise she'll know we've talked.'

James agreed, but wearily, leaving Maggie with the feeling that she really was getting too involved, and that James was bored with it all now and probably wouldn't do anything about it.

Later in the week she tried to talk to Pete about it all.

'The trouble with you and Jess is you are both alike,' he said. 'You both storm in without thinking and with all your feelings on show.'

Maggie scoffed, thrown by how quickly he'd turned the conversation on its head, reluctant to admit he might be right. 'It just makes me sad, that young women these days just feel they can take what they want, and throw a paddy if they can't have it.'

'Look love,' he said, putting an arm across her shoulders, 'the world has changed.'

'Well, I don't like it,' she said, peeling carrots and chopping them forcefully. 'There's no respect for anyone or anything. Women behaving like men, all predatory and crude.'

Pete nodded in agreement at this, but added, 'That's you getting older. Try looking at it all when you are me in another ten years. Then you'll know what the invisible man feels like as well.'

'So, you feel miserable and invisible, is that it?' she said carefully, putting the casserole in the oven.

'Maggie, I've felt invisible in this house and at work for about fifteen years,' he said, smoothing out the paper on the kitchen table. She ignored the first part of his declaration.

'Huh, work. I can't believe they haven't even rung or sent a card.'

'They have,' he said, keeping his eyes on the sports' pages. 'Rang the other day but I told them not to bother with that bloody hearts-and-flowers stuff.'

'Oh, Pete, why?'

'It's false sympathy, and I don't want it.'

Maggie brooded on the conversation, knowing there was a horrible twisted logic in it all.

It was sink or swim out in the real world, stand up and be heard even if no one wants to listen. What happened when you got older? Did you shout louder, or bow out gracefully? It seemed like Pete had bowed out, helped himself morph into the invisible man because it was easier. That a proportion of it might be down to her, Maggie saved for another day.

Laura rang to say that she'd met Liz for lunch at last, and

James had signed a contract and the builders were all set to start. That subject quickly exhausted, they talked about the party.

'I hope you didn't go overboard with Jess, I bet it's all blown over.'

'Well, yes and yes. James lent me his horse for the afternoon, that big chestnut.'

'Oh? How did it go?'

'Good. Although I'm still getting over it,' she said, 'You know he's trained O'Malley to stand still if his mobile rings?'

'Oh, wow. Even Simon doesn't do that. He runs everywhere at the moment, always several steps ahead of me,' she said succinctly.

'So... where did he get to last Saturday, in the pub like I said?'

'Oh, something like that. I can't remember.'

They'd had a row again, she could tell.

She wished Simon would get his divorce through and maybe marry Laura, make some sort of statement. Did it take five years to get a divorce? He always maintained it was because he was self-employed and Malice kept changing the goalposts. Although, when Maggie thought about it, Laura's men had always been a bit commitment phobic, or maybe she subconsciously chose that type if you believed some of the daytime television. It was all meant to relate to your childhood. In Laura's case it possibly related to their controlling, insensitive father.

'Have you told Dad about the baby?' Maggie said, determined not to do it for her.

Laura went quiet. 'I'll write to him, I promise.'

Maggie hoped she meant it. They were both proud, protective and poetic. There was more of Dad in Laura than she would ever admit, it just came out differently. Laura might play the independent career woman on the surface, and she always maintained she wasn't interested in getting married, but privately Maggie always maintained that she was. And it would be in an old atmospheric, Celtic chapel like the one in the village, all dripping with gravitas and sanctity.

Because Maggie couldn't think of anything better, she married Pete in a registry office and they danced to Abba in the pub. Everyone had had a good laugh and gone home drunk. But Laura was drawn to anything spiritual. She cried at the words of hymns, monks chanting, funeral marches and weird new age music. Even the panpipes in the garden centre set her off once. Maggie didn't know anyone who did that; it was quite beyond her. She always wanted to laugh, but it was part of her sister, and it had taken Maggie about twenty years to acknowledge and understand that everyone had a different inner flame.

Maybe if she applied that logic to Jess, she'd understand her better.

Jess came home from college later in the week to say she'd had a text from James during her lecture about Indian head massage and the power of pebbles.

'Oh?'

'Yep, he says he's missing me loads, and he wants me to have his *lurve* child.'

Maggie felt her pulse quicken. She added soy sauce to the prawn stir-fry and risked ignoring her for as long as possible. 'And the translation of that is?'

Jess looked at her phone and began reading, 'He says, I can't ride (horses) but I'm the best shit-shifter on the yard, and he can't accept less than six months' notice.'

'Well then,' she said. And breathe.

*

When the weekend came around again, Pete insisted on no visitors. He even talked about going to the pub for a salad, just the two of them. Maggie didn't think the Farmers' Arms did salad, but even so. And then Nathan rang, and everything changed. He wanted to bring his friend Chris over for Sunday lunch, Valentine's Day.

In a lather of anticipation, Maggie began to make up the guest room, adding some nice extras like fresh flowers and scented bed linen. Jess made no secret of her disdain, but watched the preparations with a smug grimace, which Maggie found distinctly unnerving. After a cryptic phone call from someone at the yard, she calmly announced she was going in to work because they were busy and she was bored.

'Good job he didn't accept your notice, isn't it?' Maggie said, pushing everything back in the airing cupboard, doing her best to keep the satisfaction out of her voice. 'Just goes to show, it pays to think things through instead of being so impulsive.'

This was ignored, like everything else Maggie said.

When she drove over later with Ellie, it was to find Jess standing on top of the manure heap, wearing a tiny white T-shirt with Shit Shifter printed across the front, a black Wonderbra clearly visible beneath. Her midriff revealed a bejewelled navel, which was new. What sort of inner flame was that? Vulgar and sexual was all she could think of.

'What do you look like?' Maggie hissed.

'*Hot*.'

'After everything we discussed.'

'You gave me your Stone Age opinion. I haven't given up on him.'

'That's my girl,' Carla said, pulling on her boots. She was in white, hopelessly impractical for normal people in a stable yard, with a fur gilet and pink riding gloves.

'Carla!' Maggie snarled, but they both just laughed, told

her to lighten up. Carla caught hold of Maggie's arm and lowered her voice. 'Don't worry, he's a very difficult nut to crack. I've already tried the Wonderbra, the sport bra, the glamour bra... and no bra.'

'Please don't encourage her, for goodness sake.'

'I'm sure James can handle her,' Carla said, as if Jess were a flighty mare.

When James saw them, his mouth twitched ever so slightly at the sight of Jess. He just said they all looked like they'd stepped off the set of Absolutely Fabulous.

*

Lunch was late but so was Nathan, and Ellie just had time to scatter heart confetti across the table before the doorbell chimed. Ellie, all excited because her big brother was home, ran to the door first, but Maggie was close behind, eager to see his friend. Nathan scooped up his sister, and there was a moment of happy chaos in the hall with bags and a hobbyhorse on a stick for Ellie. Maggie had to stand on tiptoes to kiss him because he was so tall. Goodness knows which side of the family he got that from.

'This is Chris,' Nathan said, finally standing aside.

Chris had long blonde hair, and his trousers were the same shade as the pale terracotta carpet in the sitting room. He was quite charming though, had nicely manicured nails and gave Maggie a beautiful spray of lilies. She knew then, if she was being honest with herself, but she waited till he told her. Mercifully, it was much later and they were both alone. Nathan was quite composed, well-rehearsed she supposed, but he'd always been like that, assured and sensible. Goodness knows which side of the family he got that from either.

CHAPTER SEVEN

Laura

Valentine's Day was not the romantic event Laura had envisaged.

She was cool with Simon. He was polite and caring, but it was not enough. He said he was still getting used to the idea of the baby, and he felt under a lot of pressure already with the business, the children and Alice, and no, he didn't want to consider moving to a house with a garden, he was still paying for the last family home, and no, he wasn't in the mood for love because he felt stressed.

Let me guess, he's gone all tentative in the bedroom. You poor, poor cow.

Simon was cool with *her* because they'd disagreed about a number of issues.

Firstly, Laura didn't think the holiday flats in Spain were the money-spinners Simon seemed to think they were. He wanted to take a risk and Laura didn't.

'We could be home and dry with this, get Alice off our backs once and for all.'

'And it could ruin us as well! Especially if you're using Dragon Designs as collateral.'

'Well, I've already committed now.'

'*What…?* How? Simon, what have you done?'

'I've *told you*, the money from the Morgan-Jones job will

go directly into the flats.'

'We haven't got it yet, only a goodwill deposit and a contract.'

'Good enough.'

Laura didn't think it was and fretted about the logistics, but Simon had already made arrangements to go out there with Steve. When he told her the dates and saw that it clashed with Maggie's Florida holiday, he was agitated.

'Oh, blast. I didn't realise you'd be on your own, sorry.'

'It's fine,' she snapped. 'Too late now, although I don't know why you've booked to go over half-term.'

'Steve arranged it.'

The previous Saturday night, Laura had sat at home growing increasingly worried as to where he might be. He said he'd been at Cherry Grove talking to Alice, and he was sorry he hadn't realised his mobile was switched off.

'What on earth were you talking about till one in the morning?'

'Well, we had the first sensible discussion in about six years, so I took advantage of her rational state of mind.'

'Am I allowed to know the content of the discussion, or is it filed along with the decision on the holiday flats?'

'Laura! What's got in to you?'

'Common sense,' she said, 'basically, *I'm sick to death of Alice.*'

'There's not much I can do about that.'

'Simon, you need to start treating *me* as your partner.'

'Of course you're my partner, I can't manage the business without you, you know that.'

Laura turned away, not wanting him to see her face. Seconds later, he realised his mistake, but by then it felt too late, like an afterthought.

*

Later in the week, Laura rang her sister to wish them a happy holiday. They were flying out on Thursday night for two weeks. Maggie said the central heating had broken so there was no hot water, and the wheels had fallen off the big suitcase.

'Pete can't pack a case to save his life. He put the shoes in last, *on top*.'

'Are the girls looking forward to it?'

'Ellie is sick with excitement, but Madam Jess doesn't even want to come. She'd rather work on the yard in the rain,' Maggie said irritably. 'And have you seen the pictures she's put on that space book? Lap dancing round the yard brush and rolling on the pub floor.'

Laura smiled to herself, 'You mean *Facebook*. Do you want me to get one of the contractors to look at the boiler?'

'Oh, Laura that would be great. You've got a key, haven't you? I don't know what's happened to spring, have you got sleet as well?'

Actually, Laura thought it was possibly the prelude to the second ice age, and not just on the outside. She took Simon to Manchester airport. It was very cold, grey and miserable, like the atmosphere inside the car.

'Please don't make any major decisions without speaking to me,' she said.

'Laura, just keep to your side of the business, and I'll keep to mine. I don't tell you how to design and fit.'

He'd barely got his bags out and closed the boot, when Laura rammed the car into first gear and stuck her foot down, jumping ahead of the queue of traffic waiting to depart the dropping-off area. Blaring horns followed her progress back to the motorway. Determined not to cry, she forced herself to concentrate on the road, arms poker-straight.

The whole week had been a nightmare, fraught with difficult jobs and workmen not being in the right place at the right time. Simon was doubly stressed because he was trying

Midnight Sky

to tie up anything urgent and important before he went on his trip, and Alice had had a fit because he'd *apparently* agreed to spend some time with the children over half-term to make up for the time Cameron was ill. Simon said he'd made no such promise.

Barbara was already in the office, head down at her computer.

'Bill rang,' she said. 'He's finished the plastering up at the Rowen cottages and can you take a look before he moves on to that Victoria villa? He also mentioned that because it's so cold, do you want him to get the heaters in the cottages? The plaster is taking ages to dry out, and the forecast is for snow.'

'Yes, well, they've been saying that for days.'

'And your sister has left a message on the machine, saying she thinks she's left the back door open,' Barbara said with a smile. 'I bet she hasn't. I always think I've left the oven on.'

'I'll go and check it out,' Laura said, anxious to be on the move and doing something.

Laura was back on the road and at her sister's house in forty minutes. She slid the bolt across the back door, and it felt strange being there when it was so cold, silent and empty. Satisfied the house was secure, Laura headed back out beyond the village, and the first flakes began to float down.

Cold, silent and pretty.

Mefysen looked great, and the knocked out pantry had been the right decision. Laura ran a hand over the still damp plaster. The cottages were clean and empty, ready for their new life. She found her notebook and began to take accurate measurements for kitchen and bathroom fittings.

She didn't notice the cramps at first, but then, as she stood on an old chair to hook a tape measure up to the top of the window, the sharpness of the pain caused her to gasp. She sat down abruptly on the wide window recess and tried to breathe calmly although she was clutching the edges of the sill. James was in the yard, walking with that lazy stroll he had, closing up the barn and kicking over the lower bolts on the loose boxes. In the field opposite, the Arab mares were standing subdued with their heads together, snowflakes on dark eyelashes, rumps to the wind. The snow was already covering Minas Bach, and it was becoming impossible to distinguish the mountain from the low milky sky, lit as it was by that odd lilac diffusion which precluded a lot of snow. She needed to get home.

Slowly, Laura slid off her perch, but the pain came again, and this time she was doubled over, and this time it was more frightening in its intensity.

Oh, please God, not that, not now, *not ever.*

She fumbled in her bag and found her phone, relieved to see there was a signal. Unsure what to do, she waited to see if it happened again. Laura ran through her phone index, wondering who she could call, sweat breaking out on her face, unable to remember if she'd got the number for the yard stored in her phone. It was there, and so was the pain.

It was like a contraction.

Almost crying, she pressed the green symbol. The number rang out but no one answered. When she dragged herself over to the window, Laura could still see James walking slowly over to the house, squinting up at the sky. Another agonising minute ticked by, whilst he knocked the snow off his boots, and then finally, he went inside the house. Please pick up, *come on.*

'Yeah?' he said eventually, 'Morgan-Jones.'

'James I'm at the cottages, and I think I might need an ambulance.' It all came out in a panicky rush, and Laura couldn't be sure if he'd even heard her. Suddenly, she lost the connection, or she dropped the phone. Time must have passed because she was vaguely aware of being moved around, of someone touching her face and saying her name, but it was all dreamlike and frightening. One moment she was cold and shaking, the next sweating and clammy.

She could hear James talking on the phone. He must have put her in the recovery position on the floor because when she opened her eyes, she was looking at plug sockets and the new skirting board.

'Laura? I need to take you to hospital.'

She nodded, unable to help him much as he lifted her off the floor. James carried her outside, and slid her into the passenger seat of his Land Rover. When he was pulling the belt across her, he said something about contacting Simon.

'No,' she managed to say.

The short journey to Llandudno General Hospital took forever, or it seemed that way, although Laura had little comprehension of what was going on. She must have fainted again because she was aware of her head against the passenger door, and she could hear James calling her name and squeezing her hand. She dug her nails into it, but he didn't let go until he had to negotiate the left-hand turn into the hospital, and then he was lifting her out, disentangling her from the seat belt. She felt the snow touching her face, her hair, and he carried her carefully over the deep slush in the car park.

They waited a long time in reception because there was a traffic accident on Deganwy Bridge, and there seemed to be some confusion about wheelchairs and available doctors. The triage nurse asked James a lot of questions about her, none of which he could answer, so someone caught hold of her hand and asked how many weeks pregnant she was. Laura managed to whisper ten, with tears running into her ears and mouth.

James repeated it all, losing his temper with the form filling. She had her hands locked around his neck, her face crushed into his shoulder, and she would remember the smell of his jacket forever and the fresh outside, warm feeling of it was all mixed up with her childhood and a complicated yearning for something she didn't understand.

'When are you going to give her some pain relief?' she heard him say. After a few moments, he carried her to a mumbled destination and followed someone impatiently down a long bright corridor, until they were shown into a room.

And then she was taken from his arms and laid flat.

The last thing she remembered was the sweet smell of gas and air.

*

It was all over the following day. The consultant told her that she'd had a rapid miscarriage, which was why she'd fainted and had so much pain. There was no reason for it, and she mustn't blame herself. They'd given her an ultrasound scan and confirmed that her pregnancy was terminated. She'd continue to bleed of course, but that was normal too, and there was absolutely no reason why she couldn't try for another baby in a few months' time. Laura could have written the script herself, she'd read so many books. Except that none of it really applied to Simon and herself.

On Sunday, the nurse in charge came to see her, and pulled the curtains round the bed.

'Laura, I'm not happy about discharging you for a number of reasons.'

Laura knew why. She was exhausted because she'd not slept. And she'd not slept because her bed was so close to the maternity wards. But it wasn't just the noise that kept her wide-eyed.

She couldn't sleep because her dreams were missing.

'We're also going to have to put you back on an infusion if you don't start eating and drinking.'

'I just want to go home.'

'Perfectly understandable but I'd rather there was someone with you for a while,' she said, 'Are you sure there's no one we can call?'

'No, no one,' she said, and laid back down and stared at the wall.

They brought the IV infusion over at lunchtime and left it by the bed, along with something sloppy in a bowl and a cup of tea. Laura managed to force down the tea and two mouthfuls of whatever the food was meant to be, then opened the locker by her bed and hunted through her bag. Her mobile battery was completely dead, but there was a call phone by the nurses' station. Alarmed by how feeble she felt, Laura shuffled down the ward and along the corridor, where she slumped down gratefully in a plastic chair. Luckily, there was an old smelly directory with half the pages missing, but she thumbed through it and found a full quarter page dedicated to Morgan-Jones.

The advertisement said 'horse breaking a speciality'.

Why was it called *breaking*? It didn't fit with his persona at all.

'James...?'

There was a long beat before he answered her, 'Laura?'

'I really need you to do something,' she said. 'I need you to come and collect me from the hospital and take me to my sister's. Bring the keys, I think they must be in my car.'

There was another long moment of contemplation, 'Why?'

'I really need to get out of here, *please.*'

She didn't recognise her voice, it sounded strange, desperate. The call ran out of time and Laura replaced the handset and went to find her clothes. They were in a disgusting messy heap, but she pulled them on anyway, and sat on the bed.

The nurse said, 'Where do you think you're going?'

'Someone's coming for me.'

'Where from?'

'Rowen.'

She made a snorting noise. 'You'll be lucky; Rowen is practically cut off. Need a serious four by four. Or a set of huskies.'

The nurses on duty all laughed.

It took him an hour. Judging from the state of his appearance, James looked as if he maybe opted for the dog sled but Laura could have wept with relief. She caught his eye, but the nurse in charge did too and ushered him into her office, no doubt to give him precise details about her condition and aftercare.

Whatever he said, they must have been happy with his response, and he was allowed to collect her. He led her slowly back to the entrance, whereupon he had to carry her again over the ice, grit and frozen slush in the car park because she was wearing suede boots with kitten heels. He had a seriously filthy four by four, with snow chains on three of the tyres.

The volume of snow was quite a shock, in the way it was banked up at the sides of buildings and the surface of the road was treacherous. They joined a slow moving queue of traffic and Laura watched the scenery glide past with unfocused eyes. The sea was a massive void of restless grey, bouncing up the walls, and the sky was so low in places that Conwy castle's turrets looked to be draped with wet, grey cotton wool.

'Just take me to my sister's will you?'

'They're away, aren't they?'

He drove her to Maggie's house, then stood unhappily in the hall while Laura tried to disguise how weak she felt. There was a terse message on the answer machine from Simon, left the previous day.

'Laura are you there? I spoke to Barbara on Friday, and

she said you were going to Rowen. I know there's been a lot of snow. If you're ignoring me because of what we disagreed about then it's very childish. Charging off like that at the airport! You just missed that blue Golf GTi.' A long sigh before he continued. 'The flats are great by the way... if you're interested. Try and call me, will you?'

Laura pressed delete, and the machine made a long bleeping noise. James followed her into the kitchen and leant against the units with his arms folded, watching her every move. She couldn't get the boiler to start up and the fridge was switched off and defrosted because it was empty.

'Laura, there's no way I'm leaving you here on your own,' James said, 'you'll have to come back with me.'

'I can't do that.'

She slumped down into one of the kitchen chairs, needing to be alone with her thoughts, and her body as it went through this horrible, private female crisis. She didn't want to share the experience with a man who was a virtual stranger. He was a stranger with an axe, and a shotgun! Beginning to shiver after the heat of the hospital, Laura met his eyes and realised how tiny her options were.

'I need some more clothes and things,' she said.

He gave her a small nod of confirmation and waited while she went upstairs and looked through Maggie's wardrobe but everything was too big and she'd taken anything nice on holiday with her. She was marginally more successful with the contents of Jess's room. She found tampons as well but couldn't face those, and took about six months' supply of sanitary towels out of the airing cupboard. Depressingly, they half-filled a kitchen bin liner, and she tied a big knot in the top.

'I don't suppose you've got a hairdryer?' she said dismally from the landing.

'Somewhere,' he said, mildly exasperated, and clearly more concerned with making a move before they were both properly snowed in.

The gradient up to the yard was just about passable. Laura climbed out of the vehicle and stood on the doorstep of his house with her borrowed belongings in black bags and longed for her warm, clean and comfortable home. With Simon looking after her, and Alice far away in Australia.

'What are you waiting for?' James said.

'I don't want to stay in this mess of a house.'

'It isn't that bad,' he said, kicking the door open.

Washboy, nearly knocked them both flat. Laura followed him down the scuffed hall, feeling unbearably miserable and wondering if she'd done the right thing in leaving hospital. James stopped at the threshold of the kitchen and rubbed his unshaven face, 'Okay. It is a bit of a mess.'

The sitting room was better, and Laura stood awkwardly in the doorway while he made up the fire. She'd not seen this room before. Like the rest of the house, it wasn't tidy, but it was comfortable in a worn out way, with lots of old books in glass fronted cabinets, cushions and throws on big sagging sofas, and thick stone walls decorated with oil paintings of horses. The smell and crackle of the fire as it curled around fresh cut logs was incredibly soothing, nicer than the clinical under-floor heating at the apartment anyway.

James made her a pot of coffee. He announced he had work to do because no one could get up to feed their horses, and he was already miles behind with everything else. Laura held her hands out to the fire and watched through the window as he shovelled snow, filled and emptied buckets and manhandled bales of hay into the fields, until there was only the blush of twilight to see by and for a short while the snow-blown landscape looked magically illuminated.

She noticed that James had reversed her car into the barn, and her laptop, keys and phone charger were on the coffee table. When Laura plugged in her phone it sprang to life with messages, mostly Simon. It took only seconds to reply by text, explaining she was snowed in at Maggie's, and the same message went to Barbara at the office.

She didn't want to speak to anyone, or think about anything.

After a while, Laura could hear James in the kitchen. She went to stand at the door and he was doing a manic sort of clean-up, stuffing rubbish into bin bags and sweeping cats off the table. The washing machine was busy and looked to be full of mud.

'Do you think I could have a bath?'

'A bath?'

He told her to give him ten minutes and dived upstairs. After the allotted time had passed, Laura went to find him, and he was doing another clean-up operation in the bathroom. Eventually, she got to close the door behind her and dragged off her dirty clothes. There was no lock, but she couldn't have cared less if the whole Welsh rugby team decided to march in.

It was a pretty bathroom, although the antique washstand housed only razors and shaving foam, a stack of plain white soap and two bottles of expensive aftershave, both unopened. No bath oil or shampoo, but the bath was Victorian and cast iron, a proper roll edged one with claw feet and brass fittings, and the water was deep and hot, so it kind of made up for the lack of frills.

There wasn't much hope of relaxing though as Washboy nudged the door wide open, and had a good look at her. Stick thin with a whip-like tail, the dog went through all her belongings on the floor then finally made off with a bra and padded stealthily back down the stairs. Laura poked the door shut again with the aid of a dusty, thoroughly dried out loofah and lay back in the water.

She could hear James stripping sheets and dragging something out of a cupboard. It was mildly concerning that there was only two bedrooms, and one of them was full of stuffed birds in glass cases, guns and old bridles with torturous mouthpieces. It hadn't occurred to her where she might sleep, but anywhere had to be better than the maternity unit. She would have even settled for one of the loose boxes.

Laura dressed herself in Maggie's old tartan pyjamas and a fusty old dressing gown, which was on the back of the door. It had dog biscuits in the pocket and some nuts and bolts, which she carefully put in a porcelain bowl on the windowsill. Everything was miles too big and trailed past her hands and feet, but she couldn't have cared less. When she was watching the bath water running away, and it was tainted with the blood from her body, the ordeal of what she'd been through started to hit home. And she knew when the tears started they would rip her apart.

The noise of the water drowned them out at first, but she couldn't hide them, and she couldn't stop either. Everything inside her was breaking down into rivers of blood and tears, huge gut-wrenching sobs. Everything hit her, from failing her father to failing her unborn child and everything in-between. All completely irrational she knew, but it made no difference.

When the water had gone and Laura finally emerged from the bathroom, James was waiting for her, leaning against the wall. She went to hide her face in her hands, but he caught hold of them, pulled her gently towards him and hugged her, so closely she could feel the contours of his body, as if he could somehow impart the strength of it. Considering she barely knew him, it was an intimate gesture, but it felt completely natural, to stand with her head against him while he stroked her hair. For a long time, she only needed to focus on his heartbeat and the snow dripping off the gutters outside.

'I bet you wish you'd left me at Maggie's now,' she said into his chest. 'Every time I come to your house I'm in a horrible mess. I *make* a horrible mess.'

'How does that matter?' he said quietly.

Downstairs, he'd stacked up the fire again and Washboy was flat out in the heat, a pale pink satin bra entangled under his legs.

'I want you to eat something,' James said, turning back the cuffs on the dressing gown.

'I couldn't eat a thing, not even chocolate.'

'Uh huh, so it's serious.'

She tried to smile but her face didn't work like it used to. He made her a mug of sugary cocoa and a piece of toast, and she ate it all, but it lay like a lead weight in her stomach, as if she'd swallowed it whole. James worked his way through what looked like enough food for three people, before disappearing back outside. The dog investigated the remains of his meal, spilling cutlery and rice all over the floor as it licked the plate clean, then trotted after him with a big hunk of bread.

'I know you must be disgustingly fit,' she said, when he finally came back indoors, 'but you look shattered, don't you ever stop?'

'Almost stopped,' he said, and disappeared down the hall into the shower room. It didn't seem to bother him that Laura was there, and he flung his dirty wet clothes all over the floor and walked about in a towel, flicking the television on and rubbing his hair dry.

'Do you want your dressing gown back?' she said, keeping her eyes on the television.

'No thanks. Last used it on a Welsh cob called Fancy Bred.'

Laura sniffed the sleeves and had a horrible feeling he wasn't joking.

He dressed in another tatty pair of denims, then sat next to her with two mugs of tea, and practically a whole fruit cake, hacked into doorstops.

'You can't possibly be hungry,' she said.

'You don't reckon? After ten hours manual labour?'

The evening news was all about the weather, airports closed and roads blocked, but after about five minutes James had fallen asleep, and Laura just managed to grab the mug out of his hand before it hit the floor. The dogs dived in for crumbs.

Several hours later, Laura opened her eyes thinking she must be in the hospital because of the background noise, but she was crumpled up alongside James on the sofa. He had one arm around her, one hand tangled in her hair. The fire was almost out, Washboy was in a nose to tail curl on one of the chairs and an old episode of Friends was blaring out of the television.

'I think my arm is numb,' she said groggily and tried to sit up.

'Go to bed,' he said, yawning. 'First right, top of the stairs.'

'But that's your room. I can't take your bed as well.'

'Laura,' he said evenly, 'I didn't rescue you from that fucking hospital to sleep on this fucking sofa.'

She made her way slowly up the stairs, turned first right and fell into bed.

A small white terrier got in with her.

*

Laura woke early because she hadn't pulled the curtains and the dawn light threw strange shadows into the room. She supposed it was much like the rest of the house, shabby and dusty. There was a cast-iron fireplace and the floor was stripped oak, littered with piles of clothes and dog toys. The bedside table was cluttered with books, mostly psychology, the proper heavy-going medical kind, both human and equine; a lot of loose change and an expensive watch which had stopped on the second of June at ten-sixteen. But the bed was heaven. It was soft and clean and didn't smell of hospital. Laura luxuriated in the plain white linen for a while but started to feel guilty, and pulled the horse blanket cum dressing gown back on. When she got out of bed, her feet came into contact with an empty wine bottle, and it rumbled noisily across the uneven floor.

Downstairs, it felt like she must be outside, it was so cold. She knelt next to James, still on the sofa. At least he'd got a duvet from somewhere and one of the pillows off the bed. His clothes were thrown in a tangle over the back of the sofa, and for a second or two she was distracted by his bare arms and shoulders.

'James? Please go and sleep in the bed for a while. You've got a full day's work to do, I can sleep anytime.'

He rubbed his face and squinted at her grumpily, as if he couldn't remember who she was, then turned over and ignored her. Laura shuffled into the kitchen, which was marginally warmer because of the Aga, made some coffee, and trailed back up the stairs. It was fully dawn and the room was bright.

When she looked through the window, it took her breath away.

A white, backlit wilderness, it was like pastel-coloured fondant in the rising sun, broken only by tiny threads of black where the fence line was above the snow. There were only a few horses left out in the fields, and they stood motionless in their white domain. There was something calm and safe about it though, cocoon-like and suspended in time. But it felt all right, being suspended in time.

Around mid-morning, James wanted her to have breakfast with him. He'd already been outside for about three hours, and the hotplate was full of bacon and sausages.

'How many eggs do you want?' he said.

'One.'

'Don't be stupid. That wouldn't keep anything alive.'

He made her a perfect plate of fluffy, buttery scrambled eggs and toast. It was far better than anything *she* could have done. 'How come you can cook this good?'

'It's a life and death thing. I don't think I'd have survived past the age of ten if I hadn't done something about it.'

'Didn't your mother cook?'

'Not that I can remember,' he said, loading his plate with food. 'She made a fish pie once and nearly killed us all.'

'Tell me about her.'

'She writes screenplays and fiction. If she's in character, you might not get a coherent conversation out of her,' he said, taking the coffee pot off the Aga. 'It can be funny when you don't have to live with her, but my childhood was spent trying to understand why my mother was the one running through fields of bloody poppies in her nightie. At least, since Dad died she lives in Dublin, and it takes her longer to get here.'

'Ireland?' Laura said, stirring her coffee. 'My father lives in Ireland.'

'Tell me about him.'

Laura struggled with this because it always sounded like she was over sensitive or full of self-pity when she described her childhood and how much she'd disliked the farm. Maggie had loved the life and all it represented, the bartering at livestock markets, the hunting and the basic survival of life laid bare. She'd been a superb horsewoman, could handle a gun as well as any man, and thought nothing of killing a chicken for dinner.

But Laura had found little uplifting about living with the cold, the mud and the endless round of breeding, rearing, killing and eating. She still struggled with every aspect of the life her father had so endorsed. Most people thought of him as a proud, principled man of the soil, but Laura saw him as introspective and controlling with old-fashioned views.

James listened, and she was surprised by how much information he drew out of her.

'He was just trying to make an honest living out of what he knew. Same as me.'

'Maybe,' Laura said, 'but you're more... I don't know, nurturing?'

'You're very different to your sister,' James said, pushing his plate to one side. 'How come you thought she was always the favourite?'

'My sister did everything that was expected of her,' she sighed and studied her nails, 'and I had an affair with a married man.'

'So, you're the black sheep?'

'I disappointed him. With my choice of career, boyfriends, everything really. It all started when Mum died of cancer; I was only about eight. I don't think Dad could cope with me; I was too needy. He just carried on without her, as if she never existed, and I never really forgave him.'

'Maybe it was the only way he could deal with it.'

Laura slowly locked her eyes onto his, 'Is that how you deal with it?'

'I dunno. Sometimes it relents and lets me breathe for a while, but it comes back, drags me down into the black abyss, when I'm not expecting it.'

His words made her shiver. 'I still miss my mother.'

'I know what that feels like,' he said, and lit a cigarette, almost as if it was a full stop, as if he'd closed that train of thought. 'What about the rest of your family?'

'Just one older, very bossy sister.'

'Same here,' he said, then suddenly got up and went outside. When Laura glanced through the window an hour later he was still leaning on the paddock rail, staring at the dripping ice, and throwing finished cigarettes into the snow.

CHAPTER EIGHT

Laura

The weather forecast for the west coast of Wales was pretty accurate. The wind steadily increased, bringing the wind-chill factor down to about minus twelve, blowing the fresh dry snow into deep drifts. As dusk fell and the moon rose, everywhere began to freeze over, and James said it was like walking on diamonds.

Laura took his word for it, and watched while he made something spicy with rice and chicken. All the fires were roaring, and she wore Maggie's gardening jumper with one of James' sweaters over the top. She looked like a hillbilly.

'How much heat can you stand?' he said, offering her a spoonful to taste.

'Mmm, okay, a bit more.'

He grinned and added more chilli, then promised her a glass of wine if she ate it all.

It wasn't difficult, and he opened a bottle of Chardonnay. After dinner, they moved into the sitting room, and Laura's mobile rang and rang.

'Are you going to answer that?' James said until eventually he passed the handset to her.

'Laura?' Simon said, 'At *last!* Where are you? Is everything all right?'

'Fine. I'm in Rowen,' she said, her eyes on James.

'But I've been calling Hafod House, plus I've sent e-mails and pictures of the site.'

'Something was wrong with the telephone connection and the Internet. It must be the weather, the ice,' she said, 'didn't you get my text?'

'Well, yes, it's just that I hadn't spoken to you.'

He told her about the flats, and he asked her about the snow. When she ended the call, Laura switched the phone off. 'I don't know what you must think of me. I'm not sure what I think of me.'

'None of my business,' James said, poking the fire.

'I do feel like I owe you an explanation though, if you could bear to listen.'

He contemplated Laura for a moment; with her legs tucked up on his sofa, his little white dog nestled next to her, and topped up her wine glass with a shrug. 'Other people's relationships always baffle me. I don't mind listening, so long as you don't expect me to come up with a clever analysis.'

Laura explained how Simon wanted to fund the project in Spain.

'And you don't think that's a good idea?' James said, draining the wine bottle.

'No... but he'll go ahead anyway.'

Tentatively, she got round to her unplanned pregnancy, Alice and the children. Laura left nothing out, in fact, she wondered if she'd said too much about her relationship with Simon, which was far more than she'd ever told her girlfriends; however, that was because it would likely find its way back to Alice. She found her need for atonement was mostly down to the wine and her need to rationalise it all, plus James being such a good listener without falling asleep or butting in.

'Do you think Alice wants him back?'

'How am I supposed to know that?' he said, then after a moment, 'You haven't told him... about the miscarriage?'

Laura said she couldn't over the phone, but she knew why the words were really stuck in her throat; it was because she was scared that Simon wouldn't feel the same pain, and even more momentous than that thought, was the idea that he wouldn't want to try again.

And where would that leave their relationship?

James watched her pressing a wad of tissue over her eyes and trying not to break down. The dog pawed at her arm, not understanding her silent distress. Somehow Laura swallowed it all down.

'I'm a mess,' she said, cuddling the dog. 'Confused and irrational.'

James shook his head slowly. 'You're vulnerable. Massive difference.'

*

Despite the heart-searching, Laura slept for twelve hours, her body finally giving in to the food and wine and the comfort of the bed. She was only dimly aware of the howling wind rattling through the house causing it to creak, like a grounded old galleon ship.

James disturbed her while hunting through the wardrobes and searching the floor.

'Sorry,' he said, 'can't find anything. Have you seen a shirt with a big rip on the sleeve? There's a screwdriver I need in the pocket.'

'James, all your clothes look like that.'

He explained that he was going over to the barn by the cottages to see if he could move some horses over there because they were going stir crazy with lack of exercise. When Laura finally roused herself and looked through the bedroom window, she could see James leading six jostling horses slowly along the lane, with two loose ponies trotting behind.

He'd been through the room like a hurricane. Laura went to close the wardrobe doors, but when she caught sight of the contents, slowly opened them again. She ran her hand through the clothes and watched them drop back with a lifeless swing.

They were all small sizes, mostly plain and practical, and there were some nice long skirts and jackets and a floating dress, the kind you'd wear for a summer wedding. There was even a slight perfume clinging to everything, something faint and softened with time. She looked down at the boots and shoes and saw two boxes. Under a layer of tissue was a wedding album dated sixteen years previously, with James and Carys Morgan-Jones inscribed on the front. She didn't open it, as it seemed too personal. Next was a leather journal, full of a handwritten script all about the Arab horses.

Carys had written, 'Eira my grey mare is in foal again. She still has her late summer coat, like dappled sun through the old wisteria. Cariad is still protective of her, her firstborn.'

Laura flicked through the pages, and it was deeply evocative of her life, her love for the countryside and her horses. In fact, the emotion was so intense in parts, it was almost tangible. She set it back down carefully, and saw a carved wooden box. Inside was a diamond ring, a Victorian eternity ring and a wedding band with an inscription on the inside.

The room suddenly seemed airless and Laura snapped the ring box shut, closed the heavy wardrobe door and rested her forehead against it.

For a moment, it felt like someone was watching her. It was a strange sensation, knowing that the owner of the rings, the beautiful words and the perfume was gone from this place, gone from a place where the connection was deep and rooted. It didn't belittle the sadness over her miscarriage, but the significance of the belongings in the wardrobe altered the perspective. It had been a life, which had affected the lives of others, a life which had entwined so perfectly with another.

She looked through the window again, and James was walking back, his head down against the wind, the empty halters over his shoulder. He was in the kitchen by the time Laura ventured downstairs. James frowned at her, 'You okay? You look really white.'

'Just can't get warm,' Laura said, wrapping herself in her arms, knowing full well it had nothing to do with the temperature.

*

In the afternoon, she found a small pair of boots in the porch and wandered outside with one of James' coats over the top of two of his sweaters. She found him in the back paddock making a snowman, and the black mare was watching him with pricked ears, snorting indignantly when he rolled anything too close.

'That's not work,' Laura said, ducking under the fence.

'It is, kind of.' He produced a huge misshapen carrot out of his pocket and passed it to Laura. 'I've saved the best bit for you. I want to see where you put it.'

She smiled and stuck it firmly where the nose should be.

'Classy,' he said, 'I know where there are some more carrots. You can look through them all if you're interested.'

Laura laughed, and he studied her with his head on one side. 'I've never seen you laugh like that.'

'Not felt like it, and it takes too much energy,' she said, knocking the snow off her hands and stamping her feet. 'I hate feeling so weak and weepy all the time.'

'It's only been a couple of days. You'll get stronger. All that stuff that goes on in your head takes longer to heal than anything physical, even for horses,' he said, and took hold of her hand and placed it on the mare's neck.

The horse flinched, but stood calmly, hot breath meeting the cold air. Laura could see herself reflected in a dark eye. Beneath the rug, its warm body felt like liquid silk, its coat was so fine. It had a tiny white star on its forehead, and Laura noticed for the first time a long snaking scar, from its throat down the length of its gullet. James told her it was a knife wound. The thought of anyone plunging a knife into such a beautiful animal, made Laura feel sick to the stomach.

'She's so calm, I can't believe it,' she said, stroking the flat shoulder blade and feeling the muscle and bone of the horse beneath her hand, fascinated by how it all fitted together. 'I was scared, when you had that accident.'

'All forgiven; she trusts me again,' James said.

'Why doesn't she just run away? I would, if I were her.'

'She won't do that. The need for some kind of connection is stronger than fear.'

Laura dashed the tears from her face with the back of her hand. 'Now see what you've done?' she said, trying to smile. She took a deep breath and looked up at the bright blue sky.

'What's her name anyway?'

'Midnight Sky.'

*

Later, Laura washed her hair in the downstairs shower room with washing up liquid because he was out of shampoo, and the promised hairdryer was nowhere to be found.

'I don't suppose you've got any conditioner?' she said, her hair in a towel turban, but he could only come up with mane and tail shiner or cooking oil. She pulled a face and dried her hair in front of the fire, which took simply ages, then had to trek upstairs for her hairbrush. Laura stopped in her tracks.

James was sprawled across the middle of the unmade

bed. He was in a fathomless sleep, one arm flung across her pillow, and several layers of t-shirts had ridden up to reveal a tanned stomach with a slight, natural muscle definition. There was not an ounce of fat on him. Even asleep, he looked taut, driven. He was covered in cuts and bruises, his wrist still in plaster. Laura slowly draped the duvet over him, and he never moved.

Deep in thought, she crept back downstairs and put a few more logs on the fire. After a long time of staring at the flames, Laura realised she'd forgotten the brush, but her hair had already dried and was probably hopelessly fluffy. Her reflection in the bookcase confirmed as much, and she gave it up as an impossible job. Instead, she looked sideways at the volumes of books. A lot of them about animal behaviour, and the training and breaking and breeding of horses, some Celtic poetry, a new one about autism and children. The framed photograph took her eye.

It was Carys, it had to be. Long crinkly dark hair, petite build, very pretty eyes. It had been taken in the brightness of summertime, and it was very slightly out of focus because it looked as though she'd begun to laugh or smile at the last second, accentuating the life and warmth in her eyes. There were more of her with the horses, holding cups and rosettes, one with her arms around James, his head inclined close to hers. He looked different, softer, less wired.

Laura couldn't decide if the presence of Carys all over the house was a good thing or not. James was doing the exact opposite of what her father had done, but she was deeply touched that he cared enough to put up with her being there, sleeping in their bed.

*

After dinner, she found the energy to wash the dishes, but the kitchen was like a never-ending treadmill with one job leading to six more. James came to find her, and took her by the hand, a bottle of cognac in the other. He made her sit by the fire and the little white dog leapt up onto her lap. It was cute, nicer than the Lurcher, with a soft curly coat and tiny little pink paws. James told her she was called Lambchop but answered to Choppy or Lamby.

'This will make me fall asleep,' Laura said, swirling the amber liquid around the glass. 'You were well away this afternoon, didn't move for about four hours.'

'I don't even remember lying down. Christ, how old does that make me sound?'

'Is that how you deal with it? Hard physical labour?'

He knew what she was talking about. 'I've tried most things and nothing much touches it.'

'Such as?'

He laid his head back against the chair and closed his eyes. 'Cannabis, alcohol, smashing things up with an axe, taking off round America, even some safe legal drugs from the nice doctor.'

'You missed one out. Another relationship.'

'That's the very *last* thing I need, believe me. I could drive someone clinically insane with the stuff I've got in my head.'

'Tell me about her,' she said quietly, 'Tell me about Carys.'

'I'm sorry I can't,' he said, meeting her eyes. 'I find that... just too painful.'

'So is time not even a superficial healer?'

'I don't know. I'm up to the part where it just gets tired of tending the wound. You know, it's not exactly pouring with blood, but it's still raw, gaping open.'

'What was the taking off around America about?'

'I've got a son over there.'

'A son?'

'Not with Carys. I didn't know he even existed till he was

ten,' he said, and refilled Laura's glass. 'You look shocked.'

'I am, well, more surprised than shocked.'

He told her about Sam. He was twenty-two and after twelve years of long distance effort, they had an easy-going relationship, but James said he felt cheated out of all those early years.

'Did you never want children with Carys?'

'God, yeah, we both did, but it didn't happen till the very end,' James said, then instantly regretted the words, and Laura knew she'd probed too far, too deep. He got to his feet and stood over the fire, his hands on the mantle, and the room was totally silent other than the spit and crackle of the logs and the inconsistent ticking of the grandfather clock. 'You don't need to hear all that.'

'I do,' she said, with more conviction than she felt. 'Tell me... tell me what happened?'

For a long moment Laura thought James wasn't going to say anything, then he began to talk about the day his wife died. She'd gone out riding on the grey Arab, Cariad. When it began to get dark and she wasn't answering her phone, he began to get worried. Cariad trotted back into the yard by herself, her reins broken.

'I knew then. I knew she was dead,' he said bluntly. 'If she'd been alive, I think the horse would have stayed with her. And I just had this overwhelming, crushing feeling. Like I couldn't breathe any more.'

He told her how he'd called the emergency services and even ridden out there himself, to the rolling uplands above Rowen in the January dusk. He'd been unable to find her because his searching was too frantic, too random, but the mountain rescue dogs went straight to her.

'She was just lying on the moor, not a mark on her, but ice cold. Just staring at the sky,' he said quietly. 'You know what the worst part was? She'd tried to call me. She'd got the number up on her phone, but she hadn't pressed *call*. It was still locked in her hand.'

'Was it an accident?' Laura said, but he shook his head, rubbed his eyes.

Although he'd related the story with a steady clarity, it took James a minute to feel under control again. 'The autopsy said it was a pulmonary embolism, possibly brought on by pregnancy. She was thirty-one, and five weeks' pregnant,' he said and drained his glass then stared into it. 'It's me who's got the fucking heart failure.'

The logs fell in the fire, and Laura concentrated on the charred mess on the hearth. It hadn't been what she was expecting at all. The imagery his words had created in her mind were utterly harrowing. There was absolutely nothing she could think of to say, but she felt it. She felt it all.

'I understand,' she whispered.

*

The following afternoon, James turned out the horses, and they galloped in all directions, spraying mud. The snow was running off the mountains like icing off a giant cake, in dirty watery streams. Laura watched him for a while through the kitchen window, and he turned to smile at her, despite the pouring rain.

Later, he found her trying to sort out the wet clothes on the floor.

'You should be able to get home now,' he said, rubbing his hair dry and throwing the towel onto the wrong pile.

'I don't want to,' she said, stuffing pile number two into the washing machine, 'I want to stay one more night. Can I?'

'Really...?'

'But I want us to laugh and get drunk and not talk about anything serious or sad.'

'*Laugh…?*'

She switched the washing machine on, folded her arms. 'I'm going to sort this kitchen out.'

'Right. Good luck with that.'

Just before dusk, a battered Ford Fiesta pulled up in the yard and a girl climbed out, dressed for work. She gave James a token kiss and they seemed close, talked for a long while. Shortly after, Carla's BMW purred into view, and Laura dived away from the window, feeling suddenly exposed. She certainly didn't want to go into long explanations why she was in James' house.

'Are you sure I can't tempt you to the pub?' she heard Carla shout, as she got back into her car. 'Not even for a pie? You must be tired of talking to yourself… no?'

The other girl stayed longer, helping with chores, but then her car wouldn't start, and James had the bonnet up with a torch on the engine for ages, before finally resorting to taking her home. As a result, they ate late, but Laura enjoyed the hunger pangs. James gave her a bottle of red wine to open and asked how she liked her steak.

Minutes later he was complaining he couldn't find anything in the kitchen and was part irritated, part bemused when she tried to explain that all the expensive cooking utensils were in the decorative pot by the hob, not slung all over the table, stuck in buckets of horse mash, or chewed up on the bedroom floor.

'You *can't* keep garlic, dog wormers and drill bits in a Le Creuset casserole dish either,' she said, ignoring his perplexed face. Before he could ask where she'd put them, Laura pointed to two neatly labelled jam jars.

'I need the garlic,' he said, staring at her moodily.

Laura opened the fridge, and he foraged for ingredients, then threw everything onto the table, 'I'd hate to live with you, Ms interior designer *organiser.*'

'Not a problem after today,' she said struggling with the

corkscrew. 'Who was the girl?'

'Rhian? Been here years, worked with Carys, but we're not talking about that are we?'

She watched him throw onions and mushrooms into a pan and slid a glass of Cabernet Sauvignon next to him. 'You know, we've told each other a lot of secrets these last few days, you know more than my sister.'

'Yeah, well, you know more than *my* sister,' he said, and looked at her with a frown. 'I don't know why we've spilt our guts to each other. Even Carys' parents don't know some of what I told you. I sort of lied by omission, if you follow me.'

'I follow you,' Laura said, flicking her eyes onto his. 'You did it to protect them, that says a lot about you,' she went on, finding cutlery. 'Do all these shared secrets make us proper friends?'

He threw the steaks into the pan, 'Sounds a bit girly. I suppose I can handle it if you can.'

'I don't think I've ever had a man friend before. People reckon it can't work, sooner or later sex gets in the way, unless he's fashionably gay.'

'You know what I think about all that, and since I'm *not* gay I'm sticking to drugs and drink.' He put the plates of food onto the cleared table and topped up their wine glasses, ready to clink his against hers. 'Friends, you say?'

'I'd love that.'

'So long as it doesn't include shopping for shoes,' he said, holding his glass too high for her to reach.

'I don't need you for that.'

He slowly touched his glass to hers, and Laura was suddenly, blindingly aware of how much she liked him. Despite his dark intensity, or maybe because of it, there was something honest and unpretentious about him. Funny and sad was such an attractive combination, for a friend.

She made coffee, and they took it into the sitting room with two large glasses of cognac.

'I don't know when your birthday is,' Laura said, throwing herself down on the sofa with the dogs. 'I need to know these things if I'm your friend.'

At first she was dismayed when he told her it had been last Friday, the day he'd taken her to hospital, and she had to think quickly to avoid their conversation becoming morbid again. 'You must be Aquarian. That makes you a complex, caring, free-thinking humanitarian,' Laura said, aware that she was already beginning to slur her words and wag her finger at him. 'And they can be a bit eccentric.'

'I like the idea of eccentric. You can get away with all sorts.'

'Jess told me you ride in the menage with classical music playing through the speakers.'

'How's that eccentric?'

'And you've been seen standing on that circus horse.'

'Ed? That's only when Liz has gone home. I can't get him to canter in a straight line. Safe as houses, but kind of sad.'

'So he just goes in ever-decreasing circles?' Laura said, upending the bottle, 'That sounds like me.'

'Maybe he's *fashionably* gay,' James said thoughtfully. 'Not straight, never will be.'

Laura found his comment hilarious, couldn't stop laughing until even Lambchop slid off her lap, and James said he didn't think it was that funny, he was going to get another bottle of wine.

'I don't want any more!' Laura said, but he ignored her, had the cheek to say she was a lightweight. He also managed to knock over the table lamp and trip over the cable twice en route to the kitchen.

'Did you move the lamp?' he said, 'I'm sure it wasn't there this morning.'

'James, it *was*. It's been there about ten years judging by the dust on it.'

It took both of them to work out how the shade went

back on, and it seemed hopelessly complicated. 'Is it foreign?' Laura said, kneeling on the floor and looking at it from a different angle. Eventually James just plugged it in without the shade and all the lights flashed, then fused.

'Fuck. Now look what you've done,' he said, scrambling to his feet, but Laura grabbed his arm, 'James I don't want you to mess about with the electric, you're sloshed. Leave it.'

'Oh all right,' he said and nudged the dented lampshade with his foot. 'Maybe I'll just smash it up with the axe in the morning. Never did like it much, too flowery.'

Laura agreed it was, pulled the bedding down off the back of the sofa and settled herself underneath. 'I need oblivion,' she groaned. 'Your turn for the bed.'

'Look, we're not going to get in another argument over this.'

'We will if you don't go upstairs,' Laura said, and pulled the quilt over her head. She heard him fall over the lampshade in the dark and had to stuff the pillow in her mouth.

He trapped her in the duvet first, so that she lost the use of her arms, and attempted to carry her up the stairs. The whole process was immensely protracted because of the huge bulk involved and the narrow, crooked staircase, and then because Laura kept falling out. He didn't drop her, but they both practically fell through the doorway and James more or less threw her at the bed.

'Stop now,' she said feebly. 'That's making me feel really giddy.'

James collapsed next to her and she made a half-hearted attempt to dive off, but he grabbed the waistband of her jeans and Laura had to lie down slowly, the room spinning. She remembered nothing more until waking in the night, desperate for the loo and a drink of water. When she got back to the bedroom, dragging her clothes off in a trance and getting under the covers, she was suddenly aware that James was still there. At first she couldn't remember why and felt a small rise of panic. Did they...?

The previous few days came flooding back in an emotional backlog. Of course not, James was fully dressed on top of the bed, comatose. He was just her new *not gay* best friend. They'd been drunk and laughing, although the fight up the stairs and the lamp didn't seem so funny the second time around. Not funny in the *slightest*. Laura carefully removed his arm from her side, covered him with the spare quilt, and drifted into a sickly sleep.

When grey daylight seeped into the room, Laura could barely move. She could hear horses whinnying and kicking buckets. James was completely out of it and hadn't even changed position. It took three attempts of shoving his shoulder to get him to open his eyes. '*What?*'

'You're such a heavy sleeper.'

'Uh... is that it?'

Subdued with the effort, Laura lay flat and searched out his hand.

'James... I don't feel very well, do you?'

'No,' he said, and threaded his fingers through hers.

*

It didn't take long to pack a new bin liner. James had manoeuvred her car out of the barn, and left it on the lane with its nose pointing home. He was back under the bonnet of the Fiesta, covered in oil. Laura stepped round the bits of engine on the floor and wondered what to say.

'I think I've just reconnected the ignition to the brake lights,' he said. 'It's your fault, getting me hammered like that.'

'I don't remember you stopping me. Do you think I'm over the limit to drive?'

'Keep the air con on full,' he said, and threw the tools

on the floor so he could lean against the car. He surveyed her crumpled clothes and frizzed out hair with a reflective expression. 'I never asked you when your birthday was.'

'September, that's Libra,' Laura said, 'Lover of all things beautiful, balanced and harmonious. Likes good company, hates to be alone and likes to be neat and clean.'

'You must have hated it here with me. A manic depressive with a filthy kitchen and no hair conditioner.'

She didn't smile, but dropped the bag and slid her arms around him then pressed her cheek against his cold face, ready to say all kinds of things, but all she managed was, 'I haven't hated it.'

James didn't return her embrace, didn't even watch her drive away.

When Laura checked her rear-view mirror there was only Midnight Sky watching her, ears pricked forwards, her mane and tail just catching the wind.

CHAPTER NINE

Laura

Laura drove back to Hafod House, replaced her borrowed things, and organised a plumber to fix the heating. She was home in less than an hour. Deadly tired and with a considerable hangover, Laura showered, smothered her hair in conditioner and went to bed, but restful sleep was elusive. Although her body was wrung out, her mind was full of intense, mixed-up dreams as if her mind had been in a cocktail shaker.

All she could see was Carys, lying bone white and cold on the moor, staring at the black sky. Then it was Midnight Sky, galloping across the skyline with a bloodied neck, the whites of her eyes rolling in fear. Searing white light, like the lights in the hospital and Laura was dragging her clothes off because she was far too hot, and his body was pressed against hers, hard and sensual. A woman she didn't know was patting her hand, and she felt suddenly sad, almost blinded by the darkness. Oh, there was a baby crying… Laura sat bolt upright, her heart pounding, drenched in sweat.

She grabbed her mobile from the bedside table, took a moment to recover.

There was a text from James. 'Okay, where's the cat food?'

Her hands shaking, she made the call, finally. It took a

while to connect and there was a lot of background noise, a bar maybe.

'Simon?' she said, almost shouting. 'I need you to come home.'

'Laura, is that you? I can hardly hear you.'

'I've lost the baby,' she said, pinching the bridge of her nose to stop the flow of tears. Her words took a second to register, then he groaned. 'I *knew* there was something wrong. I'll get the next flight. Laura? Are you still there? Oh, God, love, when did this happen?'

'*Please*, just come home,' she said, and threw the phone across the bed.

*

Simon was home in the early hours of Friday morning. Everything at the airport had been backed up, so he'd had a nightmare journey on a budget airline via Munich, but all that didn't matter and she practically fell into his arms as he came through the door.

He was wet-eyed when he caught sight of her, and it was all genuine; Laura had no doubt of that. Of *course* he was upset, he said. What on *earth* made her think he wasn't going to be upset? Did she think he was some kind of monster?

'I'm sorry, I feel all mixed up.'

'You're completely overwrought,' he said gently and took charge of the entire weekend.

Simon couldn't do enough for her, running baths, making her stay in bed, showering her with duty-free perfume and filling the apartment with sprays of expensive flowers, but it wasn't enough.

James had told her that mental and emotional energy moved in and out of physical form. Laura repeated it to Simon because it fascinated her, told him she'd read it in a magazine. If she was honest, he was slightly baffled with anything he perceived to be too introspective or soul-searching.

The statement made him frown for a long time. 'What's that supposed to mean?' he said, eventually. 'Laura, stop overthinking, no wonder you can't sleep.'

When Simon went in to the office, she remembered the text from James and replied, 'The cat food is in the boot cupboard. Bone to pick with Washboy. Pink bra missing.'

After a few minutes he replied, 'What cat? Starved to death. What bra? Be buried.'

Laura smiled and sent 'Bra belongs to Jess'.

After a few minutes he sent, 'Can I call you?'

Can I call you? She kept reading the text like it was a mantra. If it were a girlfriend she wouldn't think twice. In the end, Laura harnessed her mental energy and made the call herself.

'How are you?' he said.

'I don't know, actually. James the cat didn't really starve, did it?'

He laughed. 'No don't be stupid. You just took ages to text back. Don't put it in there again though, the dogs scoffed the lot and threw up in the village shop.'

'Oh sorry! You keep fading. Where are you?'

'I'm riding Carla's drama queen of a horse. It's been stood in for days, so she won't ride it till I've tired it out, only she used slightly different contextual wording.'

'James... I want to say thanks for looking after me. You were way more than a friend.'

There was a short silence, and for a moment, Laura could only hear the wind and the metal clink of the horse's footfall on stone. He said, 'You don't have to worry about me saying anything.'

'I know. That's why you're more than a friend.'

'Shut up, you'll have me agreeing to go shopping next.'

She smiled, wiped her eyes, 'Better go...'
'Bye, love,' he said and disconnected quickly.

*

More flowers arrived from the girls with a card wanting to arrange to meet up for a drink. They'd found out via Steve, and Pam and so on, but Laura couldn't face it. She didn't want to explain how she felt while they all put their sharp opinions forward. Chrissie had had lots of babies, all delivered naturally with virtually no pain relief. She'd be all clingy with Laura, urging her to try again. Trisha would find some way to be scathing about Simon, and if Pam was talking to Alice… Laura didn't want to talk to Pam.

Simon agreed it was inappropriate. 'Don't worry, I'll explain to them. I'll get a takeaway and we'll have a quiet night in, open a nice bottle of wine.'

They ate in silence. Laura had a very small appetite, and Simon wasn't much better. She was expecting him to try and talk her round to the Marbella project, and then try and talk her out of trying for a baby again. 'You're very quiet,' she prompted.

He sighed and threw his fork down, 'I'm worried we're going in different directions.'

Laura was thrown by his demeanour; he was normally so upbeat, full of ideas and quick-fire answers. 'What do you mean?' she whispered, knowing full well what he meant.

'To be honest, I feel under considerable stress, with you and Alice and the business.'

'Keep talking.'

He began to count items off on his fingers, 'Alice, Australia, the divorce, the children, it just goes on and on. Plus trying to make enough money for all of us. Marbella is *solid*, I swear to you, but you seem so down on it, and I need you with me,' he said, meeting her eyes. 'Alice is serious about Australia. You know she's gone and put the house on the market!'

'So? She can't sell if you don't sign. Maybe you should sell, get rid of the mortgage and her at the same time.'

'And what about my kids?' he said, running a hand through his hair.

'Look, you know what I think about Australia. Call her bluff, stand up to her!' Laura sighed, and distracted herself with the espresso machine. 'Right, we've talked about you, and Alice... why am I included in your stress list?'

'*Why*? First of all you lie about the abortion. It took you a *week* to tell me that it never happened. It took you *another* week to tell me about the miscarriage! Have you any idea how that makes me feel? Some things just don't add up.'

Laura slid the coffee cups onto the table, knowing there was an uncomfortable element of truth from his side of the fence. He wanted to go over the sequence of events again. 'So, you were at the cottages, and it was snowing, and it all started. And Morgan-Jones took you to the hospital?'

'Yes. And I stayed in because of the snow, and James-'

'*James?* First-name terms with the clients now?' he said, then shook his head and made her continue.

'*James* collected me, because there was no one else, and dropped me at Hafod House. I admit I didn't make much effort to speak to you because I was... well, I was scared you wouldn't feel the same and anyway you couldn't have got back.'

'So at this point, you drove home, went to pieces and called me?'

'Yes!'

*

Towards the end of the week, she did what James had done and went back to work. Simon was pleased because they were ten days behind with everything, and he'd been twitchy about it all week. Laura settled herself at her desk, and he brought her a cup of tea, hunkered down to her level. 'Are you sure you're all right?'

'What needs to be done?' she said, switching on her screen.

'Well... we could do with making a start on the electrics and the plumbing on the cottages.'

'I need to work on the interior plans a bit more first.'

'Right... I'll leave you to it,' Simon said, grabbing his phone and his car keys. 'If you get tired, promise me you'll go home?'

'I'm fine,' she snapped.

She knew why Simon was pushing for the cottages to be done, he needed the money. She'd seen a draft contract for the purchase of the holiday flats on Barbara's desk, waiting to be posted to Graham Gallagher. Laura waited till he'd gone before she studied all the e-mails he'd sent from Spain. It was a nice location, but the accommodation looked hideous, and the site was huge. The biggest worry was that the figures were tight, there was no margin for error. At the end of the serious shots was a daft picture of Steve and Simon in a bar, enjoying themselves in the early summer sun in straw hats and white chinos, like property tycoons.

She went back to the cottage plans and worked for an hour, then had to e-mail the yard for some information before she ordered kitchen units and fireplaces. She kept it business-like, asked for measurements of the chimney breast in the larger cottage and some of the windows. Barbara arrived and was horrified to see Laura at her desk and fussed around her all afternoon, and then Bill was there with flowers and more commiserations. She was short-tempered with them both, and had to apologise.

'It's all right, love, we all understand,' Bill said, not really understanding.

Just before five o' clock Barbara answered the phone and put the call on hold.

'Mr Morgan-Jones,' she said, covering the mouthpiece. 'Nice voice. What does he look like? I'll bet he's all weedy and wears an anorak.'

You wouldn't be disappointed. 'Always the way isn't it?' she said to Barbara, and picked up the call.

James said, 'What are you doing in the office?'

'Working, it's therapy.'

'It's too soon. Have you been there all day?'

'I'm much better, thank you,' Laura said loudly, glancing across to Barbara, then swivelled her chair round to face the window and lowered her voice, 'Have you found any buried treasure? As in pink satin 36CC?'

'What? Oh that, could be anywhere.'

'That's what I'm afraid of.'

'My dog's got a bone to pick with you, as it happens. You've gone and boil-washed his jumper, it's too tight. He pees on the floor if he gets cold. Even I draw the line at that.'

'It was *filthy*! I'll get him another,' she said, trying to avoid Barbara as she flitted about the office, printing off documents and sorting out the post. She turned the chair back to face her desk and shuffled some paper about. 'Okay, Mr Morgan-Jones, if you *could* just get those measurements to me I'd appreciate that.'

'If I just think breasts, I'll remember the digging job as well.'

'Both, as a matter of some urgency please,' she said curtly, mostly to stop herself laughing.

'I'm on it, Miss Brown.'

Considering they were both basically morose, it was an odd twist of human nature that the little clandestine conversations and messages she shared with him were the only things to make her smile. Maybe it was because it didn't take very much effort, and he expected nothing of her. The remainder of the time, Laura was moody and weepy.

*

Maggie came home in the middle of the following week. The first thing she did was call Laura and thank her for the welcome home of a warm house. Simon couldn't believe it when Laura ended the conversation without a mention of her miscarriage.

'Simon, she's just stepped off the plane with jet lag, I'm not going over it all now!' she said, annoyed that he'd been listening whilst pretending to read the paper, but immediately softened when she saw the concern in his face. 'I'm sorry. I know I'm being a cow, but I can't stop.'

He folded the paper and moved across to the sofa, put an arm around her. 'Laura, don't take this the wrong way, but why don't you have a chat with Doctor Wilson?'

Laura looked up at him under her eyelashes. 'You don't know what to do with me, do you?'

'I just think it might help.'

'Can she help get me pregnant again?' she said without thinking, but getting pregnant again was all she really thought about. Simon looked at her for long seconds and didn't take his eyes from hers, 'All right, this is what I think. What I'd like to do is get this Marbella project in the bag, sort out this mess with Alice, and then when our finances are more stable, we can talk.'

She knew all of that made sense, but it all sounded too much like a projected life plan.

'Talk won't get me pregnant,' she said petulantly.

'Neither will all this stress.'

But the stress was down to Simon. Just before the

exchange of contracts on the Marbella project, Steve pulled out. Laura was pleased at first, thinking it would all fall apart, but Simon decided he wanted to go it alone on the back of an even bigger loan. Laura thought he must have taken leave of his senses, but Simon insisted Laura behaved like his business partner and took a proper look.

Hoping to be the voice of reason, Laura agreed. If nothing else, the trip might claw back the lost ground in their personal relationship as well. The sun, sea and sangria effect had to count for something. What it actually boiled down to was two days of following Simon around an out-of-date concrete jungle, in a sudden wave of blistering heat.

'What do you think?' he said. 'Can you cost out some refits?'

'Simon... I *hate* it.'

'That's not a professional opinion.'

'It's my opinion. I need to feel some kind of connection to be creative.'

'This isn't about being self-indulgent Laura! It's about making money.'

After a couple of days of mostly negative bickering, Laura left him in Marbella speaking broken Spanish, trying to sort out all the finances and find contractors. There hadn't been much romance either. Although, all Laura really longed for was tenderness.

It was a relief to be home, walking through Chester town in the fresh green of a cool spring day. She picked out a few summer tops and a pair of sandals. It was easy to waste time, sitting under the birch trees and watching the street artists. Towards the end of the afternoon, Alice found her in Starbucks.

'Had an offer on the house,' she said smugly, and pulled out a chair opposite. '*Cash.*'

'Good for you.'

'Well, it might well be good for Simon too,' she said,

slurping away at a chocolate confection through a straw. 'I hear he's got himself into a tight spot. Financially.'

'None of your business.'

'Oh, but it is,' she said, and leant in closer, popping a marshmallow into her mouth. 'I've got him in a tight spot as well. *Sexually.*'

Laura stared at Alice, and Alice stared back but rather more enigmatically. 'Tell me, how does it feel? Everything slipping away…money… security… chance of a family… *love*. Not nice is it?'

'What do you *want*? You evil cow!'

'Evil? Bit strong isn't it? I just want you to *feel* what I did. Remember, it was you who had an affair with my husband,' she said, and laughed. 'Actually he still is my husband!'

'Why can't you just move on? He doesn't want you back, and you don't want him.'

'How do you know that? Si still cuts quite a dash. I might just see how he shapes up. He may have learnt a lesson, I mean, you haven't been easy these last few weeks.'

'You don't fool me, Alice.'

'Ah, but he fools you. I know how he works. Inside information,' she said and tapped the side of her nose, then finished her drink with a noisy flourish. 'I bet… I bet I can reel him in on the promise of say… fifty thousand?'

'I've got a better idea. Why don't you just fuck off to Australia?' Laura scraped her chair back and slopped the remains of her coffee over the table.

'Oh, ciao!'

Laura kept on walking, her insides shaking, her hands shaking. When she was far enough away, she fumbled in her bag for the pills and forced one down her bone-dry throat.

*

Laura drove over to Rowen the following weekend. It was March and everywhere was windblown. All the snow had vanished, leaving muddy verges studded with sprouting crocuses, primroses and narcissi. The bright, weak sunshine wouldn't last, but it was uplifting to breathe in the new growth and the soft spring air.

It had been five weeks since her miscarriage. Doctor Wilson had given her a short supply of anti-depressants and told her to rest and get her physical strength back. She'd said much the same as James had done although in more clinical terms and without the aid of a disturbed steeplechaser.

'I don't think working is a good antidote. I'd like you to take a break.'

As soon as she stepped out of her car, Maggie was there, arms around her and tugging the bag out of her hands. She'd already told her sister about the ordeal over the phone so she didn't have to lie face to face about staying in the house. She could tell Maggie hadn't quite swallowed it, but her sister had the sense to realise it wasn't the main issue. The only person to really grill her was Jess.

'So, he *carried* you into the hospital?' she said, watching Laura's face intently. 'And he came back, through all the snow?'

Laura tried her best to be honest without giving the game away, but Jess wouldn't leave it alone, probing for every tiny detail. 'Look,' Laura said patiently, deciding to play the trump card, 'I can tell you that he just isn't interested in *any* kind of relationship, serious or casual.'

'He told you that, did he?' she asked quickly, her eyes narrow.

'I think he's still in love with his wife.'

'Yeah well, that's because he's the real deal,' Jess said, with enormous satisfaction.

*

On Saturday morning, Laura gathered a few daffodils from the bottom of Maggie's garden and walked to the old church, reading all the familiar headstones. She sent James a text, 'Meet Rowen church?' Laura was poking the flowers into the old pot on her mother's grave when he arrived.

'Last time I arranged to meet a woman here it was to get married.'

She got to her feet and smiled, shading her eyes from the sun. 'Carys?'

He nodded. 'How are you?'

Laura took the tablets from her pocket and rattled them. He read the label with his head sideways. 'Citalopram. I've done those. Couldn't string two sentences together after a while. They just mask everything.'

'You're probably right,' she said and looked up at the old apple trees. There were tiny pink buds on the gnarled branches. 'I'm afraid I've got you here under false pretences; I don't want to marry you. Can I buy you lunch to make up?'

'Yeah, okay,' he said easily. 'It's going to have to be good though, to make up for jilting me. If we're going to the pub, I'll have meat and potato pie, then jam roly-poly and custard, and two pints of real ale.'

'Is that all?' she said and patted his washboard stomach.

*

The following day at the yard, Liz homed in on Laura. After the usual commiserations, Liz was anxious to say how furious she was with James for leaving her at Maggie's house. 'He should have brought you to me! He just doesn't think. I've told him what I think of his *bloody* inconsiderate behaviour,' she snarled. 'He must have been on one of his downers that week. Nothing much got done. I don't think he set foot in the office. Lord Brixton-Smith is on the phone every day wanting his weekly report about Midnight Sky, from *five weeks ago.*'

Laura looked miserably at her boots, suddenly unable to string two sentences together, while Liz laid in to James again, telling him exactly what she thought. He took it all calmly, including the stabbing finger. Jess, her antennae immediately on full alert, sidled a bit closer. 'Back off, can't you?' she said haughtily to Liz. 'If auntie Laura is okay with it, what's it got to do with you?'

James put an arm across Jess' shoulders and wheeled her away in the opposite direction.

Laura sent him a text, 'Lifesaver. *Sorry* X'.

His reply came back as, 'Twice now. XX.'

Later, Maggie suggested a walk down the beach so they could have a proper talk without anyone earwigging. The tide was turning and there was a flat expanse of hard sand, broken only by mussel banks and groups of oyster catchers. They climbed up through the sand dunes and found somewhere sheltered to sit and watch the trawlers on the azure horizon.

'So, how are you really?' Maggie said, chewing a stalk.

'Not sure,' Laura said, letting sand run through her fingers. 'Doctor says it's normal to feel low, but I feel like I'm losing Simon as well. Going in different directions I think he called it.'

'He wants to be careful he's not losing *you*,' Maggie said, keeping her eyes on the sea. Laura took a deep breath of the salty air and tried to focus on the gentle swell of the breaking tide as it rushed at the shore. The sea was meant to be healing.

'There's a beach ride on Wednesday,' Maggie went on, leaning back on a clump of marram grass. 'James says I can ride his horse.'

'So, why don't you? I wish I had the bottle to do it, blow

the cobwebs away.'

'Jess will think I'm spying on her. She's still in lust.'

'Actually, I think it may well be more than lust, and I may have made it worse,' Laura said. 'I just seem to make everything worse.'

'Tell me about this direction you're going in.'

'Downhill?' she said, then when Maggie scoffed, continued. 'I just want a child. Simon wants a holiday complex in Spain. To him, it's all about his finances and his ex-life. Apparently, when all that's finally sorted out and world peace is in sight, we can have unprotected sex.'

'Well, I suppose it's kind of promising, a compromise,' Maggie said carefully. 'Can't blame him for being cautious. I know it's not a big yes, but it's not *no*, is it? It's something in-between.'

'It's called stalling, that's what it is.'

Laura had the feeling Maggie was stalling as well, tiptoeing around her feelings in an uncharacteristic attempt to stay impartial.

It wouldn't last.

*

In an attempt to do something positive and catch up on their long-ago cancelled meeting, Laura arranged to meet Liz for a drink before she drove home, and at long last, they managed to discuss the cottage interiors.

'I think the larger one is family accommodation, and I think we should stick with practicalities. But the small one, Mefysen, is it? It's a couples thing. How do you feel about putting a small four-poster in?'

'Great. Just go ahead,' Liz said, sipping her gin and tonic. 'Look, there's no rush if you don't feel on form. I had a miscarriage once, knocked me for six, to be honest,' she said, chewing her lip. 'And there's me laying into my little brother. I was too hard on him, wasn't I?'

'It must be a struggle to live with something like losing a partner.'

'God, yes, she was far too young. They were inseparable. The shock was like nothing else. Part of me feeling angry is me feeling helpless, I think. I don't know how to help him,' she said emphatically. 'If it's not something practical I'm useless.'

Laura looked into her gin and tonic and wondered if any of that logic applied to Simon. 'She's not buried in the local church, is she?'

'No,' Liz said, and for a moment Laura thought she wasn't going to expand on the answer. Liz swirled the ice round in her drink first, kept her eyes on the glass. 'He took her horse up to the moor and scattered her ashes at dawn. Wanted her spirit to be free, where it was always happiest. His words, not mine.'

'I think that's quite... liberating.'

'Well, took some guts,' she said, and downed her drink. 'Sorry, it gets me every time. It's this bloody menopause. Let's have another drink shall we?'

Simon rang while Liz was at the bar. 'Hi, love, are you still in Rowen? You couldn't just check the electrics at the cottages could you?'

'Yes, I suppose so... be a couple of hours in that case. What are you doing?'

'Meeting a cornice specialist at that Victorian villa. He's late.'

She ended the call just as Liz put another drink in front of her. Laura said something about checking the electrics. 'Oh don't bother,' Liz said. 'I know it's on because James has been cutting the grass in the back, and he took a kettle up there.'

It could have been the antidepressants kicking in, but

Laura felt a chink of hope lift her spirits on the drive home. Simon, Liz and Maggie were a bit similar in a crisis. When she thought about Simon and everything they'd survived together in their relationship and the business, it was a testament to how solid they really were. What were those words Jess had used?

The real deal!

She rather hoped the Victorian villa was the real deal as well, relieve some of the financial pressure. A dilapidated rambling place with six bedrooms, Laura had only seen pictures, so on impulse and partially to avoid some roadworks, she headed along Cherry Road. When she passed the end of Cherry Grove, she slowed down for the speed bump and out of the corner of her eye, saw the For Sale board in Alice's garden... and Simon's car.

Laura carried on, found the villa and parked outside. It had a massive crack down the gable end, but Bill would sort that out. It was fabulous really, a substantial family house, if anyone bought those kind of properties any more. It would probably be better divided up into three flats, which was kind of depressing in one sense.

Laura must have stared at nothing for about five minutes, then called his mobile.

'Laura! Where are you?'

'On the A55... where are you?'

'Oh, so you'll be a while... meet at home?'

Laura stared at the empty property for another five minutes, before driving slowly to Cherry Grove. Once there, she parked outside and looked at the house It was a traditional three-bed detached in a good residential area but shabby from lack of love and care. Tara's cycle lay propped against the sidewall, one of the wheels had a flat tyre, and there was a broken slide on its side. The spring grass was about a foot high and gave it an air of haunted neglect.

She walked passed Simon's car, stood in the dusty porch,

rang the bell and looked at the mess of post, papers and empty bottles. Alice answered, mildly surprised but not in the least flustered.

'Oh, Laura, come in. Are you looking for Si?'

Laura ignored the obvious and stepped inside the hall, just as Simon was coming down the stairs. He did a sort of disguised double take at her. 'What are you doing here?'

'Same question to you. I've just been to the villa.'

'You *said* you were still on the A55.'

'So I lied,' she said coldly, hardly believing the words coming out of her mouth. 'Why are you here, Simon?'

'Waiting for the children. Would you believe that guy never turned up?' he said, coolly.

'The children won't be home for hours. Why were you upstairs?'

'I've just used the bloody bathroom, is that all right?' Simon said, his eyes flicking to Alice and back again. He found his shoes at the bottom of the stairs and sat on the bottom step.

'You *implied* you were at the villa.'

Alice was enjoying this immensely, arms crossed under her big boobs, looking from one to the other as if she were watching Wimbledon. The top button of her dress gaped open, but that was normal for Alice. The loose hair was unusual though.

'Just what are you accusing me of?' Simon said, and got to his feet. 'Meet me at the office, and we'll discuss some more obvious *implications*.'

A cold shiver tightened across her scalp and left Laura almost breathless with the injustice.

She followed Simon's car into their parking space in a trance, and followed him wordlessly up the office stairs, whereupon he dismissed Barbara. When they heard the door close behind her, he told Laura to log on to her computer. She knew what was coming. Simon scrolled down all the messages between James and herself with a sanctimonious expression.

'Here we go, this is the best one,' he said. '36CC still on the loose! Why does our current major client know your bra size? Not forgetting all the texts on your phone.' He snatched her mobile off the desk before she could reach it. He said, 'Oh there are new ones. Meet Rowen church...Twice now, followed by kiss kiss.'

'You're making something out of nothing. Everyone does a cross at the end of a text.'

Laura watched him go through the drawer in his desk, slapped a pile of plumbing quotes onto the top. 'Here's another question for you,' he said, sliding an invoice out of a folder. 'Hafod House. The replacement of a copper coil and an ignition switch, it's the date that's interesting. It happens to fall right at the end of that same week, the week that doesn't add up. You know the week you had a miscarriage and spent it in a freezing cold house by yourself? *That* week.'

Less than an hour ago she'd been almost happy.

Though it had no substance, it was false emotion, wishful thinking collapsed in an instant by his harsh accusations, its foundations as shaky as the subsidence at the villa.

CHAPTER TEN

Maggie

Maggie lay on the bed trying to pull a new pair of stretchy pants over her legs and a huge pair of padded knickers. The top of the pants met the lower waistband of the new no-bounce bra. She gritted her teeth with exertion.

'I'm furious with Simon.'

'I've told you before he's a prat, but you wouldn't have it,' Pete said, frowning. 'Those trousers are too small for you, Maggie. Your sister could run that business single-handed. All he does is ponce about with a clipboard.'

'Not at the moment she couldn't, she's like a zombie. She's so sad, Pete, all she wants is a baby, love and security. I'm going down there to tell him exactly what I think. Laura needs a proper man,' she said, finally standing on the bed and clenching her fists in the mirror. 'We need a Mr Brown to look after our Paddington.'

'Maggie,' he said wearily. 'I've told you this before as well. Stop getting involved in other people's business. And that goes for our Jess.'

'So it doesn't bother you that your daughter is *intent* on seducing a man in his forties?'

'If she makes a mistake, she'll learn something. She *won't* learn if you keep stopping her from living,' he said, seemingly pleased with his little speech and left her jumping up and down on the bed in what Maggie hoped was a good simulation of O'Malley in full gallop.

Maggie thought about his words all the way to the yard, knowing he was right but knowing she wouldn't be able to stop voicing her opinion if an opportunity arose. There was a lot she needed to get off her chest, but the timing was never right. She hadn't even told Pete about Nathan yet, and she hadn't told him that she thought Jess could be suffering from middle-child syndrome, which would account for her outrageous attention seeking. Then there was Ellie, due to start secondary school later in the year. It was vital she continued with James through the summer, but Pete was getting so tight with money, Maggie was starting to get cross with him, cutting the plugs off appliances and taking fuses out of things, pretending they were broken. The latest fad was a fuel-consumption gauge.

A good gallop down the beach was just what she needed to help her feel less uptight.

James was loading horses into the lorry when Maggie arrived, and they were all keyed up, whinnying to each other. When James spotted Maggie, he called out to Rhian to bring out O'Malley. He looked bigger than ever and spooked at everything. Maggie felt her stomach sink. If she needed to get airlifted to hospital off the beach, how would she explain the XXL equestrian knickers? She'd probably be declared incontinent and popped on a commode.

A wooden partition went in after O'Malley, followed by the horse James was going to ride. They could hear it lashing out at the horsebox walls with its hind feet. Liz watched with a scathing look. 'Is that the one that bites and kicks? The one the knacker's yard *paid you* to take away?'

'What gave you that idea?' James said, lifting up the ramp and knocking the bolts home.

'Make sure you've got NHS Direct in your phone. I'm going shopping.'

James drove the lorry over to the beach car park, and Maggie followed in the Toyota trying to feel light-hearted. It was like a summer morning with the lightest of breezes rippling over the sea to make tiny white crests, and the sky was the pale duck-egg blue of early spring.

It took a while to get everyone mounted up, but finally they picked their way through the dunes and over the shingle, the horses jogging and excited.

'Why have I got the slowest horse?' Jess said, kicking on her mare to keep up.

'It won't be in a minute,' James said, 'it's got a thing about the beach. Like I said before, needs strong riding, but you wouldn't listen.'

'Yeah, right,' she said, thoroughly fed up with him.

Maggie was pleased; she needed knocking down a peg or several.

Once on the hard sand close to the edge of the sea, James told Maggie to keep O'Malley at the front, and follow the tide line for about two miles.

'Ready when you are,' he said, 'No one come near me. Give Cutie Pie a wide berth.'

Maggie did her best to set the pace but the horse was stronger than last time and within seconds they were flying, four distinct hoof beats followed by a moment of suspension. As she approached Penmean Head, the incoming tide curved across her path and made a natural barrier with a deep inlet. O'Malley slowed, blowing at the long run, and Maggie easily pulled him to a halt, exhilarated with the whole experience. For a while, there had been nothing in her head except the horse and the vista of the beach.

When Maggie wheeled O'Malley round, she saw James galloping erratically along the edge of the sea, but Jess and her mare were intent on just ploughing through it, sending up huge sprays of water. As they approached the inlet, rather than slow to a gentle halt, the mare suddenly had a burst of speed and rushed straight into it then stopped dead and deposited Jess in about two feet of sea. Ears pricked, it trotted into the deeper water, sank to its knees, and lay down with a satisfied grunt.

Everyone shrieked and laughed, but Maggie was horrified. It wasn't that Jess had hurt herself; it was because her shirt was rendered mostly see-through. Remarkably, Jess was speechless, and for a long moment she was freeze-framed with her mouth open and her hair dripping.

James shouted, 'Catch hold of Kestrel before she rolls... Jess!'

She still didn't move, so James had to wade in, seawater up to his knees, and drag the horse to its feet. It came up like Neptune with all the tack dripping wet, and shook violently, like a huge dog. While he held the horse at arm's length, Jess suddenly sprang to life and tried to pull him over, first by clutching his hair then by grabbing hold of the front of his jacket, but she was nowhere near strong enough to get any leverage so she kicked sprays of water at him instead.

Carla found a cigarette. 'Look at those two love puppies.'

Maggie watched, aware her mouth was forming into an unattractive shape, like a pig's snout. Jess looked like Barbarella with a Floridian tan and a barely-there bra judging from her in-your-face-nipples show. Not for the first time, Maggie wondered how a seemingly celibate man resisted her when she lolled all over him and put her hands up his shirt at every opportunity, even if on this occasion it also involved several gallons of cold Irish sea water. There followed the farce of helping her back onto her horse. Jess pretended she didn't understand the principle of a leg-up and kept falling into him, milking it for all it was worth. Somehow, once back on the horse, she even managed to get the maximum wobbling effect out of her chest, caused entirely by her grossly exaggerated chattering teeth.

'I'm *freezing*, Jamie...' she pouted. '*Look.*'

James sort of looked, but on spotting Maggie's face, busied himself with untying his horse from the breakwater, where it was energetically digging a hole in the sand. 'Right, last one back to the lorry gets the drinks in. Wait till I get on though, or it doesn't count.'

A good vicious sixteen and a half hands, Cutie Pie danced away every time he got a foot in the stirrup, teeth bared, ears flat to its head, suddenly terrified of the water filled hole it had created beneath its hooves.

Jess said, 'Hurry up can't you? I'm dying from fucking exposure here!'

'Come on, it's only a leg over,' Carla said.

After a couple of attempts of jumping off a carefully positioned rock, James managed to get across the mare's back. He was just at the point of lying across the saddle, a second away before he got his leg over the other side and took up the reins, when Jess rode alongside and kicked Kestrel into a gallop. The chestnut lifted into a gentle rear but then changed its mind and performed a sort of drunken bunny jump instead. Somehow James managed to stay with the horse. Thoroughly overwound, Cutie Pie bolted off to the right towards the caravan parks and the championship golf course, the bit firmly between her teeth, her eyes rolling.

Everyone cantered back in the general direction, but the ride was spoilt for Maggie. Not only had Jess managed to flaunt herself in her usual style, but she was irresponsible as well. At the lorry, Jess was standing in her stirrups, scanning the horizon and chewing her bottom lip, as well she might. James did eventually appear, but on foot, leading a thoroughly sweated-up horse, its flanks heaving with the bridle all twisted and the mouthpiece halfway up the side of its head.

Rhian said, 'You're not thinking of selling that one on, are you?'

'Why did you go the long way round?' Jess said, back to

being cocky once she knew James was safe. When he was in full view, she pulled her sopping wet shirt over her head and flung it in his direction. Everyone laughed. James did give Jess his jacket, but it slightly spoilt the gentlemanly effect when he said, 'Okay, you win, Miss wet... no t-shirt. I mean... oh, I don't know what I mean.'

'I think you mean *not a novice ride*,' Carla said.

Jess hugged the wax jacket around herself and even managed to remove her wet boots and jodhpurs as well. The jacket just skimmed her frilly red backside. Maggie watched her climb in the lorry and put her long brown bare legs up on the dash.

O'Malley safely loaded, she drove home, marched through to the sitting room and without saying a word to Pete, downed a large brandy and on purpose left her used glass next to the bottle top. The house was in the same man mess as earlier. In fact, Pete had added to it with papers, his kicked-off shoes and mugs. He was, in fact, fit enough to go back to work. Goodness knows what he'd said to the council to keep them quiet for so long. Whenever she tackled him about it though he was evasive, shifty. It didn't make sense, like a lot of things. Resisting the urge to refill her glass, Maggie sorted out a set of clothes for Jess and drove back to the yard in time to help unload the horses.

Liz wanted to know why Jess was only wearing underwear, riding boots and a wax jacket, but Jess and Lucy were in high spirits by then, more interested in logging the highlights on their mobile phones. She tackled her brother instead, swerving out of the way as Cutie Pie barged backwards down the ramp.

'James, I've just had Conwy Golf Club on the phone,' she said darkly.

'Oh? I'm not interested in a membership. I keep telling them.'

'They say the seventh green is almost totally destroyed

with deep hoof prints and skid marks,' she said. 'And apparently, there's a trashed picnic table in the caravan park. Care to enlighten?'

'Actually,' Maggie said, 'Jess isn't entirely blameless.'

'Thank you, Maggie, but Jess wasn't in charge, nor was she riding that nutty thoroughbred.'

After giving it some thought, James said, 'I think it was the umbrella that started it.'

Bursts of laughter and chatter; knowing when to retreat, Liz secreted herself back in the office, eyes narrowed on James, phone in hand. Maggie pushed the bag of clothes at Jess, then went to untack O'Malley. She was just trying to find the right peg to hang the bridle on when James' grey Lurcher suddenly appeared out of the hay store. He had something in his mouth, and when her eyes got used to the gloom, Maggie saw it was a bra. The dog took a bit of persuasion to give it up but she proffered a chocolate drop and the deal was done. On further inspection, it took only seconds to recognise the grubby, pale pink satin as part of a set she'd bought Jess for her eighteenth.

What the...?

Unable to decide what it signified, other than something else that needed explaining, Maggie walked briskly over to the house, her pig's snout firmly back in place. Liz was in the office, persevering with an apologetic conversation over the phone and waved Maggie through to the kitchen, where she found Jess drying her hair, and James making drinks. He asked if she wanted a cup of tea, but Maggie just stood there, swinging the bra round on one finger, hoping its weighty presence would be enough to finally put a stop to something.

Jess barely looked at her. 'You look like the fat controller, waving the engines out. And you've already brought me a bra and a *polo neck*.'

'Oh, I didn't bring this from home,' Maggie said. 'This

was in the hay store.'

James, just about to lift a mug to his lips, lowered it slowly instead.

Jess looked at the bra a bit closer and frowned. 'Actually, I wondered where that had gone. Ugh, why is it all chewed? It's disgusting.'

'Oh, you could go into acting.'

Liz appeared in the doorway. 'All right, what's going on now?'

A beat. 'What?...why are you all looking at me?' James said.

Liz looked pointedly at the bra. 'Well, it's a known fact that Jess is smitten with you.'

'*Smitten?*' Jess said, 'Are you two fresh out of Wuthering Heights or something?'

Maggie felt her hands curl into fists and her nails dig into her palms. 'So, you've no explanation whatsoever?'

'Unfortunately not, my dearest Mama,' Jess said sarcastically, pretending to swoon. 'I dearly wish it had been ripped from beneath my bodice and cast asunder, but alas, it is not to be.'

James maintained that Washboy must have stolen it from somewhere, and that's all there was to it. But just for a second, he looked uncomfortable, shifty. 'Got stuff to do,' he said suddenly and pushed past his sister. He went into the office and shut the door.

Maggie got into the Toyota, rammed it into third gear by mistake and jerked down the drive, Pete's 'driving badly' face hovering into her subconscious. What was wrong with them all? Pete was useless, Simon was useless, she wasn't sure about James; he had more brownie points than the other two, so he was on the back burner.

Pending useless.

And several things needed getting to the bottom of. They might be all connected. Sometimes the smallest most obscure clue led to the truth, according to Detective Bergerac anyway. After forty minutes of speeding along the A55, blowing the maximum petrol consumption she was allowed for the whole week, Maggie parked up in Chester City centre and staggered about a mile to Dragon Designs in her riding boots, which were crippling to walk in. She hobbled about in reception, treading straw and sand into the carpet, waiting for Simon to finish his meeting.

Presently, he said goodbye to his client and gave her a warm smile. 'Maggie!'

He kissed her cheek. Nice smell, nice smooth skin, expensive shirt.

'Have you been riding? Laura's at home, resting.'

Oh, he was good, he was very good, and less showed on his face than the other two, but it didn't mean he wasn't just as shifty. 'I'm not after Laura. I want to speak to you.'

'You'd better come through. Is there something wrong?'

Maggie let him have it with both barrels and told Simon exactly what she thought of him. Five years of suppressed opinions came gushing out. 'My sister's been through hell. If you were any kind of a man she wouldn't need any pills!'

'The doctor prescribed them,' he said, puzzled.

'Yes, I know that! But this goes back further than the miscarriage. Trying to get her to have an abortion when she didn't really want one! If you spent less time around that bloody ex-wife of yours or... or jetting off to Spain she might feel more... *cherished*,' she said, suddenly overwhelmed by a wall of emotion. She plonked down tiredly onto a chair.

Yes, cherished was a good word. Old-fashioned and under-valued.

When he was sure she'd run out of steam, Simon went to the computer terminal on Laura's desk and switched it on. 'Why don't you take a look at this?'

Maggie found her reading glasses, and peered at the screen. It took a few minutes for it all to make sense; e-mail was not something Maggie was familiar with.

'36CC still on the loose...' she read slowly. 'That bra is at the yard, but it belongs to Jess; I've just come from there and James claims to know *nothing* about it.'

'Didn't Laura borrow her clothes during the week you were away? The week that doesn't add up?' Simon said, and slid an invoice for her boiler repair in front of her. He stabbed a finger at the date, and Maggie felt suddenly deflated. She had niggling reservations about that week herself.

He slid Laura's mobile phone onto the desk.

'Take a look. It makes interesting reading. Meetings at Rowen church and so on.'

Maggie was horrified, 'Are you saying she's having an affair? With *James?*'

'I don't know all the facts yet...' Simon said carefully, 'but at least now you can see what I'm dealing with.'

No wonder Laura wouldn't answer her phone, no wonder she wasn't in the office.

Maggie drove back with her mouth opening and closing like a fish needing air. She pulled in to the yard to see James and Jess sitting on an old wooden bench, drinking bottles of beer. They were watching the Arab mares grazing in the late afternoon sun, the sweet smell of last summer's meadow hay in the air, early spring flowers along the hedgerows. It was a perfect love setting, all serene and romantic.

'Here she comes,' Jess said under her breath, 'Miss Marple investigates.'

'I owe you an apology,' she said to Jess. 'Sorry for grilling you.'

'And James! He hasn't done anything wrong.'

'Can I have a word in private?' Maggie said to him.

She followed him into his house, feeling her daughter's eyes boring into her back like heat-seeking missiles. He offered her a drink, a chair. Maggie politely refused both, she was far too agitated, and besides, she'd never get back up off the sofa without his help, which would considerably reduce the impact of what she had to say.

'So, I got it wrong about you and Jess,' she said tightly. 'It's right under my nose, it's too public but it's a good smokescreen. What you're actually doing on the quiet is breaking up my sister's relationship!'

'How's that?'

'I've just seen Simon, and I've just seen dozens of messages, all from you, and yet earlier you denied all knowledge of that bra.'

That got a reaction, but only in the smallest intake of breath. On the whole he was incredibly calm and measured, and his gaze didn't leave hers, but that was quite unnerving, the way he stared at her with his gypsy eyes and his... well, that didn't matter.

'I can't explain anything till I speak to Laura.'

'Well you can't. She's not in the office and Simon has her mobile.'

He looked down at his hands, and Maggie left him sitting there, turning his wedding ring round and round.

*

Pete saw her pull on to the drive, and he was all exasperated and tapping his watch. But Maggie flapped her hand at him and went next door. She asked Linda if her sister had stayed in the house when they were on holiday.

'Laura? Oh you mean the really pretty one? She's got a look of Jennifer Aniston hasn't she?'

Maggie simpered, 'Well yes, but did you *see* her? When you were feeding the hens?'

'Well, no I can't say I did. Any particular reason?'

'No. Thank you for looking after the hens.'

'You're welcome, any time.'

Investigations complete, Maggie thought she'd feel satisfied to arrive at some kind of result but what she actually felt was horribly let down. Her own sister had lied to her! Pete snatched the door open as she trailed miserably up her own path, aware that there was probably another pair of eyes boring into her back.

'Where have you been, all this time?' Pete said, 'Why did you go next door?'

Wordlessly, she sat on the bottom stair and made Pete tug her boots off, desperately trying to hold on to the stretchy pants and the padded knickers.

'Maggie, are you going to say anything?'

'No,' she said and burst into tears. She'd not cried for about eight years, not since Ellie had been diagnosed.

'What's all this about?' he said carefully, following her up the stairs.

'It's about everyone keeping me in the dark and leading me up the garden path!'

Pete was remarkably patient to start with, but he listened to the story with an expression reminiscent of Stan Laurel, and Maggie had to admit when it was all strung together there were areas where it was patchy.

'Simon says this, Simon says that as per bloody usual. Then it's *Linda* says. Have you heard what Laura says yet?'

'No. She won't answer the phone at the flat,' Maggie said, wiping her eyes.

'And this James, he says nothing?'

'Guilt written all over him,' she said sullenly.

Pete was thoroughly exasperated. 'I'm going to make us a cup of tea,' he said, and opened the bedroom door, to find Jess sitting on the landing. She sprang to her feet and pushed her way into the room, tearstained and wild.

'Jamie and... *Auntie Laura?* Just what have you accused him of?' she said to Maggie, 'How much more embarrassing could you be? You're like some kind of frustrated old witch.'

Unable to stop, Maggie had a fresh bout of sobbing, which threw Jess slightly, but it was Pete's reaction, which threw them both more. He actually raised his voice in quite a commanding way. 'Jess that's enough! Stop eavesdropping and start apologising to your mother. *Now!*'

She didn't, of course. She ran down the stairs, slammed the front door, and reversed off the drive with a dramatic screech. Pete looked through the bedroom window. 'That's about six months' wear off the bloody tyres, that is,' he said, turning to Maggie. 'Be all over the college, all over the village and all over the bloody Internet now because of your interfering.'

*

Maggie lay awake half the night straining to hear the noise of Jess' car, but she didn't come home. Pete took Ellie to school while Maggie lay in bed, crippled with two hours of galloping on O'Malley and the strain of everything else.

She heard Pete come back in the house and sling the keys across the table instead of hanging them up. They'd be lost by lunchtime, and she'd be expected to know where he'd left them. She waited for sounds of the television, but Pete came back up the stairs and sat on the bed.

'Right. If you can stop trying to be your sister's saviour for a minute, and if you can stop thinking about the kids for a minute; *I* want to talk to you. Me, Pete.'

Maggie knew what was coming. He wanted her to go round and apologise to everyone. She'd already thought about it but everyone's phone was on message only. Well there's a surprise, no one wanted to talk to her. Maybe she should drive over to Laura and Simon's flat...

'...so even if I wanted to, I can't go back to work,' Pete said. 'They made me redundant back in January. Maggie are you listening?'

'Redundant?'

She had to listen again then while Pete explained how he'd pretended to go to work for a while in the hope he'd find something else, rather than face telling her. He'd tried all the leads he could think of, but the fact was he was too old, and since the heart flutter, too much of a health risk. The years of experience he'd had with the council counted for nothing. She was stunned.

'They've put a wet-behind-the-ears graduate in my place with a fancy title and changed everything round so they can pretend my job doesn't exist,' Pete said.

Maggie went over the implications in her head, tried to make her dry mouth work properly. 'I can't believe it, after all the years you've been there. Tell me the worst. Have we got debts?'

'No, but we might have to consider selling the house. Not yet,' he added quickly, 'but perhaps by the end of summer if nothing turns round.'

'Oh, Pete no!'

'It's a money pit, Maggie,' he said, and she knew he was right. A small mortgage was all very well, but the running costs and renovations of a big Victorian house was never-ending. He talked about unnecessary costs, mentioned the dinner parties and all the entertaining she loved so much. And Ellie's riding lessons.

'I'm sorry, love, I'm the one who's kept you in the dark, led you up the garden path,' he said, and he looked suffocated with it, ground down with the burden of guilt and responsibility. All the time she'd been procrastinating about everyone else, Maggie had taken her eye off the ball at home, taken it for granted that Pete would just carry on, day in day out trudging in to the council offices. He was the one person in the house who underpinned everything that happened there, simply because he funded it.

Bergerac would never have missed so many clues. Maggie made a conscious decision to give up detective work and put her arms around her husband.

The one person she never had time for, her invisible man.

*

Jess came home later that evening. She slammed her car door, slammed the front door and slammed her bedroom door. Maggie looked at Pete. 'I think Jess is home.'

'Leave her.'

'Don't you want to know where she's been?'

'When are you going to learn that she does all this to wind you up and get you running on overtime?' he said, his eyes on the football highlights.

Maggie crept upstairs on the pretext of having a bath, but Jess had already beaten her to it, and the hot water was gushing out, the bathroom full of steam and some exotic fragrance.

'You could have phoned me, let me know where you were,' Maggie said evenly.

'Oh, here we go,' Jess said, going into her room and pulling things out of the wardrobe, hangers falling down everywhere. 'I followed your trail of destruction if you must know. Saw Jamie, then stayed with Auntie Laura. She's like, a proper nervous wreck.'

'So... did they say anything?'

'You mean did I like, cross-examine them?' she said sweetly, then pushed her face close to Maggie's. 'I asked Jamie if he'd *ever* slept with my aunt and he said... NO.'

Maggie followed her into the bathroom. 'That's only half the story.'

Jess turned the water off. 'Auntie Laura said she borrowed

some stuff and stayed at his house for a couple of days and they stayed in touch, you know, like friends do? Oh, but you don't know, do you? You haven't *got* any friends!' she said, and slammed the door in her face.

Pete thumped on the hall cupboard, like a jungle drum warning, and Maggie slunk back downstairs, still stinging with her daughter's comments and her rudeness.

'Do you think Jess is suffering with middle-child syndrome?' she said.

'There's nothing wrong with Jess.'

'No,' she said, 'we have quite challenging children though, don't we?'

'Where's this going, Maggie?'

Tentatively, she told him about Nathan, and his reaction was what she'd expected really. Explosive.

'You mean to tell me he's shacked up with that poof, and you're worried about Jess chasing a fella?'

He wouldn't discuss it, probably because there were so many other issues juggling for supremacy. At least everything was out now, good, bad or indifferent… mostly bad.

Later in the week, they had a talk about money. 'I'll have to get a job,' Maggie said.

'Doing what?'

'Well… anything!'

Pete lowered the paper, 'What are you going to put on your CV?'

'Not that kind of job, an ordinary one.'

'They don't exist, love. You need a degree these days just to get an interview for the bloody corner shop.'

Maggie scoffed, but when she looked in the North Wales News there were just two employment opportunities. The first was, 'strong person required to help with lambing', and the second was for a sex chatline.

Right, so that was on the back burner.

When Sunday morning came around, Maggie felt torn in

two. James had promised Ellie a different pony to ride, called Seren. 'Seren means star,' she said, making a star shape out of her cereal because she was too excited to eat it.

'Come on, let's see this riding you've been doing,' Pete said to Ellie, but his eyes were on Maggie. When they arrived though, James wasn't on the yard, and his vehicle wasn't there. Ellie dragged her father away to see Mr Ed, and Maggie sat in the office, unsure what his absence might mean.

'I've no idea where James is,' Liz said.

'We don't mind waiting.'

'Did you get that silly incident with the bra cleared up?'

'Oh, yes...' Maggie said. 'Teenagers huh?' She rolled her eyes and tried to smile but it all came out false, as if she'd had plastic surgery. It was much more difficult than a real smile, and Maggie wondered how the likes of Linda and Malice managed it all the time. Liz looked as if she were waiting for some kind of explanation, but ironically, James chose exactly the right moment to arrive. He marched into the office with a bag of tools and a chequebook, both of which he slung across the desk.

'Where have you been?' Liz said, 'Ellie's waiting.'

'Fixing the picnic bench and paying for the seventh green, like you told me to.'

'Oh,' she said, glancing down at the diary. 'You've got... I don't know how many unreturned calls logged in here, 'Annalise, the Mare and Foal welfare society, Paddy, the chairman of the RDA, and Lord B, *again!*'

'If the caravan park calls, the kiddies' roundabout was nothing to do with me,' James said, ignoring everything she'd said, and ignoring Maggie. They watched him stride back across the yard to where Jess was waiting in the menage with Seren, and Pete was leaning on the paddock rail.

Maggie stayed in the office and watched James as he patiently tried to teach her little girl how to canter, placing her legs and hands in the right place. Maggie could tell

Ellie was struggling to combine the mental and physical co-ordination, but it all suddenly came together, and Maggie's heart was dragged up from her boots. Ellie went twice round the menage by herself and brought the pony to a controlled halt.

Even Pete looked across to the office and gave Maggie a sort of serious smile and a nod. She wondered if it would make a difference to his household budgeting now that he'd seen it for himself, but if she were honest, Maggie would sell her soul for Ellie to ride like that. Ten minutes later, she steeled herself to eat her share of humble pie and found James repairing halters in the tack room.

'James, can I just...'

'No, sorry... don't want to hear anything,' he said, not unkindly, but there was no eye contact, no smile, real or otherwise.

CHAPTER ELEVEN

Laura

It was like being in prison, but it was of Laura's own making. She didn't want to go out, and she didn't want to answer the phone. The feeling of being locked up was all in her head, because she'd twice opened the door, before calmly closing it again. She'd also picked up the phone a dozen times, but replaced it without dialling.

The fact was Laura didn't really need to go out or make calls to find out what was happening in her life. Simon, and Jess, had both kept her well informed. On Monday afternoon though, she purposefully picked up her handbag and car keys. Simon knew exactly where she was going because Laura didn't want to be accused of anything. She couldn't hide away any longer, she wanted to see her sister, and more importantly, Laura couldn't let the one person who was the most innocent of all go on taking the flak for her own shortcomings.

It was cold and windy, and once off the main roads and into the countryside everywhere looked torn and breathless, and other than the different birdsong, the promise of spring had vanished. The hedges along the lane up to the yard were budding, intertwined with long tendrils of honeysuckle and wild rose.

He was fitting a new catch on the paddock gate, but

stopped when Laura walked across. The wind was tearing at her hair and jacket, and she had to wrap her arms around herself to stop her teeth chattering. 'James, I'm *sorry*.'

'All got in a bit of a mess, didn't it?'

Laura nodded slowly, followed him inside and watched him hunt for clean cups. Lambchop came to her, and she couldn't resist picking up the dog for a cuddle. The kitchen was almost back to its original condition, but it was the first thing to make her smile in ages.

'He's not going to come crashing through the door and land me one is he?' James said. 'He's bigger than me.'

Only in height and girth, Laura thought.

James studied her wan, impassive face. 'I know I've got a shotgun, but I only keep that handy for Discount Double Glazing and the bloke from the golf club.'

'It would more likely be Maggie crashing through the door.'

'She's already been and crashed,' he said, stirring a lot of sugar into his drink. 'They're all baying for my blood.'

'I know. I should have realised how it would look to Simon.'

'Why did you keep all the messages anyway?'

'I didn't think I needed to hide anything. Naive of me.'

'Laura, I can't do this friends thing anymore. I'm not messing up your relationship.'

Laura hid her face in Lambchop until the dog squirmed to get down. 'I knew you were going to say that,' she said.

'So, have you sorted out everything at home?'

'That's a big question.'

'Very small answer required.'

'Can I get back to you on it?'

There was an awkward silence, punctuated by a dripping tap. James seemed to look right inside her head, but he suddenly dropped the eye contact and rubbed the bridge of his nose. He looked tired and unshaven, and his hair was slightly too long, but he easily got away with the bohemian look. 'I'm going away later, over to Ireland,' he said, and reached up to remove an envelope from the dusty plate rack, which he handed to Laura. 'Do the horse sales and play the prodigal son for a while. I can't move round here without someone making a deal of it.'

Laura slid her finger under the seal, her eyes back on his. It was a banker's draft, for the full amount due. 'You don't need to do this... the job isn't even finished.'

'I don't want to cause any more hassle for you.'

'Forget what I said about Marbella.'

'It's not just about that,' he said, 'I don't know how long I'll be away.'

'Oh... do you need a receipt?'

'No.'

All matters discussed, he walked back to the car with her, and Laura passed him a bag off the back seat, which he took from her and opened suspiciously. 'What's this?'

'It's a jumper, as promised, for Washboy.'

'Laura, it's pink, he won't wear that.'

'Why are all men colour-blind? It's *not* pink, it's dark rust and salmon, and it's a Gucci.'

'It's... a *what*?'

But she'd already started the engine. James stepped back and watched her pull away. At the end of the drive, Laura dared to look in her wing mirror, and he was still there, holding the bag, the wind messing up his hair. Up until that point, the pills had been pretty good at stemming tear flow, but Laura struggled all the way to Hafod House. When Maggie opened the door, it all started again, and they both had to have tissues.

Pete said Maggie was suffering from severe meddling syndrome, but he was quite good humoured about it and even poured them both a Christmas sherry. He left them in the sitting room with a box of tissues. Maggie was sore about all the confusion and the false accusations. For her own part, Laura knew it would be taxing going over the week of her miscarriage. The miscarriage had been the catalyst really, that awful time when she was lying in the hospital with everyone else's crying baby around her, and all she had in her head was a dreamless, loveless landscape. It brought home how much she wanted what the majority wanted, a family life, and yet she'd fought against it for years. It seemed her entire existence to date, past and present, was under the microscope. Her future though, was like looking through binoculars the wrong way around.

Then there was James. After a lot of thought, Laura explained it as being simply a shared empathy, the way he'd had part of his soul dragged from him, and at the time he was... well he was just *there*. Plus, it had been another, smaller revelation in that she'd liked being in his house. In the past, all of that country stuff represented too much of her father and the negative aspects of her childhood, but the tide had turned, challenging her feelings, and she found it was comforting, that there was a thread of joy buried beneath the harsh memories.

It wasn't all about death; it was about growth as well.

Maggie listened and nodded, understanding up to a point, but Laura could tell, as with Simon, she hadn't truly exonerated herself. 'You're a complicated little soul, aren't you?'

'I don't make sense to you, do I?'

'Course you do,' Maggie said, but there was a sigh in her voice as well. 'Well, it's nothing like the fixation Jess has got on him. She just wants his body. And you... just want to talk to him?'

Conversational intercourse. 'I've just said that, haven't I?'

'Course you have.'

While Maggie was in the kitchen, Laura took out the

cheque and looked at it again. Unusual signature, in that the James part was just scribble and the surname was like interlocked initials, but she wasn't really dwelling on that. It was the fact that he'd made it out to her, to Laura Brown, and *not* Dragon Designs.

*

Jess came home from college in a white tunic, struggling with a case of aromatherapy oils and numerous heavy files, all of which she dumped in the sitting room.

'I've just had a text from Carla,' she said, waving her phone. 'Listen to this… she's on her way to Holyhead with James to catch the ferry across to Dublin! *The cow!* She says the waves are like the sides of houses, and it's really rough. Well, I hope she's as *sick as a dog.*'

'And how did the exams go?' Maggie said evenly.

'What? Oh, passed with two distinctions.'

'Well done,' Laura said, forcing out a smile. 'What were they for?'

'Identify the major muscle groups and a full body massage.'

When Jess had left the room, phone clamped to her ear, Maggie said, 'Huh, no prizes for guessing whom she'll want to practice that little lot on?'

'Let's change the subject,' Laura said. 'Pete looks well; he must have lost about a stone? And that holiday tan suits him. You must have *some* news I haven't spoken to you for a week.'

'What can happen in a week?' she said airily. 'Pete's been made redundant. Oh, and Nathan's come out gay, did I mention that?'

'Redundant? Oh, Maggie no!'

Maggie hadn't much to say about Nathan, other than Pete

had almost had another coronary, and it would all take some getting used to. Laura commiserated with the job situation, privately horrified that it could mean the loss of Hafod House. When Ellie came home from school, no one wanted to even think about it and the subject was dropped.

Laura stayed for dinner, a half-hearted joint effort of a roast chicken salad, appreciated mostly by Pete and Ellie. Jess ate the salad, and two tiny potatoes in between looking at her notes on waxing and tinting, and responding to her phone. There was another bulletin from Carla to say they'd only been sailing for twenty minutes, and James was already hanging over the side.

Pete laughed. 'Only two hours to go.'

Driving home, Laura found herself checking the time, trying to ascertain if James had crossed the Irish Sea. She felt at sea herself, not being able to talk to him.

'You should be able to talk to me!' Simon had said, and she had agreed.

They'd argued about James, and Simon had been jealous and angry, not wanting to understand her explanations. In the same way they'd argued about Alice, and Laura had been jealous and angry, not wanting to understand *his* explanations.

Simon had eventually calmed down, even apologised for some of the things he'd said to Maggie. Maggie had apologised for some of the things she'd said to Simon, but Laura hadn't wholeheartedly apologised to anyone, except James.

She might be a complicated little soul, but she was no fool.

Simon was waiting for her at the apartment. It was immaculate, even the granite was polished, the kitchen bin had been washed, and the curtains were hanging in equal symmetry. It was all shiny on the outside but quite soulless, a little like their relationship really, when she thought about it.

'Did you see him? Did you tell him it was no go, this *friends* idea?'

Laura threw her coat and bag down, 'He said it before I did, and anyway, he's gone away,' she said. Two and half hours since they'd set sail. He'd be on Irish soil at last.

She had a vision of him lying in a star shape on the grass.

'Really?' Simon said, pleased with the information. 'Good. Now let's just try and keep it professional, shall we?'

*

Simon was trying to be professional too, but even he was starting to struggle with the almost daily escalation of problems in Spain, exaggerated by the logistics of the distance and the language. For a while, he was a human dynamo, totting up columns of figures, phoning contractors and promising money to contacts in Spain. Laura kept her head down.

He declared he was going to employ an on-site project manager.

'Can the company handle another salary?'

'I need someone who can speak the lingo. There's a convention on at The Empire Hotel in Manchester next week, all about working abroad, so I thought I'd set up interviews down there,' Simon said, then stood behind her chair and squeezed her shoulders. Laura kept her eyes on the mood board she was working on for the villa. 'Oh... I see.'

'All we need to do now is get the cottages sewn up and hit them with the invoice.'

'I don't want a rush job doing.'

'I do.'

The painters were finished in record time. Simon had Laura arrange for the tiler, carpet fitter and wooden-floor specialist all lined up for the middle of the week; after which it was the furniture and kitchen equipment, and finally the soft furnishings.

*

On Sunday morning, they both travelled down to the cottages, her car crammed with the final tools of her trade, the finishing touches. Normally, the fruition of the end product was her slice of job satisfaction. This time Laura felt mostly unexcited by the prospect, but when she opened the door of Morwydden Cottage, she couldn't stop the smiles coming. It looked like a solid family home at last with polished oak floors and a huge open plan kitchen; a continuation of what James had started really, with a comfortable sitting room and French doors overlooking the mountain stream. Laura threw open the doors for a moment and looked at the tumble of garden with its broken stone wall, and breathed in the wet spring smell. The hawthorn hedge was in abundant green leaf, and beneath the daffodils there were clumps of pale yellow cowslips and primroses, violets and tiny white stars of wood anemone. She could hear the mares tearing at the new grass and the lambs bleating on the mountain. The natural earthiness of it all reminded her of the journal, and Laura hoped it was all how Carys would have wanted it. She would hate to trample over anything quite so deeply revered, if only in memory.

Its little neighbour, Mefysen, was a lot more traditional with the original open fires, and in the bedroom she'd gone ahead with the four-poster bed. The walls were cream, and she'd chosen a dark red for the carpet and the drapes around the bed. A small chandelier added a touch of opulence without feeling fussy. It took most of the day to hang curtains, pictures and mirrors. Simon left her to finish off just after lunch, satisfied that James wasn't around, and anyway the placing of logs and candles wasn't his thing. More importantly, he was taking Cameron to the cinema and after that Tara wanted to go ice-skating.

'Why don't you come with us?' he said.

'Oh, no thanks....'

Liz came to find her as it was getting dark, and the look on her face gave Laura the edge of satisfaction she'd been missing. 'Oh, wow!' Liz said, looking around.

'Come and see the bedroom, it's my favourite.'

'Oh, *wow*,' Liz said again, feeling the cream chenille throw across the bed. 'I'm so impressed. You've done such a wonderful job, so quickly as well.'

The grand tour done, Laura locked both cottages and handed the keys to Liz with a sorrowful smile. 'Well... that's it.'

'Oh, but that's so final. Come over to the house and have a celebratory drink. Redman Estates think they've already found us a tenant for Morwydden. Isn't that amazing?'

'Oh... fantastic.'

Laura followed Liz's car over to the farmhouse, and it was strange without him being there.

The kitchen had been cleaned up again, and Washboy was wearing her old Gucci sweater.

Liz went through the wine rack, and after some deliberation passed her a glass of Cabernet Sauvignon. Laura sniffed it tentatively to see if it evoked any memories. The enveloping cold snow... the warm silken feel of the mare... feeling drunk... his fingers threaded through hers...

Lambchop licked her fingers under the table, and Laura opened her eyes. 'So, have you heard from him?'

'Only to see if his dogs and horses are all right,' Liz said, then spotted Carla outside in the yard and tapped on the kitchen window. 'I'll see if she knows any more than I do.'

But Carla wasn't much help. 'Well, it took him a day to

get over the crossing. Just wanted to lie down on the ground, very still. So I went shopping in Dublin,' she added brightly.

'So, no indication of his return?' Laura said, 'I want to buy some riding lessons for Ellie's birthday.'

'Now, how did he put it?' Carla said, lighting a cigarette and energetically wafting the smoke. 'He said something along the lines of... he's not getting back on that fucking boat, until the sea is a fucking mill pond.'

Liz said, 'What am I meant to do with Midnight Sky?'

'Oh, he says you must leave her quietly, at grass. She needs thinking time.'

Liz made a loud tutting noise, 'And I'm supposed to tell that to Lord B am I?' she said, vigorously wiping down the kitchen worktops. 'So where is he now?'

'Your mother's, I think.'

'He won't last there long. She'll have him doing fifteen years' worth of DIY and filling the freezer with meals,' she said, topping up their glasses. Jess peered through the window, her face pressed to the glass. She waved at Laura, and stuck her tongue out at Carla.

'She hates me, bless her,' said Carla.

Unable to resist, Jess came in and helped herself to the remaining wine. 'What are you all talking about?' she said. 'And where's all the mess gone? It's not the same.'

'In the bin, mostly.' Liz said. 'I know he can cook and turn the washer on, but that's about it.'

'Well, he can't be good at *everything*,' Carla said, and fluttered her eyes at Jess. 'We all know James has considerable skills... not all of them lie in the kitchen. Go on, you're dying to *grill* me.'

Jess twirled a long tendril of hair. '*So* not interested.'

Laura swirled the wine around her glass and felt a curious parallel with Midnight Sky.

Thinking time out at grass sounded so lovely, peaceful and healing.

Early on Thursday morning of the following week, Laura watched Simon pack a bag for two days of interviews on his quest for a site manager. Although she had her back to him, Laura could see him moving about the bedroom through the dressing-table mirror.

'No sign that Morgan-Jones is back yet?' Simon said, folding his shirts carefully. One of them was the terribly expensive shirt Laura had bought for Christmas. She watched with interest as some brand new underwear went in the bag and a weighty pack of toiletries. His best shoes, for his clay feet, went in a separate bag.

'No, Maggie says not,' Laura said and applied some blusher to her washed out complexion. 'It's a shame because it's Ellie's birthday on Saturday, she'll be eleven. We've bought her some riding gear, if you're interested.'

'Oh, he's taking the piss now! Phone that sister of his and get a contact number.'

'Why should I do that? He's not even due to pay yet. Simon, you can't delete numbers from my phone one minute then tell me to chase him the next,' she said, pausing with the mascara wand, then she twisted round on the stool. 'And you can't get me to use my convivial relationship with him to force him to pay because it suddenly suits you.'

'Don't be ridiculous,' he said. 'It's called chasing money owed.'

Laura turned back to her reflection and outlined her eyelashes with cocoa brown. 'I thought you had a loan?'

'It costs a fucking fortune!' He threw something else into the bag, ripping the zip along in a temper. 'You know the company needs that money!'

After a lot of sighing, Simon apologised for shouting and kissed her goodbye.

When she heard his car pull away, Laura swallowed her

pill. Her nerves were shattered, and her body felt like a husk, everything pulled out and replaced with doubt and deceit. She went in to the office as normal, chatted to Barbara, worked until four and then calmly drove to Six Cherry Grove.

The For Sale board said it was sold, subject to contract. Laura looked at the house and took in the overgrown garden and the smeared windows. Steeling herself, she went and knocked on the door. When she felt certain it was empty, she peered through the lounge window, and it looked as neglected as the outside, with the usual jumble of electronic games around the television. It was where someone lived, but it wasn't a home. It couldn't speak, but it told a story.

Next, she drove to The Empire Hotel in Manchester.

Laura felt a bit ridiculous pulling a long coat over her suit, donning sunglasses and a scarf, but she couldn't think of any other way of looking as anonymous as she felt. In the huge glossy reception area, she was aware of several trade stands and advertisements with sectioned-off desks. Laura ignored all the buzz and walked into the bar with a large newspaper, ordered a soft drink and prepared to wait. It was all over in less than an hour. Although it was exactly what she was expecting, she hadn't reckoned on feeling so sick to the core. It was the shirt that hurt the most, the dove grey silk she'd chosen with such love and care.

And he was wearing it for *Alice.*

Laura stayed sitting, staring at the paper but aware of their every move as they looked at the dinner menu. They looked ordinary, like the married couple they were. When they moved into the restaurant, Alice linking his arm, Laura made a move to go. She stole a backward glance, just to be sure of what she'd seen. Now that it was actually in front of her eyes, her brain had to acknowledge it as cold fact, and it had been all the indecision, which had almost defeated her. She'd needed to see something tangible instead of a vague feeling. She had no idea who was using who, but Laura had arrived at a point where she didn't actually care. If Alice genuinely wanted him back, or if she wanted to destroy him out of bitter spite, then Laura was happy to let her. The certainty was that she wouldn't be dragged down with either of them.

'Bye, Simon,' she whispered, tired of fighting, tired of all the denial, tired of loving him.

*

At home, it didn't take long to pack, and Laura was in no hurry. She used all their good suitcases for her clothes and found some cardboard boxes for all her stuff out of the bathroom, her books and music CDs. Then there was her sewing machine and her laptop. It didn't amount to much and it all fitted quite easily in her car. It looked like she was going on holiday, everything pushed up against the windows. She did a similar clearing job in the office, even composed a short note to Barbara and made sure she had her old address book, all her original contacts. The only real pang of regret, was leaving the office, where Dragon Designs had begun.

Driving to Rowen, with the late spring sun still flickering through the side window, Laura was filled with a calm resolution, knowing exactly how she felt and what she wanted to do. Maggie was surprised to see her, and Laura apologised for landing on the doorstep. 'I've left him,' she said, but with no emotion or tears. 'I've left Simon, the business, everything... I don't like my life any more.'

Pete gave her an almost triumphant hug. 'I'll get your bags love, you get inside.'

There wasn't much to say about it all, other than between the holiday flats and Alice, Simon was set to bankrupt both the business and what was left of their love and respect for each other. The house sale would fall into the same dark pit, smashed with the wrecking ball that was Simon and Alice's twisted relationship. Although when Laura picked over it all, Alice had never actually lied to her. It was Simon who had so many different faces, so many different hats.

Jess came out of her room and watched Laura unpacking. 'What's he done?'

'Simon? Promised me a nervous breakdown.'

'Has he cheated on you? Why is it that good-looking, successful men and *all* footballers, turn into like, such knobheads?'

'Don't generalise,' Laura said. 'You're too young to be so cynical.'

'Yeah, but they don't need to try, do they?' she said. 'He must be like, *pure* knobhead to not want you, you're so smart and like, *proper* stunning.'

Laura gave her a weak smile, touched by her clumsy flattery because it was so heartfelt.

'So, how did you like, catch him out?' Jess said.

'Ah, well, I made the leash so short, it was only big enough for a noose in the end.'

Jess held up her hand for a high five, 'Woah! *Total* respect, sister.'

*

Laura received Simon's agitated call just before ten that same evening, having read the note she'd had hand-delivered to his hotel room. She'd done it more by way of letting him know that she had been there, seen the film, got the t-shirt. Personally hand written with her old fountain pen was only slightly more sophisticated than being dumped by text, but there was a measure of satisfaction in its simplicity, an old-fashioned flair perhaps which had complemented her disguise with the scarf and the broadsheet newspaper.

'I'm sorry, Simon, I've heard it all before,' she said, and at two minutes past ten, Laura switched her phone off. She kept it switched off the following day whilst she trawled around all the local estate agents looking for short-term property to rent. Back at Hafod House, Laura leafed through all the details, and in the Redman Estates' pile was Mefysen Cottage with an 'interested party' stamp across the picture. Mefysen meant strawberry and she wondered if there were any at the bottom of the garden. After staring at the picture for a long time, Laura screwed it up and put it in the bin.

*

Ellie was eleven on Sunday, and it was mildly uplifting to have something happy and ordinary to think about. Laura presented her with a new riding hat, boots and a sweatshirt. It had a galloping horse on the front with fake fur for the mane and tail.

'You shouldn't have spent all that money,' Maggie said.

'I didn't,' Laura replied. 'I put it all on Simon's credit card. They tried to judge each other's reaction, then both grinned at the same time. 'Maggie don't be cross, but I've paid for six lessons as well.'

'You shouldn't have!'

'Why the hell not? I wanted to.'

'Is that on his credit card as well?'

'No. From me to you and Ellie.'

Maggie squeezed her sister's arm, 'Thank you.'

Ellie went off to the yard for the day, with a sulky Jess weighed down already with the responsibility of taking her sister to the yard for a pony-club day with Liz bellowing orders.

Later in the afternoon, Laura and Maggie busied

themselves with party food and balloons. Maggie had made a horseshoe cake and because her sister was tipsy already, Laura took on the responsibility of poking eleven candles into the soft icing. The house slowly filled with guests, and Maggie was in her element, her hands full with sausage rolls and another glass of red. When the doorbell went, Maggie yelled at Laura, 'Can you get that? It'll be Liz dropping off Ellie. Ask her in for a drink, will you?'

Laura went to snatch open the door, and Ellie ran in, stopping only to show her an old shoe worn by Seren, with daisies poking through the nail holes, but it wasn't Liz on the doorstep, it was James. After a moment, Laura said, 'Oh… you're back?'

'I'm back.'

Ellie dashed back to give him a party hat, but Laura couldn't think of a single thing to say. Maggie, a glass tilting in her hand, more than made up for it. 'Oh, James! You're back! Liking the long hair, you know, you look like that Long John Sparrow? Minus the eyeliner, of course! Oh, and the sea legs, I heard all about that. Hey, Pirates of the Irish Sea!' she gabbled on, tugging at his sleeve. 'Come on, come in for a drink. I want to apologise for all those stupid misunderstandings about you and Jess, and my sister. I mean, *as if.*'

'All forgotten,' he said but allowed himself to be coerced off the doorstep.

They followed Maggie down the hall, chattering then about getting Ellie bathed and changed and would Laura watch the food in the oven and get James a drink? He followed Laura into the messy kitchen, but she was glad of something to do and began to stack dishes and run the taps.

'Who's Long John Sparrow?' James said, pouring himself half a glass of wine.

'She means *Jack* Sparrow… Pirates of the Caribbean?' she said. When he carried on frowning, Laura smiled and added, 'Don't worry it's quite flattering.'

He watched her move about the kitchen for a moment. 'So... how are you?'

'Oh you know, the usual. Homeless, weary of heart,' Laura said, and concentrated on adding some lemon oil and a handful of olives to a French bean salad. 'I've left Simon.'

Next door's teenagers barged in and helped themselves to drinks, mentioned that they could smell burning, and Laura pulled open the oven door just in time to rescue the pizza. She slid it on to a wire rack, replaced the bottle top off the Coca Cola and hunted through the drawers for the pizza cutter. When they were alone again, James said, 'Homeless? What's wrong with Mefysen?'

'Nothing. I don't know!' she said, flustered. 'It's got an interested party.'

'I can make it uninterested,' James said, twisting a key off a huge bunch.

Laura stopped in her tracks. 'James, that's not fair.'

'Life's funny like that.'

Laura stared at the key on the table, then picked it up and slid it into her pocket. 'Thank you,' she said, and met his eyes properly for the first time, and in doing so, realised just how much she'd missed him, how much his close proximity made better sense of her day. She was about to risk a smile when he said, 'Laura, there's smoke coming out of that oven.'

All the downstairs alarms were triggered, and Party Hits Fourteen was temporarily drowned out. Pete wafted a towel at the device in the hall, but in the end, James had to take the battery out. Maggie opened all the doors and windows. 'It's all right, don't anyone panic!'

'Maggie, no one is panicking, only you,' Pete said, grabbing the wine glass out of her hand.

Jess arrived, still dirty from sweeping up the yard and spotted James as he was trying to leave. 'Jamie, don't go yet! You've got to have a drink with me.'

'You always get me into trouble at parties.'

'But there's a fire. I might need to be rescued and given mouth to mouth.'

'It's only pie,' he said, but James couldn't leave if he wanted to.

He couldn't leave because Simon's car was blocking him in.

CHAPTER TWELVE

Laura

James asked Simon quite reasonably to move his car. He didn't smile, but he wasn't especially hostile, and climbed into the driving seat of his vehicle and started the engine with his usual slow nonchalance.

'You're not going anywhere Morgan-Jones,' Simon said. 'You owe me a substantial amount of money.'

James wound down the window, a pink paper crown still on his head and an unlit cigarette dangling from his lips. 'I don't owe you anything. Are you going to move it, or do you want me to squeeze past? I don't intend going up the bank. Some of those field poppies are quite rare.'

'You touch my car with that *fucking* heap of scrap, and you'll get more pain than just the cost of repairing it!'

James slowly lit his cigarette, and Laura was aware that Jess was hovering right behind her, mesmerised by the scene, itching to have her say, and Pete was peering behind the curtains ready to leap to her defence. It was tempting to let Jess loose on Simon, but Laura thought better of it and walked part way down the drive, 'Simon, just *move* the car,' she said. 'I've got the money.'

'So why didn't *he* say that?' he said, throwing James a mutinous glance. Simon got back into his car and reversed it so violently, the wheels made deep trenches in the gravel.

James drove past with a curt nod, and Simon got back out, slammed the door and marched back up the drive. 'What the hell's going on, Laura?'

'Well, for a start it's Ellie's birthday party, so stop shouting and swearing.'

He followed her into the dining room and pushed the door closed. The muffled hum of laughter and music was still discernible from the sitting room, and Laura thought it somehow epitomised the last few months of her life, that feeling of being on the wrong side of a closed door.

Presently, after looking at her with an expression of exasperated hurt, he said, 'So are you going to tell me why you've left me?'

'You have to ask? After everything I put in the letter, how I *felt?*' she sighed. 'You haven't read it, have you?'

'Laura,' he began patiently, 'you spied on Alice and me having dinner and made the leap in your head to us having sex! We were merely discussing the house sale.'

She sank down onto one of the chairs and rubbed her eyes. 'You've always got an answer.'

'Precisely! Doesn't that tell you something?'

'It tells me you're a snake.'

A long silence fell while he gazed out of the window. 'Alice has got to you, hasn't she?'

'We had a conversation a while back.'

'What about?'

When she didn't respond, he pulled out the chair opposite her. 'All right, so... where's this cash?'

Laura put her hands on the table. 'In my bank account. It has been for some time.'

'*What...?*'

'I need it to live on.'

'Just a minute, let me get this right. You've had all this planned? You and him?'

'I had it planned, just me.'

Simon leapt to his feet. 'You... *calculating bitch! Why?*'

'I'm *tired*. I feel used, unloved, and I don't want a secondhand family, a secondhand life.'

He stared at her, and Laura struggled to hold the eye contact, but she was determined not to back down.

'And what about me?' he said.

'It's always about you, Simon,' she said darkly, and before he could get another word out, went for the jugular. 'I don't love you anymore.'

Laura heard herself say the words knowing it wasn't strictly true. If it were strictly true, she wouldn't feel so bad watching him walk back to his car and sit there for a good half an hour before he drove away. Damage limitation, that was what she'd done, self-preservation was what it all boiled down to. Yes she'd played a bit dirty along the way, but so what?

*

The following morning, Laura pushed open the door to Mefysen cottage again and dumped her suitcases on the mat. It still smelt new, with the faintest trace of furniture and floor wax, cut logs and lavender. Through the French windows she could see right down the long cottage garden. James was there, straddling the stream as he tried to repair the dry stone wall, which separated the lawn from the steep slopes of the open mountain, and the sheep. The dogs were paddling in the water.

She watched for a moment as he heaved the uneven grey stones into place beneath a tangle of blackthorn and wild strawberry. As Laura walked across the hewn grass, James stopped to wipe his brow across his arm. 'Are you the new tenant?'

'Only if you're the old landlord,' she said, and looked at

the pile of stones he was working with. 'My father used to love rebuilding the walls. He'd say that the centuries of men's hands on the same stones put feeling into a place.'

'He sounds... poetic,' James said, striding across the stream. 'You've got more in common with him than you think.'

'Maybe,' she said, shielding her eyes against the sun. 'Can I buy you lunch?'

It was the end of the Easter break, quiet and blissfully sunny in the pub garden. James didn't want a big meal because he couldn't lug rocks around on a heavy stomach, so she bought sandwiches instead, and only a half pint of beer.

Laura swallowed a pill with her orange juice, and James picked up the remaining pills, read the label and stuffed them in his back pocket. 'You don't need any more of these.'

'I do,' she said, mildly alarmed, 'just for a while longer.'

'I'll keep them. When you feel desperate you'll have to come and find me.'

'You could be anywhere!'

'So call me,' he said, in such a way that Laura obediently slid her phone across the table to him. She lit a cigarette and watched as he began to put his number back on her directory, then he grabbed her cigarettes and put them in his jacket pocket as well.

'James! That's not fair. Everything will end up being boil-washed.'

'You never used to smoke.'

'I've got to have *something*.'

'You can have me,' he said, his eyes still on her phone. 'You can have a friend again.'

'I missed you... when you were in Ireland.'

James returned her phone with a cautious smile, but it wasn't awkward, not in the least. The words had just fallen out of her mouth, glad to escape because they'd been there for such a long time.

*

Laura decided to hold a cottage-warming party before the weather broke.

She invited everyone from the yard, Pete and Maggie, and her new neighbours. For half an hour, as she wandered around the old market town, buying bread, cheeses and wine, plus the ingredients for making chilli con carne, everything felt happy and normal, a bit like she was on holiday. However, when she called in to Redman Estates and tried to use her business card to pay for the cottage, she discovered Simon had cancelled it, and when in the bank, Laura wasn't too surprised to discover he'd also cancelled her salary.

She called James. 'Do you know a good solicitor?'

'No. They're all fucking useless. Better off with a shotgun.'

'I need one. Come on think!' she said, grinning. 'What sort of friend are you?'

'I'm the best kind, an honest one? What do you need a solicitor for?'

'I want my half of the apartment, and I want Simon to buy me out of Dragon Designs.'

'Like I said… better off with a shotgun.'

She did get a name out of him eventually, and even managed to make an appointment, but the process was so long and protracted that Simon would have plenty of time to manoeuvre. Laura held out little hope of clawing anything back, but she had to try.

Just before seven, she laid out the food on the oak dining table and changed into pale suede trousers and a black silk shirt. Through the tiny leaded bedroom window, she could see James still moving rocks about, determined to finish the wall before the light vanished. She envied him his mostly self-sufficient way of life, the way he relied on no one except himself. If something cropped up which threw him out of his comfort zone, he simply learnt how to do it.

All afternoon, Laura had tried to get her head around making money and thought she might start by placing an ad in the local paper for making and repairing soft furnishings, but she'd spent a lot of time staring out of the window, taking drinks out to James, or just sitting on the grass watching him. Since he'd cleared the weeds and brambles away, the remains of what used to be a cottage garden were slowly emerging. Down the slope to the stream, where the ground became soggy, there were marsh marigolds and lady's smock, and between the two cottages there was an overgrown hedge of yew and laurel, happily combined with a sweet briar rose, wild honeysuckle and clematis.

Towards the end of the afternoon, when they were both lying on their backs on the grass, Laura had her eyes closed and she could hear woodpeckers in the ancient fir trees and the distant bleating of lambs on the hillside, and it evoked a sudden rush of memories, mostly of her mother who had loved her garden.

'You've gone all quiet,' James said.

'Thinking. My mother...'

'...and you've got a tear escaping from one eye.'

'I need a tablet,' she whispered, her eyes firmly closed, but he didn't give her a tablet. She felt him kiss the tear away with slow, infinite gentleness. When Laura dared to open her eyes, he was back building the wall.

*

Liz was the first to arrive. She was pleased that Laura was in the cottage, but unhappy about the circumstances, 'I'm so sorry, after everything you've been through, with the miscarriage and everything. If there's *anything* I can do.'

'Thanks,' she said lamely, knowing there was nothing

anyone could do.

'Is that James still doing the wall?' she said, peering down the garden. 'Jamie!' she bellowed, 'Give it a rest can't you? Go and get changed.'

But he couldn't hear her properly so just scowled, then because they were looking at him, yelled back, 'WHAT? What have I done now? Gone and taken a fucking breath without your permission?'

Liz grunted with amusement. 'We love each other really. He's not going to be able to move tomorrow because of a bad back, and he's got all those horses arriving from Ireland, and the front pasture still needs aerating.'

'Best leave him. He's happy getting wet and dirty.'

Jess and all the other girls arrived. Carla brought the vet, followed in by Maggie, Pete and Ellie. When the family from next door arrived too, the cottage was full, spilling out into the garden. James finished the wall just as dusk fell, and Laura was lighting the garden torches. Liz wouldn't let James inside because he was filthy, but by then, some of the guests were smoking outside anyway. There was a glorious sunset and it was still warm.

Jess whispered to Laura. 'You can tell they haven't had sex.'

'Who?' Laura said, blowing out matches.

'Jamie and Carla... the body language is all wrong. She's still winding me up about Ireland.'

'She's got the vet now, anyway,' Laura said, lighting the final candle. 'She likes them hunky, doesn't she?'

'Yeah, but the vet is like, serious overkill? He's way too fat. If he were to fall on you with his animal passion, you could be killed outright. Be like a barn door falling off its hinges.'

Laura laughed, and Maggie wanted to know what they were whispering about.

'Sex,' Laura said.

Maggie glared at Jess. 'Have you got *no* other

conversation?'

Jess sidled away to where James was sitting on the floor, his back against the cottage wall, rubbing the back of his neck. She kicked his foot. 'What you need is a massage.'

He squinted up at her. 'And that's where you come in, is it?'

'I'm fully qualified now, but I'm supposed to practice,' she said, exchanging a secretive look with Lucy. 'According to my expert eye, I reckon you're the perfect guinea pig. I've got all my kit in the car,' she said, then when he didn't say anything. 'Oh, *go on,* Jamie, I don't know anyone else with the right muscle groups. You can have all the exclusive extras.'

Next door's teenage son, who was built like Hercules, tapped Jess on the shoulder. 'I'll have the extras. What are they?'

'There you go,' James said, flipping open a can of lager. 'Ben can help you out.'

'Yeah. I've got big muscles,' he said proudly.

'They're artificial,' Jess snapped, looking him up and down.

'No they're not,' Ben said, and tensed a bicep under her nose for closer inspection. 'They're real, go on have a feel.'

'I'm *so* not interested in what your pumped up, baby flesh *feels* like. Do you drink that chocolate build-up powder, as well? I think I can see it on your top lip,' Jess sneered. She shoved him out of the way and went to dance barefoot on the lawn with Lucy, a bottle of vodka in one hand and a cigarette in the other. Laura had an idea the gyrations were for someone else's benefit but when she looked across, James had his head back against an old planter full of spent geraniums, his eyes closed against the sun. Ben was a lot more appreciative and stood just a few feet away from the girls with a big grin.

Her sister didn't mix well with the vodka generation.

'Stop glowering at the young ones, you'll get wrinkles,'

Laura said.

'Too late,' Maggie said. 'look at this face.'

They were on the little patio, balancing plates of Welsh cheddar and hunks of warm bread on their knees, watching Pete and Ellie down by the stream with the dogs. Lambchop was digging up stones and taking them to James, dropping them in his lap and barking till he inspected them.

Maggie said, 'So, how do you feel? Now that you're footloose?'

'Better now that I've made the decision, but a bit overwhelmed by all the change,' Laura said thoughtfully. 'I think I just need to find me again, find some peace of mind.'

'What you need is a straightforward man with no baggage, no ex-wife, no kids, old-fashioned values.'

'I can see them forming a queue.'

'Well, they will. Just you wait.'

Laura tried not to roll her eyes and downed her drink. 'I'd settle for simple old love.'

'There's nothing simple about it. That's where you're going wrong.'

The sun dropped and the air cooled dramatically. Everyone moved inside for a nightcap.

Jess, hopelessly drunk, caught sight of James, 'Aw, look, Luce,' she said, throwing down her shoes and bag, 'aw... poor baby he's so worn out.'

'I'm not, I can go all night,' Ben said.

Jess hitched up her dress, knelt on the grass next to James and carefully removed a lit cigarette out of his hand, which was perilously close to burning a hole in his thigh. She took a long drag on it before handing it to Lucy and then covered James with the picnic blanket. Encouraged by the depth of his slumber, Jess was about to put her mouth on his, when Maggie's strident voice shattered the ambience.

'Jess! What are you doing?'

'Keeping him warm, otherwise he'll be really stiff in the morning.'

Maggie's reaction was slow but predictable, mostly in the form of a beetroot scowl. Liz took one look at her brother and told Laura not to worry about leaving him in the garden overnight. 'He's perfectly hardy,' she said briskly, as if he were some kind of perennial or native mountain pony. 'Never ill, constitution of an ox.'

'But he does get seasick,' Carla pointed out.

'How does that count in a fucking garden?' Jess said, trying to put her shoes back on. Ben offered her a meaty arm to lean on, 'Yeah, but he might *dream...* he's in a boat.'

'Can someone please get *him* out of my *face*?'

The party broke up in a noisy cluster of farewells but it didn't matter, there were only the Arab mares for neighbours, and they were mostly interested in all the commotion, strung out in a shadowy line with their ears pricked.

When Laura found her way back into the garden, James had woken of his own accord. 'Where is everyone?' he said, struggling to get to his feet. He stretched himself upright with a fair amount of groaning and a lot of small stones fell to the ground.

'Gone home,' Laura said, collecting stray plates and glasses.

'Oh, sorry... I'm starving, is there anything left?'

'Look at the state of you,' she grinned, 'I've saved you some chilli.'

He looked longingly at her for a moment then declared he was going home to get cleaned up first. 'Don't throw anything away,' he said, pinching a bread roll off the tower of crockery in her arms.

An hour later, Laura went to close the curtains upstairs. Outside, the horses moved like ghosts between the trees in the dark fields, and there was a pale moon in the sky. She'd just about given up on James returning, when Laura saw him clamber back over the field gate with a black bin liner and tap softly on the front door.

'Sorry,' he said. 'Fell asleep again in the bath.'

The bin liner was full of dirty washing.

'You don't mind, do you?' he said, stuffing several pairs of muddy jeans into her washing machine. 'I think the motor's burnt out on mine.'

'Most guests bring the host flowers, or chocolates.'

'Bit naff, isn't it?'

'If you say so,' she said, handing him the washing powder.

She reheated the chilli. For a long while James didn't speak, just pointed at the food and made appreciative noises. Eventually, he pushed the plate to one side and allowed her to pour two large glasses of cognac.

'Did you bring my tablets or cigarettes by any chance?'

'Uh huh.'

James removed a squashed box from his jacket and rattled it in front of her, which was hugely annoying. 'Tell me why you need them first?'

'You know why!' she said, rubbing her clammy forehead. 'And I feel jittery without them, I feel like I'm going to have a panic attack.' Laura knew she'd over-egged it, but he still only gave her half a tablet, which he cut up painstakingly on the breadboard.

'Give me the rest of it!' she said, but he'd already secreted it away to his back pocket. Laura tried to snatch the packet back, but he clamped her arms down. Defeated, she tried to smile, but her insides turned into that horrible wobbly mess which hovered between laughing and sobbing.

Slowly, James dropped his grip and slid his arms around her instead. She hadn't been in such close proximity to him since the week of the miscarriage, but Laura remembered the bone crushing way he'd held her in his worn out clothes. He was leaning against the kitchen units, and the angle of his stance meant she could feel the full length of his body against hers, and this time, there wasn't a thick dressing gown cum horse blanket forming a safe woolly barrier. He'd changed into a clean pair of denims and an astonishingly well-laundered shirt, if she didn't count the missing button on one of the cuffs, but she loved the plain clean smell of it, of *him*. Odd that such a simple thing could be so intoxicating.

She allowed her hands to slide across his back and up to his shoulders and discovered how much she loved the solid strength of him as well, the uncomplicated warmth of being in his arms. She drew away slightly and looked at her feet. 'You're such a good shoulder to cry on.'

'You're not crying.'

'I am. I'm just good at hiding it,' she said and went in to the sitting room and lit the log burner, then curled up on one of the chairs with her cognac. She studied the man opposite, sprawled across her sofa and considered his alternative therapy. Such intense physical contact had the potential to be just as addictive, just as dangerous as the drugs she craved.

'Am I allowed a cigarette? Half, maybe?'

'You're getting the idea now.'

'You're too strict,' she said, and tried to think of something a little more eloquent, but could only come up with serious and sensual, which were inappropriate. 'And you're too scruffy...you must be short of dozens of buttons.'

'*Buttonless?*'

She ignored his horrified expression, 'If you only had to use three words to describe me what would they be? A sad, delusional junkie?'

'No. Free-spirited and emotional,' he said, more or less straight away, then thought for moment before he added, '... lost?'

'I could use the same three words for you, and yet I'm desperately seeking, and you're desperately running from it.

How does that make sense?'

He shrugged. 'One of us must be wrong,' he said and finally lit the cigarette for her. He asked her what had made her call time on Simon. When she began to talk, Laura hated the way her relationship sounded. Like a game of emotional chess, and she was acutely aware of trying to justify her feelings, her actions.

'Why did you make that banker's draft out to me?' she said.

'It's all my fault now, is it?'

'No. It gave me an escape route, for which I'm very grateful for.'

'Well... I just reckoned you'd done the majority of the work. Look, I get the feeling you bent over backwards to hang on to the original idea, the ethos of the place... whatever you want to call it. I admire that.'

'Would it be fair to say you just don't like Simon?'

'I don't like insincerity.'

She looked away from him at this, finding a reason to poke the fire and add another log.

'Were you and Carys faithful to each other?' she said suddenly, knowing what his answer would be. Even so, he took time to consider the question, or maybe he was thrown by the change of tack.

He nodded. 'Yeah, without a doubt.'

'I kind of envy that, what you had. It's so... untainted. Don't you want to find it again? Or do you believe we only get one chance of a soul-mate?'

'You're full of big questions,' he said, refilling his glass, but Laura sensed he didn't really want to answer her. After a moment, when James realised she was still expectant he said, 'The problem with that is, I've no real feelings for anyone beyond a token affection and no sexual feelings whatsoever. I live in never-never land.'

'You feel trapped?'

He sighed, tired of her probing. 'Quite possibly... or maybe it's the fact I just don't want to do anything about it.'

Laura knew when he'd closed the subject. She made a conscious decision not to wander along the same conversational path again, unless he initiated it. Her curiosity with his bereavement partly stemmed from her own need to understand her father, but when Laura mentioned this, James just told her to stop beating herself up.

'Why don't you just go and talk to him?' he said, as if it were simple.

Soon after, Laura watched him climb back over the gate and disappear into the black field. Washboy leapt the gate easily and followed him, but Lambchop had to find a hole in the hedge.

Seconds later, the little dog ran back and leapt into her arms.

*

In the morning, Laura discovered three pairs of creased denims in the washing machine, some shirts and what looked to be a set of horsey-looking leg bandages and a sheepskin noseband. The rattling noise left behind turned out to be small change and nails. There was also a soggy mass of paper which had to be scraped out of the seal, until Laura recognised a twenty-pound note folded into a square and covered with phone numbers. She left it on the windowsill to dry, slung his clothes into the drier, then realised she had absolutely nothing to do.

She couldn't even sit in the sun. When she looked outside, it was blustery and damp with fine mist and rain obscuring the mountains. The cherry and magnolia blossom flew in the wind like confetti. Even Lambchop was bored with her and whined to be let out, then eventually scampered back across the field when she thought Laura wasn't looking.

When his clothes were dry, she replaced all the missing buttons and repaired some of the rips. Laura left it as late as possible before she wandered over to the yard. It was one thing having nothing to do, but she didn't want to broadcast it. She certainly didn't want James to think she'd be forever on his doorstep, begging for pills and cigarettes. She needn't have worried; there was no one around other than Rhian cleaning a saddle in the tack room.

Compared to the rest of the staff she was quite a lot older, and positively dour. Although she'd come to the party, Laura had the feeling Rhian didn't like her very much, but Carla had said she was curt and suspicious of absolutely everyone, and fiercely protective of James. She'd been at the yard for donkey's years, knew everything there was to know and was very much in charge if James or Liz were absent.

'You know the sort,' Carla had said, 'lives for the horses and the yard is her second home.'

'She's awful hard work to talk to.'

'She has a very grim home life, apparently.'

Laura tried to remember the grim home life and placed the bag of laundry onto an old armchair. 'James not here?'

'No.'

Laura looked around, not entirely surprised to find that everything was far more clean and orderly than anything in the farmhouse. She trailed a hand across the racks of saddles, all in beautiful condition.

'Look, he won't be back for ages,' Rhian said.

There was a feeding chart with all the horses' names across the top. Cutie Pie, NO OATS, it said, underlined in red marker pen. The Arab mares had a separate chart and the writing was different, all in the same flowing neat hand.

'You knew his wife, didn't you?' Laura said, keeping her eyes on the wall.

Rhian carried on oiling the leather, as if Laura wasn't

even there.

'Worshipped the ground,' Rhian said eventually.

It didn't directly answer her question; it was more a statement, delivered in the same monotone voice. Laura knew it was her warning cue to leave, but rather than take the short cut across the field, she walked all the way around on the lane, in case she stepped on something sacred.

CHAPTER THIRTEEN

Laura

Lambchop had adopted Laura.

She frequently ran across the field from her master's house to check on her, sometimes sleeping in a ball at the end of the bed. James had told her that she went in and out of the cat-flaps and knew just the right amount of bite pressure to wake him if there was an emergency. She wondered what he classed as an emergency. Laura was pretty sure that large spiders wouldn't count, but the idea that his dog would run across the field and alert him was such a nice concept, Laura thought it was almost worth faking it, just to see if it worked. On the other hand, she was tired of faking, she had to get real.

The solicitor she'd been to see was a bit too real, in that his initial prognosis appeared to be bleak. Basically, he envisaged it would take a good while for Laura to be released from the business and the apartment. However, the wheels were in motion with preliminary letters, politely asking for Simon's response to providing financial details.

Predictably, the morning she received a copy of the letter sent to Simon, her mobile rang.

'More solicitors?' Simon said. 'Don't you think I've got enough on my plate in that department?'

'It's not just about you.'

'If you want anything out of the business, you're going to have to come back and help me run it till I get someone else.'

'It would never work!'

'Look, you've left everything in a mess here! You're part way through the villa project. What am I supposed to do with that?' he said, then made an exasperated noise. 'How about I e-mail it to you? Same salary.'

'Simon, I've *resigned!*' Laura said.

Despite her resolution, work was elusive. She posted her advertisement to the local paper, promoting her skills, and she spent hours on the phone and the Internet seeking out all the smaller clients they'd lost when they'd become a company and made themselves too big, too busy, too expensive. In a way it was worse than struggling to get on to the bottom rung of the ladder the first time around, because everyone she talked to was actually more interested in the downfall of Dragon Designs and her love life.

Love was so hard. Her sister had married at nineteen, and Laura thought Maggie had got it all wrong, but Pete and Maggie must have got something so right, and then... even if you were lucky enough to get the real thing, it was so easily lost. Laura looked at James sometimes, and it seemed like he was tied up in knots. A couple of days ago she'd come across him by accident. He'd been sitting with his back against a tree, his face in his hands. Laura longed to put her arms around him but something about his isolation made her walk away. The real part of his grief was intensely private, and she kind of admired him for that.

Some ten minutes later, he'd caught up with her, just as she was pulling off her shoes to try and climb over the fence.

'I've made a decision about the mares,' he said.

Laura knew exactly what he meant, but stopped to face him. 'What do you mean?'

'I'm going to sell them.'

'Oh,' she said, knowing it was a massive deal, but he didn't seem to want or expect anything further from her. He even helped her over the fence, but walked back in the opposite direction.

She wondered what really kept him going, was it the same blind hope she had for herself, or did he just exist? Laura decided it was neither; it was more likely that he swayed uncertainly between the two dimensions. Yet he had the strength of mind to be there for her, to the point where she'd ditched the anti-depressants, and then she was horrible to him because she couldn't sleep for a couple of days. Laura had tossed and turned all night until dawn, until the willow warblers and the chaffinches stirred noisily in the elder tree outside the bedroom window. She must have slept eventually, because she was woken by someone knocking on the door.

When Laura went groggily to answer it, there was blinding daylight, and James was astride a huge chestnut horse. It seemed to fill the small doorway, champing its bit and foaming at the mouth.

'Are you all right?' he said.

'James I'm fine, I was trying to get some sleep,' she snapped. 'Why are you checking on me every five minutes?'

'I didn't think I was.'

'Just leave me alone.'

'All right,' he said with a shrug. 'Only asking.'

She closed the door but went to peer through the curtains and watched him ride back down the lane. Washboy gave her a mutinous look and peed on the daffodils.

*

Laura found him later, still trying to repair his washing machine. Its innards lay all over the floor in the kitchen, the metal back propped against the kitchen table. She stood there an age, watching him frown at an old yellowing manual, then stare at an old oily motor. It was balanced on the bread crock, with a lamp over it, as if it were having some sort of surgical procedure.

'James, I'm sorry I was in a bad mood before. I didn't mean any of it, about you checking up on me. I like you checking up on me,' she said, leaning on the doorjamb.

'Forget it.'

His eyes flicked onto hers for the briefest of seconds, he seemed much more interested in poking the mass of nuts and bolts on the table. It annoyed the hell out of her. She went across the room and kissed the side of his face to get his attention.

'I *was* listening,' he said, reading her so easily, 'and I knew you were there. I saw you actually, running across the field and falling down all the rabbit holes, and you a farmer's daughter.'

She ignored his speech. 'Come to dinner, will you?'

'What, *now?*'

'An hour… is that long enough to get rid of all the oil?' she said, wrinkling her nose at the rag in his hands.

'Can I bring some washing?'

'No! Just buy a new one!' she said crossly, annoyed that he was laughing at her, annoyed he'd seen her running, but by the time she'd got back to Mefysen, she was grinning, and felt practically light-hearted, marinating the wild salmon and mixing a salad. Then she went upstairs and more from habit than any devious planning, pulled out her little black dress with the built-in plunge bra. When Laura caught sight of herself fully dressed with her hair all carefully tousled, she suddenly realised what it looked like and frantically undressed again, hastily wiping all the make-up off and smoothing her hair down. The last thing she wanted was for James to think she was trying to seduce him.

After a few attempts at trying to dress down, Laura decided the only real solution was her old jeans and a shirt she used for decorating, with her hair caught back in a ponytail. She ran downstairs, frantically blew out the candles on the table, and changed the music from Dido to U2.

When he arrived, he looked at her with a slight frown, head on one side.

'What?' she said.

'Nothing,' James said and went in to the kitchen with two bottles of wine. Laura followed him. 'No, come on. Why are you looking at me like *that*? Should I have dressed for dinner?' she said sarcastically, looking at the back pockets falling off his denims and the frayed hems.

'No,' he said, jamming a corkscrew into the bottle, his eyes on the garden. 'You look gorgeous.'

Laura went over the exchange of words several times, coming to the conclusion that since he had no sexual feelings, and since she was so crabby he was likely just being placatory, but then he wasn't the sort to drop a comment like that, just to appease her.

It was so much trickier having a man as a friend.

*

Partly out of having nothing much to do, Laura watched him a lot with Midnight Sky.

She found herself taking a sketchbook and some charcoal outside. Drawing for pleasure was something Laura hadn't done since her university days, but there was tremendous satisfaction in capturing the complicated movement of the horse with a few simple strokes.

Not that it was any kind of hardship wasting time outside. The long days of late spring bled into early summer with an almost continental dry heat, turning the tracks to dust.

The brown bracken covering the slopes of Minas Bach had erupted into a sea of green fern, and the hedgerows were bursting with ivy, honeysuckle and wild rose.

Only Rhian ever watched James and the mare. The other girls always claimed he'd be hours doing the same thing over and over, and it was boring; but then they missed that crucial second when it all came together, the culmination of hours of psychological manoeuvres. He'd spent a week sat on the floor hand-feeding the mare out of a bucket with the bridle draped over the side, the mouthpiece covered in molasses. A few days later he'd quietly slid the bridle into place, fastening all the tiny buckles, and Laura was caught out by how humble it made her feel. Rhian had exchanged an odd smile with her. It was a bit like the Mona Lisa, but Laura had the distinct feeling she'd earned some kind of acceptance.

It was just a few days later when she was astonished to see James had the mare at the end of a long lunge line, fully tacked for riding and trotting sedately in beautifully controlled circles. Even to her untrained eye, Laura could see there was a different spirit about Midnight Sky, that fluid energy that said she was alive again, shining.

When James brought the horse to a halt, she ducked under the paddock rail and walked across.

'I can't believe the change in her. Is she ready to leave?'

'No. I want you to sit on her.'

'*Me?*' Laura said, her blood running cold as she watched him tighten the girth on the saddle. Her knowledge of horses mostly amounted to a procession of wilful ponies in her childhood, with Maggie barking instructions at her and then giving up in disgust.

'Why me?'

'Because you're so small and unthreatening, and you're nervous of her,' James said and held the stirrup steady for her. 'Trust me.'

Laura hauled herself on to the horse, but paled when it jostled about.

'Don't let go of her or I'll never speak to you again. I *mean* it.'

'I'm not letting go of her. This horse is worth more than all my worldly goods,' he said and walked slowly around the perimeter of the paddock. 'She belongs to one of the lower echelons of royalty. Lord Brixton-Smith? He wants her fit to go into training for next year's Grand National. She came fourth two years ago,' he went on, then brought the horse to a halt and sighed. 'Laura, you can open your eyes now.'

She kicked her feet out of the stirrups, and James lifted her down easily. 'Amazing what trust does.'

'I trusted you, not the horse.'

'I know... so did the horse.'

*

Pam said, 'Where do you find a man you can trust? They're all taken. Except maybe Christy's brother. He keeps asking for your phone number. Can I let Christy pass it on?'

They were in a smart wine bar on a Thursday night, in the centre of Chester.

'Oh, I don't know. I'm not looking for a relationship,' Laura said. 'I need to sort myself out with some work, that's my priority.'

'But surely you're entitled to *something*? I know what you put into that business.'

'I'm working on it, trying to follow up loose ends.'

'Speaking of loose ends, Simon's closed the office, gone to work in Spain full-time,' Pam said. 'Those flats are a nightmare, they're costing twice the agreed amount to do up.'

Laura stared into her almost empty glass.

'Okay,' Pam said, 'if this is an insult, please just say.' She passed some headed notepaper across the table with a contact name scrawled across it. 'It's a small hotel, sixteen pairs of curtains? Steve's doing an extension for them.'

'No, it's just the thing,' Laura said gratefully. Her mobile alerted her to a message from James. Something about breakfast, and Lamby had been shivering on her doorstep for hours, guarding a special stone, where was she?

'Care to share?' Pam said, watching her text back.

'Oh, just a friend. My landlord actually.'

'Why are you grinning like the Cheshire cat?' she said, stirring her gin and tonic. 'What does he do, this *friend*?'

Laura glanced up briefly. 'Horses.'

Pam pulled a salacious expression. 'Oh... a bit of rough?'

'He's not rough at all.'

'*Hunky*, then?'

Laura put the phone back in her bag, 'Look, we cook for each other and talk.'

'So he's married?'

'Umm... not really, no.'

'What does *that* mean?' she said. 'Laura, speaking as a friend, don't get into something even more complicated, will you?'

'Like I *said*, he's just a friend.'

Pam gave her a narrow look. 'Friends don't make your eyes light up like that.'

When she got home, Laura scooped up the cold little dog and looked in the hall mirror to see if she looked any different, but Lambchop kept licking her face.

*

Laura presented herself for scrambled eggs at the allotted time on Friday morning, and told James about the curtain order, but he was subdued and distracted.

'I know men are mostly unmoved by fabric,' she said, buttering toast, 'and I know you find the whole concept of matching cushions and braid trims incredibly tedious, but you could show a tiny bit of interest.'

'Sorry... what?'

Eventually, he removed an envelope from the plate rack and showed her a letter with an elaborate logo. When she looked closer, Laura saw it was a stud farm in Cornwall. A price had been agreed for each mare following extensive veterinary reports, except that James had crossed Cariad off the list.

'Why's that?' Laura said.

'She's not for sale,' he said. 'She's staying.'

'When?' she said. 'When is all this going to happen?'

'Tonight.'

'Tonight?'

'Better for traveling the horses,' he said, getting to his feet. He stacked their plates in the sink with a clatter. 'And there's no one around. No one to see me fall to pieces or bottle out.'

'You want to do this on your own?'

'Yeah,' he said but then turned and met her eyes and shrugged.

*

A while later, when Laura was making coffee in the tack room for staff break time, Maggie called in looking for her. 'Could do with a chat,' she said. 'Fancy coming over for dinner?'

'Oh, yes all right,' she said, pouring hot water onto teabags into a selection of chipped mugs.

James appeared with Ben and introduced him as the new recruit on the yard. He didn't know anything about horses,

Midnight Sky

but he was going to help out with some of the heavy work and drive the tractor and the horsebox. 'Starts next week,' James said, 'so don't give him a hard time.'

'No, but we're rather hoping he'll give *us* one,' Carla said, but only Lucy laughed.

'Heavy work?' Jess said. 'Like a big dobbin cart horse?'

Ben grinned. 'Yeah, you can even put me in a harness, if you want.'

'Give you a chance at like, *pulling* something?'

Ben looked around at the female audience and was slightly incredulous, as if he'd landed in totty heaven. When James and Ben took their drinks outside, Maggie said, 'That Ben seems nice.'

Jess stuck a finger in her mouth and pretended to retch behind her mother's back.

'No, but he is pretty cute,' Lucy said.

'He's just a baby, a starter pack,' Jess said, flicking through her magazine. 'He couldn't give anyone a hard time. I'd rather have the full six- pack thanks.'

'As in old man Jamie?' Lucy said sarcastically.

'Uh-huh,' Jess said, a manicured finger on her cheek. 'Let's see, skilful, sensitive and serious against just strong and stupid. Mr Bed versus Mr Ed. Benny boy must be related to that circus horse somehow, same teeth, big rubber lips and like, *no brain*. Yep, it's a no-brainer.'

'Jess, why are you hanging around here on a Friday?' Maggie said. 'Haven't you got more important stuff to do?'

'God, Mother, how many times?' she said dramatically. 'Stop bugging me about my life!'

'Don't start yelling. I've got a proper headache,' Lucy groaned. 'Feel dead fat today as well.'

'Lucy's pre-menstrual everyone,' Jess shouted across the yard. '*Red alert!*'

'Tell the world, why don't you?' Maggie hissed. When Ben and James glanced over, she hastily closed the tack room door and pressed her back against it, in case they came across to see what the problem was. 'Lucy's time of the month should be private.'

Jess said, 'Mum, it may come as a shock, but men actually *know* what periods are. Only in Victorian times it was...' she dropped her voice to a whisper, 'a certain time of the month.'

'Yes, well, men know what crude is as well,' Maggie said huffily, then snapped at Laura to be at Hafod House for dinner at six *sharp*.

'Yes, okay,' she said, but by the time Laura had walked back to the cottage through the Arab mares, there was a lump in her throat, and her feet had turned to lead. She really was a hopeless case.

James was only doing what everyone had nagged him to do for the last two and a bit years. As she showered and changed to go to Maggie's house, Laura could see the horses standing in a group beneath some huge ancient oak trees. The scene looked like an old master's oil painting, the kind of picture that had tiny cracks and abrasions across the surface and needed to be restored. Laura rested her forehead against the window pane and cancelled dinner.

'I'm not feeling very well,' she said to Maggie on the phone.

'Oh... I thought you were quiet earlier. Can I get you anything?'

'Just a tummy upset. I'll be fine.'

There was a text from Christy about pizza and a film. She responded to that then switched her phone off. A couple of hours later, Laura watched James catch up all the mares. They all trotted to him when he rattled a bucket, and he put head collars on them all and they followed him out through the gate. They were so *trusting*.

A flash-looking lorry came next and reversed into the yard. Laura looked at the empty field with the gate hanging open and grabbed her sweater, tying it around her waist as she walked, quickly at first, as if she had a plan, then slower and slower, not really having a clue what to do. Lambchop barked at her indecision. James and another man were leading the horses into the lorry, and they were all calling to each other as their hooves thundered up the ramp, their nostrils all wide and wary, blowing at the unfamiliar smell. There was something wrenching about the way they communicated to each other.

James caught sight of her. 'Laura! Do me a favour will you? Take Cariad round the back somewhere before she breaks loose.'

He pointed to a dark grey mare tied to a ring in the wall, not rugged for traveling like the others, but twisting one way and then the other, whinnying her heart out because she was left behind. Her hands trembling with the responsibility of it, Laura walked the mare up and down, holding on to her as if her life depended on it. Cariad was frantic, long loud neighs resonated through her body, talking to her offspring and her sisters, her little ears flicking to and fro, straining to catch their replies.

She saw James push the ramp home and sign something for the driver, after which the lorry pulled away. James watched it bounce slowly to the end of the drive in a cloud of white dust. He stood there for long minutes, staring at the bundle of paperwork in his hands, but Laura knew he wasn't reading it. He was thinking about Carys. He'd sold her soul and her dreams, sold out the very essence of what was left of her. Wordlessly, he took the quivering Cariad and set her loose in the paddock with Midnight Sky, the documents rolled up and stuffed in his back pocket.

By the time he came to find her, Laura had tears streaming down her face. 'Sorry, it all just got to me,' she said, going through her pockets for tissues. 'Look at the mess I'm in. I wanted to be here for you, and look at me, I'm worse than you...'

Still without saying a word, he searched her eyes and wiped the tears from her face with his thumbs. 'Wait here.'

Laura watched him go into the house and return minutes later with a bottle of champagne. He took her hand, and they walked along the track rutted with hoof prints, to the top of Minas Bach. There was just enough light to make kaleidoscope patterns beneath the trees and send pale dapples across the steep wooded slopes where the curlews were circling.

They stopped by an outcrop of rock as the dying sun bled into the sea.

James stood the bottle in an ice-cold, singing stream and Laura threw herself down onto the grass and stared at the moving sky. It was dusk, and she could hear the soft burr of wood pigeon and a single cuckoo, somewhere in the copse behind. When James sat next to her, she rested her head on him because the grass was peppered with sheep droppings, and she didn't want them in her hair. And when the champagne was cold, James showed her the label, as if they were in a fancy restaurant.

She smiled at last. 'What are we celebrating?'

'Two things,' he said, passing the bottle to her. 'Everlasting love...'

Laura drank thirstily, and it went to her head with a delicious intoxicating rush because she hadn't eaten for several hours.

'You're spilling half of that down your face,' James said.

'And...?' Laura said, poised to take another gulp. 'What's the other thing?'

'I've finally bought a new washing machine.'

She lowered the bottle and laughed, then had to hold her nose. It was one of those strange moments again when laughing was close to something else. How was it that he could make her cry and laugh almost simultaneously?

Sometimes, he was almost too intense, but Laura loved that hypnotic darkness, she could find a home for her emotions in his vast heart. In return, she could love away all the hurt out of those eyes. She knew at that moment, knew she was on the brink of falling in love, but this time it looked so far to fall, further than she'd ever been dropped before, and he just might not catch her.

After all, she wasn't his everlasting love.

James placed the bottle down carefully, nestled it in a bed of gorse. He still held her eyes, then he held her, as if she were made of porcelain. It was different to the other times, in that she was very aware of his heart hammering against hers. When he pushed his hands into her hair and began to kiss along her collarbone she almost stopped breathing, it was so exquisite. Then he traced along her throat, every nerve ending on fire until lips touched lips. She opened her mouth to his. The soft hardness of his body, and the funny sadness of his mind were both finally in her arms.

CHAPTER FOURTEEN

Maggie

The idea came to Maggie the minute Jess discovered she'd landed a plum job in a posh beauty salon in Chester. Jess was quite pleased so far as Maggie could tell, until the reality set in. The reality was leaving home, finding somewhere to live in just two weeks, and handing in her notice at the yard.

Handing in her notice at the yard seemed to be the biggest stumbling block.

Maggie had thought she might have plucked up courage when she'd been hanging around the tack room, but her daughter's glare told her obviously not, but that was clearly nothing to do with courage. More importantly, Maggie had wanted to see if Laura knew of any house shares or flats for Jess in Chester, hoping it might galvanise Jess into action, but of course Laura had cried off dinner, and as usual, nothing got sorted out. She waited until Jess had gone in to work as normal on Saturday morning, then drove over there herself.

Maggie parked up and walked over to the office, seconds behind Liz; but no one was really aware that Maggie was even there because there was so much going on inside. Jess, Lucy, and Rhian were all in various stages of distress.

'All right what the hell is going on?' Liz said, plonking her bag and keys down on the desk. She snapped at James,

'Why are all the livery horses in the front paddock? Where are the mares?'

'He's sold them all,' Rhian said, her face all puffy from crying. 'They've all gone, hundreds of miles away. Last night.'

'Is that right?' Liz said to James, 'Without telling anyone?'

'What the fuck do I need to tell anyone for?'

'Well, what about me... and her parents?'

'What's it got to do with them?' James said. Liz put up a placatory hand. 'All right we'll talk about it later,' she said, and looked at the girls. 'And what about Jess and Lucy?'

'That's down to me as well, is it?'

'It usually is!'

'Jess has just handed in her notice,' James said, then looked at Lucy bent over double on the chair and frowned for a moment. 'Oh yeah. Lucy's got period pains.'

'She looks like she's giving *birth*,' Jess said.

'Is *that* all?' Liz said, disgusted. 'Pull yourselves together *all* of you, and get the ponies ready for the ten o clock, and I don't want dirty stable marks on any of them.'

Jess and Rhian slunk outside, and Liz marched after them, telling them who, what, where and when. Maggie crept into the vacated chair by the desk. James gave her a wary look, searched through the desk drawers, and passed Lucy a packet of painkillers. They waited till she'd shuffled down the hall and into the kitchen.

'Is it not a good time?' Maggie said, already knowing the answer.

'Depends what you're going to say.'

'With Jess gone, you'll be wanting someone else.'

'Got someone in mind?'

'Me.'

'You?' he said slowly, obviously wondering how he was going to get out of another sticky situation. 'Maggie, what the girls get paid amounts to petrol money and getting plastered on a Saturday night, and all the riding they want.'

'I know, and that's fine by me. Except I'll forego all my riding for Ellie,' Maggie said, having worked it all out in her head. 'You see, I don't go clubbing any more, but I really need the petrol money.'

Maggie could see him wondering how to tell her she was too old and pretty boring eye candy, but he was too polite. 'It's a really hard slog, especially in the winter.'

'James, I grew up on a farm in Hiraethog. It was like a wilderness, and we had to pull water out of a well when we first moved there, and hack rocks out of the ground to make a patch to grow spuds.'

'I know,' he said, leaning back in his chair. 'Your sister talks lovingly of it.'

'You don't know where Laura is, do you? I've been trying to call her. She wasn't well last night, she cancelled dinner.'

He put a cigarette to his lips. 'She was with me. She's okay, we went for a walk.'

'Oh... a walk?'

'Not a problem, is it?'

Maggie forced out a hysterical laugh, 'Of *course* not, don't be silly! So... am I in? I promise not to jump down your throat when Jess larks about. Or you take my sister... for a walk.'

James looked backed to be into a corner if she were honest, but he told her to shadow Jess for a couple of half days to see what she was letting herself in for, before she agreed to anything. Maggie felt as if she'd been elected to run the country. It had been twenty years since she'd had a job and she couldn't wait to do something different other than hoover under Pete's feet.

'I'll start now,' she said, rooting through her pockets for gloves.

On the way to the tack room, her sister's car pulled in,

and James' little white dog pushed its head out through the window. Laura said, 'Maggie, what are you doing here?'

'Feeling better?'

'I'm fine. I'm really sorry about dinner,' she said. 'Can I come tonight instead?'

'You might have to bring the food with you,' Maggie said and told her about Jess and their new jobs and how it would mean Ellie could carry on riding forever. It gave her a good feeling, knowing she had something under control. All the time she was talking, Maggie couldn't help noticing how well her sister looked, sort of serene and a little more fleshed out. She was wearing washed out denims, a white shirt, and with her hair all loose, she looked fresh, natural and sexy. Maggie tutted. 'Look at you. Simon must have had a white stick, and that was something else he never told you.'

Laura laughed and pointed at the sample books on the back seat. 'I'm on my way to estimate a curtain job. James is going to give me the directions to the hotel.'

'Well, good luck, we'll talk later,' Maggie said.

The moment she'd stepped aside, James went over to her car and leant in through the window. He was showing his Levi-clad backside to its best advantage and giving Laura the full benefit of his moody, come-to-bed-eyes, not that Maggie could see those because she was walking slowly backwards, but she could see her sister's eyes, and they were like melted chocolate. It was obvious why she hadn't come to dinner now. She'd been in on the secret horse sale.

Liz was in full flow in the tack room, tapping a riding crop against a feeding chart on the wall. Maggie hovered, waiting till James caught up and explained why she was there.

'Oh super! Welcome aboard,' Liz said.

Jess said, 'Is this some sort of sick joke? I have to work with my freakin' *mother*?'

Lucy's white face craned round the door. 'I feel like shit,' she said in a little voice, 'I want to go home, please.'

'Why do you put up with that all the time, Luce?' Jess said. 'I told you to, like, go on the pill. If you take them continuously, you don't even bleed.'

Maggie, already ruffled with the awful language let alone the subject matter, dared to look at James, but he didn't bat an eyelid, just handed his keys to Lucy. 'I'll run you home, go and sit in the Land Rover,' he said, then to Rhian, 'Have you got ten minutes? I want to talk to you. In private.'

'Well, thank you very much,' Liz said, hands on hips. 'Take all the staff, why don't you?'

'You've got Maggie now.'

'I'm sorry about this, Maggie,' Liz said. 'It's not normally so disorganised.'

'Yeah, it is,' Jess said, picking her nails.

Jess and Maggie had twelve horses to skip out. 'These are all the full managed liveries, like Carla's, and the school horses that don't live out,' Jess said, already bored with telling her what to do and where everything was kept. Maggie grabbed a wheelbarrow, a fork and a bale of straw.

Maggie managed the first two, but she had to have a breather after that and hung over Mr Ed's door.

'Is that all you've done?' Jess shouted from the opposite row, 'We've got the muckheap after this, then it's rugs, morning feeds and grooming. *Then* we get a break.'

'I'm fine,' Maggie said, lifting another forkful of wet straw. Jess was so fast, Maggie had to go and look at what she was doing so differently but came away feeling demoralised. She had to admit Jess had fantastic muscle tone in her arms. Maggie lifted the water buckets with a bit more gusto.

At break time, there was another argument brewing in the tack room. Maggie tried to concentrate on filling the kettle and washing the dirty mugs, but it was interesting, and their voices were getting louder.

'Hold on, let me get this straight,' Liz said to James. 'You've *given* Cariad to Rhian?'

'Yeah. I know you find it difficult to understand.'

'Damn right I do!'

'I don't need any more money, so I based the decision on something else,' he said, putting saddles away onto the top row of the rack because no one else was tall enough. Jess kept passing him more and more, watching his bare torso every time he reached up until James realised several of them belonged on the lower row and started to shove them back at Jess.

He glanced at his sister's face. 'Liz, it's just a middle-aged horse.'

'It's an Arabian mare with a championship bloodline, not a riding-school hack.'

'Too old for more foals, she deserves a nice life.'

Liz made a derisory noise, 'Don't we all? Why do you have to do everything on the quiet, that's what I want to know?' she said, and began to count down on her fingers. 'Leasing Mefysen, selling all the horses, employing staff, gifting Cariad.'

'It may have escaped your notice, but I no longer have anyone to discuss this stuff with!'

'I'm meant to be your business partner. Those mares were a massive asset.'

'An asset? *An asset!*' he yelled. '*You fucking insensitive cow!*'

Liz stared at him, astonished by his vehemence. Even Maggie stopped running the taps, a custard cream poised between her teeth, but she didn't dare bite it. Jess lowered her bottle of mineral water with her mouth slightly parted, her phone ready for action.

For a moment James looked as if he might rip the entire iron rack off the wall from the way he grasped hold of it, but then he relented and just rested his head on it. 'You just don't get it, do you?' he said quietly, 'Does it *never* occur to you that it's the only way I can deal with it? That the only way I can move forward is to base my decisions on *her*? On what she might have done, on what she might want me to do? Something of her legacy belongs here, and Rhian was part of that.'

They all watched him leave and go across the yard. Liz was crestfallen, without words. She looked around at everyone, before following James meekly outside.

'You lucky fucking cow,' Jess said to Rhian.

Maggie gulped some strong sugary coffee out of Lucy's mug and sank down into the old sofa next to Rhian and patted her hand. 'Do James and Liz always argue this much?'

'Pretty much,' Jess said, furiously texting.

'It's never been that bad,' Rhian said miserably.

But when Maggie looked through the dusty window a few minutes later, Liz had her arms wrapped around her brother, and he was hugging her back.

*

Laura brought a Chinese takeaway, two bottles of wine and some beers for Pete. Maggie could barely move, let alone cook a dinner. She had two, My Little Pony hot water bottles strapped to her lower back, held in place with a dressing-gown cord. She felt like she'd been through a mangle, everything stretched to its limit and left out to dry.

'You're going to do yourself a mischief, Maggie,' Pete said, watching her hobble about, 'You've only been there a couple of hours. How are you going to manage a full day, love? You'll be like Quasimodo by next Friday.'

'I don't understand it. James and Liz are both older than me,' Maggie said, spooning special fried rice onto the plates. Pete laughed at this and flipped open a can of lager. 'She might look a bit like a woman, but that sister of his lugs hundredweight sacks round like they're full of bloody candy floss, and most folk would have needed a mini digger to do what *he* did with that dry stone wall,' Pete went on, stabbing a fork in the chow mein. 'I wouldn't mind if you were getting paid more than pocket money.'

'Pete,' Laura said evenly, 'she's doing it for Ellie.'

'Oh, I know, I know she is.'

'James wouldn't have offered Maggie the job if he didn't think she was capable,' Laura went on, and it was nice that her sister wanted to stick up for her, but Maggie was beginning to think that running the country might be a better option after all. There was a lot more sitting down.

'I think it's more that he's scared of me,' Maggie said. 'He's just waiting for me to keel over so he can put me in a barrow and tip me on the muck heap. Job done, problem solved.'

'Stop running yourself down,' Laura said. 'You've got years of experience.'

'Yes, but it's mostly in difficult child-rearing, husband and hen-keeping. I so envy you having qualifications, you can always fall back on them,' she said. 'Did you get that curtain job?'

'Yes, and when I saw the place, I had an idea about Hafod House.'

They both waited till Pete had cleared the plates and refilled the water bottles before they took the remainder of the wine into the conservatory. Maggie was grateful for the change of subject but listened to her sister's idea with an inward groan. Laura was on her favourite subject: that of turning dead rooms into profit.

Her idea was to turn Hafod House into a guest house.

She had this crazy idea that Pete could cook breakfasts and change beds.

'You may as well stop right there,' Maggie said. 'Pete has no idea where clean sheets come from. He thinks the house fairies come when it's dark.'

'So teach him,' Laura said. 'Just think about it Maggie.

You could both run your own business instead of selling up. When Jess leaves, you'll have four double bedrooms empty.'

They talked about Jess leaving. Laura even had that all sewn up, but again she was in her comfort zone and knew where to look for house shares that would appeal to Jess, even offered to take her down there. Maggie was grateful and said so, but expressed concerns about a lack of commitment in that direction because of a *certain person*.

Confident that she had her sister's attention, Maggie popped a chocolate almond into her mouth and sucked it thoughtfully. 'They had a right ding-dong today. Him and Liz.'

'What about?'

When Maggie related it all, with the emphasis on his dead wife, she imagined Laura would do some sort of cover-up job again, but she talked about the secret horse sale like she'd starred in some kind of epic block buster. It sounded like Wuthering Heights had merged with Black Beauty. There was a bit too much running across fields and sobbing for Maggie's taste.

Even the cute dog had a walk-on part. 'James said… you went for a *walk*?'

A beat. 'Yes, we went for a walk,' she said, then Laura got to her feet and looked out at the garden, all silent and serious. Maggie thought that was the end of it. She managed to shuffle to the edge of the chair and was just about to make her excuses for a bath and an early night, when Laura took a deep breath and started to speak again.

'We drank champagne,' she said softly. '…and watched the sun go down.'

Maggie nearly choked on the almond, 'That's what lovers do.'

'We're not lovers… but we did kiss.'

'*You kissed?*'

Maggie's glass flew in the air but she fumbled to catch it,

spilling the contents in her lap. As she reached to put it on the table, both hot water bottles flopped to the floor. One of them must have been leaking because there was wet patch on one of the velvet cushions. 'What kind of kiss?'

'Proper, full-on kind.'

Maggie was a bit taken aback at her honesty.

'I know what you're going to say,' Laura said, still staring at the garden in the twilight. 'He's unstable, I'm on the rebound and it's a disaster.'

'*Yes!* Yes, all that, and can you help me up please? I'm stuck.'

*

In bed later, although her body lay inert, her mind was far too over-active for sleep. Jess had come home from the pub and laughed till she cried when she saw Maggie on all fours in the bedroom, Pete trying to get her on the bed.

'How like, seriously weird is your sex life?' she said, mascara streaming down her cheeks. On the plus side, she offered to give Maggie a massage for a tenner. They both rolled her into position, and Pete paid up, glad to escape back downstairs to A Question of Sport.

'Do the one you wanted to practice on James,' Maggie said, face down on the bed.

'Problem. Jamie's got like, proper hard muscle not a big wobble of fat.'

'All right you don't need to be rude.'

Jess half-heartedly began a back and shoulder massage. It was quite soothing but not quite there for Maggie. First of all, Jess told her she had the biggest pants *ever*, and there were so many interruptions with bleeps and ring tones off her mobile, it was a bit like lying in a call centre. Since the phone was mostly cupped under her chin, Maggie could even hear both sides of the conversation. 'Luce? You missed some mental stuff after you'd gone home. Sex on Legs and Sergeant Major Cow had this like, mega bust-up row.'

'Yeah? Bout what?'

'He's only gone and given Rhian one of those mares... Cariad?'

'No fuckin' way! *Cariad?*'

'Yeah. She'll be swanking around on it all the time now.'

'*So* not fair!'

'He's such a sweetheart though, don't you think?'

'S'pose. When does Ben start?'

Maggie had wanted to use the opportunity for a bit of a talk about leaving home, but she might have known it wouldn't happen. She knew very little about the career path Jess had chosen, other than it was typically very personal and hands on. It suited her really, it was sexy and physical and Jess had no inhibitions whatsoever in that department. When Maggie had told her about Nathan being gay, she hadn't batted an eyelid although she had detected a hint of smugness. 'Golden boy let you down, has he?'

'No one's let me down,' Maggie said. 'I'm proud of you all.'

Regardless of what Pete thought, Maggie still had an idea that Jess was suffering from middle-child syndrome. 'I'll miss you when you go to Chester.'

'Yeah, right, no one to yell at?'

She tutted and pulled her dressing gown back on. 'What's it called, this salon?'

'In the Pink.'

'I don't know what magic you've used on me, but it smells lovely.'

'*Lovely?* It's Ylang Ylang, it's supposed to be, like, an aphrodisiac not a spray-on from the pound shop,' Jess said, and closed up her case of oils. 'Might get Dad going for you.'

Pete did ask her what the funny smell was, then declared the only thing it was turning on was his asthma. She mentioned Laura's idea, just to see what his reaction was. There wasn't one, he carried on reading his book. Maybe she could start very gently with the airing cupboard and work up to the hob.

'You'll never believe what else she told me?' Maggie said and waited till his eyes had moved to her left. Admittedly, the story lost a lot of its impact without her sister's gift for description and drama, but Pete cut her short, just before the climax. 'Maggie, I'll say this once,' he said, putting his book down this time. 'Would you agree that they are both, well over the age of consent for sexual relations?'

As usual, he'd missed the point.

*

Maggie got another session in on the yard a couple of days later, on the premise that afternoons might be a bit easier. Liz, about to start a lesson with a group of novice adults, told James that he needed to go through the health and safety requirements with Ben and Maggie.

She pushed a couple of manuals at his chest with a stern look. James thumbed through one of them with a deadpan expression. The second Liz was out of earshot, James pointed to the pitchfork and a sack of pony nuts. 'One is very sharp, and one is very heavy. They both hurt if you handle them wrong.'

Ben said, 'I know which one is sharp.'

'Well done, you've passed,' James said. 'Sign this, then we can get some work done.'

Maggie laughed but quickly realised there was no joke. She had the distinct feeling that James was unsure what to do with her and whose side she might be on. He came up with covering the office. That way it kept Liz off his back, and Maggie could take a look at the booking-in system while she read all about health and safety. Maggie settled herself happily in the big leather chair with a mug of coffee and opened the manual. She began reading, Handling the Wheelbarrow.

There was only one call, from Lord Brixton-Smith's secretary, confirming a meeting about Midnight Sky, which sounded pretty important. Maggie scribbled it all down on a bit of paper. After a while though, the computer got the better of her. She managed to open the appointments file and saw that there was an extensive diary for James. It was crammed full of dates and times, contact numbers and reminders. Maggie carefully entered the information, but instead of hitting the save key she must have done something wrong because the whole lot collapsed into a line, and disappeared. If a puff of smoke had come out of the back, she wouldn't have been surprised. She played around with it for a while, until the screen went black and every tiny light faded away.

Blast the stupid thing. Even a simple stable job had a highly technical side these days. Why couldn't everything just be written in a book? Even the new pumps in the petrol station conspired to make anyone over the age of thirty-five look completely stupid. This morning she'd discovered that instead of simply sticking the nozzle where the petrol went, there was now a complicated keypad to negotiate before any fuel was issued. Maggie thought it must have broken, until a young, bored voice had come over the tannoy. 'Pump six, the lady with the blue Toyota? Could you press reset and enter the fuel code type?'

Maggie read section four, Handling Horses. It was all plain common sense really. There was nothing about handling computers, petrol pumps, or husbands and daughters. At four o'clock, Maggie was grateful to be carrying buckets of water again and stuffing hay nets. Ben and James came back from doing something manly in the fields, Ben sporting a purple bruise on his shin.

'He's learnt which end bites, and which end kicks,' James said.

'I didn't even feel it,' Ben said.

At the end of the day, Maggie had turned out all the ponies, and she was walking back across the fields swinging the halters over her shoulder and feeling mellow when she saw Laura's car. Liz came out of the office and helped her with some wallpaper books and swatches of curtain material. There was only James around by then, and he was sort of sweeping up and hosing down, but mostly watching Laura pull things off the back seat of her car because she was wearing a short skirt. She looked all summery, with bare, tanned arms and legs, and she'd swept her hair up into a messy tumble.

As she neared the yard, Maggie slowed down and watched as her sister walked across to James, stepping round the piles of horse droppings in her heels. They were in deep conversation in no time, and Maggie wondered what on earth they talked about. Laura wasn't really interested in horses, and she couldn't imagine James being interested in Laura's soft furnishings, at least not the material kind, and anyway it was Liz who was decorating her lounge.

Her sister was telling him something funny and using a lot of hand gestures and eye contact. Laura obviously didn't mind him being all dirty and sweaty in the vicinity of her linen jacket because she frequently put her hand on his arm when she wanted to make a point.

'You look gorgeous,' Maggie shouted across. 'Is that outfit new?'

'No, no, I wore it last year. Don't you remember?' Laura said, then looked at her watch and said something about the traffic around Chester.

'Oh yes,' Maggie said. 'I'd forgotten you had a *hot* date

with Christy's brother.'

Laura frowned. 'It's nothing of the sort,' she said suddenly all hoity-toity with her, but managed a beautiful smile for Mr Morgan-Jones, before getting into her car. James went back to sweeping up, but Maggie noticed he was going over the bits he'd already done until eventually he stopped altogether and leant on the brush and stared at the floor.

*

The following weekend was an absolute scorcher. Everyone was saying it was summer come early and to make the most of it. Maggie was in an especially good mood for a number of reasons. Pete had been on to his old council buddies to make enquiries about Bed-and-Breakfast regulations. It would take careful handling not to interfere or cajole him in any way. She wanted it to be his project, his baby. Laura had planted a seed, now all Maggie had to do was water it.

Liz had asked Maggie how she was getting on. 'Are the girls driving you mad?' she said. 'Some of the things they talk about turn your stomach... and the language!'

'Don't worry I've heard it all before.'

'Good, we'd like you to stay on in that case.'

In direct contrast to her high spirits, Jess was in a foul mood because Saturday was her last day on the yard. They travelled in together, an hour earlier because they were having an extra long break over lunch rather than work in the midday heat.

'You've got a face like a wet weekend,' Maggie said, parking up.

'Don't start on me.'

'Why can't we just have a nice day working together, and a nice little send-off party in the pub after? No drama, no swearing, no getting drunk?'

She pushed her face up to Maggie's and pointed to her temple. 'Kill. Me. Now.'

Jess slid out of the Toyota and slammed the door. She was wearing a pink bikini top with an MP3 player lodged in her cleavage, black jodhpurs, a white shirt slung round her waist, a bottle of water in one hand, mobile poised in the other. Maggie gritted her teeth. One day, that was all. Laura had spent two days going back and forth to Chester with her, sorting out somewhere to live, so that was encouraging, but Maggie felt distinctly unnerved by her. She didn't dare read the riot act, not yet anyway.

The first part of the day was glorious because it involved an early ride down on the beach with Rhian and four clients. Ben drove the horsebox and got paid for sunbathing while Maggie got paid for riding the new Irish horse. 'Is Jess your daughter?' Ben said on the way back.

'Yes. I know that's hard to believe.'

'Is she seeing anyone?'

'Don't ask me, I don't get to know anything.'

At lunchtime, everyone threw themselves down in the field except James who was chopping logs and sawing wood. Jess removed her shirt and hitched up her tiny bikini top.

'I think it must be sexual frustration, all that log chopping.'

'He might need them all for his fires,' Ben said with a big smile.

Jess looked at him with a curled lip. 'It's nearly eighty degrees you *knob*.'

James did eventually join them, and Liz brought out some beers, but everyone felt too hot to be sociable and mostly just lay there and watched the bone-white gulls circling high in the sky. Jess said, 'There's this woman at college, right. She's had her Mary pierced with a diamond so she can, like, have a twenty-four-carat orgasm when she's riding her bike.'

Maggie sat up far too quickly. She lay back down slowly

because she felt incredibly dizzy, but no one else seemed bothered by the conversation. James was lying on his back with one arm over his eyes, a slight smile playing on his lips, and Liz was engrossed in reading the paper, a pair of ready readers perched on her nose.

'Have you got one?' Ben said, and Maggie almost stopped breathing.

'Nah, I've got a car,' Jess replied. She and Lucy glanced at each other and collapsed with laughter, rolling around on the grass, shrieking and falling out of their bikini tops.

'I told you. Don't say anything unless you've got a really smart answer,' James said to Ben, then turned onto his front to answer a text. Seconds later, he got up and wandered down the field.

Laura met him halfway, with a sheet of paper or a letter in her hands and James put an arm across her shoulders as he read it. After a few minutes, they both sat across a fallen tree, and he lit a cigarette for her. Maggie felt a bit put out that she'd not come to her first with whatever problem she had. Even Liz looked over the top of her paper with an enquiring look. Jess watched with slit eyes, like a cat hunting prey.

Ben said, 'Is that Laura over there? She's well fit she is, proper classy.'

'That's my auntie,' Jess said. 'She wouldn't look at you.'

'No, but I look at her. She lives next door,' Ben said, trying his best to engage Jess in a conversation. 'So, are all the birds round here after the boss?'

'No. Lucy and Rhian aren't interested,' she said, and inclined her head closer to his. 'That's because one of them has no taste, and the other one's a lesbo,' she said. 'See if you can work out which is which.'

Ben nodded sagely. He looked bewitched by her.

As the afternoon wore on and the temperature rose, Jess managed to argue with everyone until Maggie was cringing every time she opened her mouth.

'Mum!' she yelled, 'Don't lift that sack. You'll give yourself a bloody prolapse.'

'Well, come and help me!'

'We're supposed to leave them for Jamie. He can lift them easy,' Lucy said.

'No, Jamie's better *in* the sack,' Jess said.

'How would you know that?' Ben said, coming to Maggie's aid. 'Hey, there's carrots in this one,' he said to Jess, 'we could count out... twenty-four.'

'Good idea, then you can share them all with Mr Ed.'

At the end of the day when they were clearing up and turning out the horses, Maggie could hear Lucy laying into Jess. 'Why did you tell Ben I'm a lesbian?'

'I didn't!' she laughed. 'Oh, here he comes now, the village idiot. Actually, he's got a look of someone famous in that green t-shirt.'

'Yeah?' Ben said. He ran through dozens of celebrities, until he finally made Jess come up with a name.

'Shrek,' she said, and flicked a catapult of dung in his direction.

'I love Shrek,' Lucy said. 'Just because you like them old and miserable. Except, what a surprise, Jamie wants someone closer to his own age.'

'Like Auntie Laura?' Ben said, and Jess's face darkened.

'*Piss off* will you?'

That was it. Maggie had had enough. They'd all suffered nine hours of her acid tongue. She was about to erupt when Jess turned on her heel and walked straight into James. Although he had no idea what the bickering was about, he grabbed hold of her and lifted her easily over his shoulder in a fireman's lift.

'Stop mouthing off,' he said, then grinned at Ben and walked towards the water trough. 'You need cooling down.'

'Hey, boss,' Ben said. 'Is this a health and safety demonstration? Handling something hot?'

Everyone laughed except Jess. When James suspended her over the water, she was like a rag doll, no fight in her, and no wise cracks.

'Jamie, *please*. Just put me down,' Jess said, her voice and her face starting to wobble. He dropped her gently to her feet and she darted into the tack room.

'What's going on?' James said, but Ben, Lucy, and Rhian just stared back like the three wise monkeys. Maggie shoved the yard brush at Ben and went after Jess, to find her in floods of tears. So this was it; breakpoint had finally arrived.

'What is it, what's the matter?' Maggie said, knowing full well what the matter was.

'I thought I'd like, hate working here,' Jess managed to say, a soggy tissue pressed against her eyes. 'But it's a right laugh. I don't want to leave now.'

'Don't be silly! You've got a brilliant new future starting tomorrow,' Maggie said, and passed her a fresh tissue. 'New job on Monday, new people to meet.'

'I'm not going,' she said sullenly. 'I've changed my mind.'

'Well, at least come to the pub,' Maggie said, testing her new tactic. Calm acceptance.

*

Jess came to the pub. She even accepted a large glass of wine from James, but her beautiful eyes were so sad when she looked at him, and Maggie felt a stab of helplessness. What was a parent supposed to do now? Let her give up everything for a man who would never make a move on her? But Pete was right; losing her temper was counter-productive with Jess.

When her husband walked in the pub, Maggie didn't recognise him. From a distance, Pete looked ten years younger, mostly because he'd lost so much weight, but there was a spring in his step as well. '*Corr*, is that your dad?' Maggie said, nudging Jess.

'No. I tell everyone I was adopted.'

Despite this bombshell, Pete bought Jess another glass of wine, then brought one over for Maggie and kissed her on the cheek.

He was wearing *aftershave*.

'What have you done?' she said, immediately thinking about the cheesecake in the fridge.

'I've done something to get my bloody life back,' he said, slapping the newspaper and some council paperwork on the table. Maggie was a tiny bit nervous, but quite a bit thrilled by his sudden takeover.

'We've got the go ahead on the guest house.'

'Oh… so we're doing it?'

'I think we're down to Hobson's love. We'll have to get our heads down and talk, and I need to get decorating,' he said, giving her a reassuring nod and a smile. 'After Jess has gone.'

Maggie told him about Jess, but he said it was just last-minute nerves. Happy to go along with that, she chinked her glass against his. 'To Hobson's House.'

When Laura arrived, Maggie tried to catch her attention to share the news, but James got there first. He found Laura a stool at the bar and bought her a gin and tonic. She still looked upset, and he listened attentively to what she had to say. Then, she slid an arm around his waist and inclined her head to his shoulder with a defeated little sigh, and he kissed her hair and squeezed her hand, with his fingers threaded through hers. The whole thing took less than a minute, but it was terribly endearing. If she were a film director, Maggie would have shouted, 'Cut, it's a wrap!' or whatever they did when it was a perfect scene. Instead, she glanced across to her daughter's face and felt the shadow of fear.

After a few minutes, Laura left James talking at the bar

and looked around for her sister.

'Are you all right?' Maggie said, as she made her way over, but Laura obviously didn't want to share her news with anyone other than James, so they toasted the guest house *again,* and then it was all about Jess's cold feet.

'Do you want me to talk to her?' Laura said, but Maggie looked across at Jess bouncing around in her bikini top and cut in quickly, 'No, no leave her, she's drunk now.'

James brought more drinks over, so they had *another* toast to the guest house, and Laura brightened up, even chatted about what they could do with the rooms. Maggie felt a bit excited; it meant she could decorate and entertain without Pete tapping on a calculator.

Jess sauntered over with a sassy smile.

'Can I buy you a drink?' she said, looking around the table. James and Laura had their backs to her, so Pete said, 'I'll have a pint if you're buying love, so will James.'

'What about me and Laura?' Maggie said.

'What *about* you and *Laura?*' Jess said, and flounced off in the direction of the bar.

'Well, that's charming,' Maggie said.

Jess returned with the beer, slopping some of it on the way, then stood swaying behind James and Laura.

'You know what you said to me this afternoon about me needing to cool down in the horse trough?' she said to James.

'What about it?'

Maggie stood up seconds before it happened. 'Jess, NO!'

Too late, she tipped both full pints of best bitter over James and Laura.

It was like one of those daft Saturday morning kid's programmes where someone gets dunked in water or covered in goo, except Maggie couldn't shout 'Cut!' James did manage to avert some of the beer intended for Laura, but a good deal of it went shooting across to the next table instead and soaked a woman in a pale blue dress.

'Oh *shit, sorry,* sorry,' James said, dripping with beer and trying to tip it off the table before it soaked Maggie's lap as well.

Pete said, 'What a waste of bloody good ale.'

Laura sat like a statue with her eyes closed while it slowly dripped down her hair and soaked through her silk shirt. Someone from the bar brought them a handful of towels and a mop bucket.

'Where's Jess?' Maggie said crossly. 'She can clear this up!'

'I think she's throwing up outside,' Ben said. 'She's proper feisty.'

'Takes after her mother,' Pete said.

'Impossible,' Maggie snarled. 'She's adopted.'

CHAPTER FIFTEEN

Laura

'She's gone too far now,' Maggie said, passing a towel to Laura so that she could twist her hair up into it, while she slopped the mop vigorously round the floor, 'Showed me up all day she has, and now this!'

Laura wrung out the bottom of her shirt and looked around for Jess. She found her sitting outside on the car park wall with Lucy. When Laura approached, Lucy made a well-timed exit and Laura took her place.

'Has mum sent you?' Jess said, white and shivering.

'No. What was all that about?'

'*Everything*,' she said dramatically, 'This stupid place and all the stupid people in it.'

Carla pulled in and saw Jess sat on the wall in her bikini top and Laura with a pub towel round her head. 'Oh... is it fancy dress?' she said, a bit crestfallen, and took a closer look at Jess. 'Is this over a man? Is this about who I think it is?'

'What's it got to do with you?' Jess said, barely able to look at her.

'He's not worth it, sweetheart, none of them are,' she said, lighting a cigarette. 'I'll be honest with you, he was only five and a half out of ten in bed.'

'You think it's fucking funny, don't you?' Jess said and suddenly made a lunge for Carla's hair. There was an undignified grapple for a few seconds before Laura managed to intervene, only for Jess to collapse sobbing over the wall, knocking Laura's arms away like a whirling dervish.

Somehow, Laura persuaded Jess to come back inside the pub, but that was a mistake.

Liz arrived with a leaving present and a card but stopped in her tracks when she saw all the mops and towels. 'Has there been a flood?'

'Tears or beer?' Maggie said, then spotted Jess and Laura. 'Oh, there you are! You've got apologies to make and dry cleaning to pay for.'

James was wringing out his shirt into the mop bucket, not too concerned about putting it back on again. 'Don't bother about me, I haven't got anything worth dry-cleaning.'

'Have all these waterworks got something to do with you?' Liz asked him.

'Oh yeah, I remember now, it started with me minding my own business.'

'Shut the fuck up all of you!' Jess said, and the whole pub turned to look and tut. She looked at James with a downturned mouth and glittery eyes. 'I thought you'd not slept with Carla! She said you were five and half out of ten.'

There was a long suspension of shocked silence. Someone even had the consideration to turn the music down. Everyone in the pub slowly dragged their eyes from Jess to James. He dragged his eyes from Jess to Carla. 'What the hell did you say that for?'

'What's the half for?' the landlord shouted, and there was a huge well of laughter as various suggestions were put forward.

'Hang on a minute,' Maggie said. 'Why are you all discussing your love life with my daughter? No wonder she's *sex mad* and all mixed up.'

'Maggie, sit down,' Pete said, tugging at her sleeve. 'You're making a show.'

'It's Mr Morgan-Jones making the show! He's got three on the go.'

A beat of silence. 'He must be way more than five and a half then,' Ben said cheerfully.

'Oh, for Chrissakes, I've had enough of this!' James said and made for the door, shoving upturned chairs out of his way. The whole pub tittered with speculation, some of them even clapped as if it was a little cameo play.

Laura went in to the ladies' toilets and leant her head against the mirror. She slowly unwound the towel and let her sticky hair loose. By the time she dared to re-emerge, the bar was full of noisy chatter again, and she slipped out unnoticed.

At the cottage, Laura threw her shirt into some cold water and stood under a hot shower for as long as she could stand it. Feeling marginally better bundled in a towel, she called James and tried to apologise for Maggie.

'We'll laugh about it next week,' she said.

'I remember Carla saying the same thing about that fucking boat, but you know it still doesn't make me smile.'

'Come over, bring the Cognac,'

'No, sorry, I'm in a really bad mood.'

Laura rung off, disappointed. She flicked through the television channels, then idly flicked through all the messages on her phone, stopping at the one James had sent to her the morning after they'd kissed on Cefn Bach. 'What's a X between friends?' It reaffirmed the boundaries of their relationship.

She was pleased in one way because she loved what they had, and it was reassuring that he didn't want to lose it either, but when Laura couldn't sleep at night the memory of being in his arms would come back to her. For a long while afterwards they'd been careful not to be physical with each other, but the last few days they'd slipped back into touching and everyone had noticed the smallest gesture.

Christy's brother, Mike, rang just before seven and invited her for dinner at the Roebuck.

Laura looked out at the garden. It was a Saturday night, still early and a gorgeous evening, too nice to be wasted feeling fed up and alone. She'd had too many of those. Mike was a good match for Laura, but that was according to everyone else. The previous time they'd been out was a casual foursome with Christy. When Laura arrived, her chair had already been pulled out for her, the wine chosen and chilled. There was something slick and controlled about it that reminded her of Simon. At the end of the evening, when he'd paid the entire bill with a rather exclusive credit card, it made Laura think about James and his roll of cash and how unpretentious he was, and how attractive that was. And later, when Mike had kissed her goodbye in his designer clothes, James had come into her head again, and she remembered how much more real it had felt when he gave her a bear hug in his worn out shirts.

But James wasn't available, and she couldn't hide away forever. It was just dinner she didn't have to pick over everything Mike did, or thought, or represented. Laura deliberated what to wear, half-heartedly picking out some pale coffee and cream silk lingerie, with stockings, and her brown silk shift dress, the same shade as her eyes. The outfit usually made her feel a bit special, but the despondency in the pit of her stomach wouldn't lift. She left her hair loose, grabbed a jacket and went to her car.

Laura sat there for five minutes, then went back inside and cancelled. That was two dinner dates he'd made her cancel. She flicked through the television channels again. She was trying to make herself not go through her phone messages when there was a soft tap at the door.

It was James with a bottle of something.

She contemplated him for a moment, took in his dark eyes and his shower-damp, messed up hair. 'Are you still a grump?' she heard herself say.

'Pretty much,' he said, and followed her through to the kitchen. She could feel his eyes on her back. 'You're all dressed up, are you going out?'

'No, I always wear Ralph Lauren around the house,' she said with a smile, and passed him a glass. He took it from her but placed it down again, and took hold of both her hands. 'Laura, you look...'

'I know... *overdressed?*'

She'd meant it as a joke, but something in his face made her stomach feel as though she'd suddenly been turned inside out, and her smile slowly dissolved. She grasped his hands tighter and even said his name, but it only came out as a strangled whisper.

'I don't want to talk to you,' he said quietly. He closed his eyes seconds before she did and touched his mouth to hers. Laura couldn't help but respond. It was impossible not to, impossible not to want to feel his hands over the delicate silk of the dress, firm and insistent over her back, his fingertips glancing the top of her stockings.

When he stopped, the truth of how much she wanted him was laid bare, and Laura knew that the fragile boundaries were blown apart forever.

'If you don't want to do this,' he said, 'now would be a good time to say.'

Unable to say anything, thankfully not needing to, Laura led him up the stairs. He removed her silk dress, and she unbuttoned his clothes in a dream, watching his face as he laid her across the bed. She moved back into his arms, and then the same kiss, but horizontal this time with every inch of her touching every inch of him, and the heady rush of skin on skin. She was excruciatingly aware of every kiss and caress, sometimes gentle, sometimes more insistent; at times, almost crushing her pelvis and her spine into the contours of his body with such strength that she almost cried out. The duvet came off the bed, and the bedside lamp fell with a soft thud onto the floor. Some of the underwear came off.

She loved the slightly out-of-control way he initiated their lovemaking. He left her in no doubt, left her with no choice, but she didn't care about that. All she wanted was for him to be buried deep inside her body in the same way he'd taken over her mind, and when he finally moved into her, it was almost too fast and frantic, the climax a breathless free fall. Afterwards, she felt as if she'd been on a roller coaster, unsure if she was still maybe upside down.

'Sorry,' he whispered into her neck.

'What the *hell* for?'

'Oh… bit mad.'

'I *love* bit mad.'

A long time must have passed in a hazy suspension of sleep, because the room was dark, but she was still wrapped up in his arms, and slowly, he began to kiss along her breast bone, her throat, her slightly upturned mouth. She pushed her fingers through his hair, surprised how soft it was, liking the untidy way it settled just beyond the nape of his neck.

He began to shift the softness of her body onto the hardness of his. Much gentler this second time, but as sweetly intense. Laura wouldn't let him move for a long while, not wanting his body to leave hers. She wanted the heavy feeling of his limbs, the musky smell and taste of his skin and his hair to be with her forever.

James slept heavily as always, breathed so slowly. Eventually, Laura shivered and had to drag the duvet back up off the floor. She pulled his arm around herself and studied his hand. Like the rest of him, it was strong and capable. She could see where his wrist had been broken it was slightly misaligned. Was it possible to love someone's arms and hands as much as she loved his? She turned his wedding ring round and round until it came off with a small tug. Inside, the inscription said, hyd angay gwneud ni rhan.

Till death do us part.

She pushed the ring back on to his finger, and she placed his hand back on to her breast where it lay like a golden promise, only it had been made to someone else.

*

Laura's mobile woke her. It was Maggie. 'Are you still speaking to me?'

'Course I am, don't be silly,' she said, and tried to sit up without disturbing James but he was lost in sleep, sprawled across the middle of her bed, one arm thrown out across her pillow and the other across his face.

'Have I woken you?' Maggie said briskly. 'I don't suppose Jess is there, is she?'

When Laura thought about some of the things he'd said to her when they were making love, the memory of it started as a fizzy feeling in the pit of her stomach, travelled slowly down her legs and ended somewhere in her toes. He said funny little things as well, like how tiny her bones were. He was like no one else she'd ever been with, but then she'd known all of this. She'd known well before she'd even arrived at Mefysen that there was something happening, something she'd been trying to deny for a long time.

Maggie's impatient voice, 'Laura are you still there, or am I talking to myself?'

'Sorry... what?'

'I'll see you on the yard, I'm working,' she said impatiently, 'I'll talk to you later.'

Laura made a huge effort to get out of bed, switched the shower on to warm up, and padded downstairs to make coffee. By the time she'd returned, James had pinched the shower and was covered in a mass of foam.

She grinned. 'Hey! That better hadn't be my goat's milk

soap.'

James wiped a porthole in the condensation on the door. '*What?*'

He obviously couldn't hear her chattering away, so chose instead to pull her in with him. She shrieked at first, almost slipping as he dragged her sodden wrap off and flung it down. Laura tried to say something but quickly gave up; it was easier to kiss his wet face and hold on to his brown body. It was easier to let him cover her with suds on the pretext of being washed, his hands pushing all over her breasts and down over her buttocks. Losing ground with the mechanics of the space and Laura's giggly hysteria, James carried her out of the shower, and she fell onto the bed her hair plastered down. 'I'm soaking wet,' she gasped.

'Good, that's good.'

She locked her eyes onto his and within seconds, what had started as funny became deadly serious and erotic. Gorgeously slow and seriously sensual, and what had started in the middle of the bed, ended very close to the edge. Laura was vaguely aware of a phone ringing under the mass of bedding, towels and clothes, which slid to the floor with them. She dashed the hair out of her eyes and untangled a mobile from her bra. She handed it to James.

It was Liz, and she shouted so loudly that Laura could hear the conversation.

'*At last,* where the *hell* are you?' she bellowed. 'Have these damn dogs been fed? They've dragged the bin over. Ragged it to *bits.*'

'Have they?'

'What's the matter, are you ill?'

'Huh? No, I don't think so,' he said, yawning and rubbing his face.

Liz said, 'Well you sound spaced out to me... are you smoking cannabis again?'

'Why don't you shout that a bit louder?' he said, a tad

incredulously, then searched Laura's eyes. 'I'm with Laura. We sat up late, drinking and talking.'

'Oh, so that's it. You're hung-over? Look, just get your arse into gear. I'm meant to be on a plane tonight. Remember that concept called a holiday?'

'Right...' he said and slung the phone back across the bed.

Sobered by the idea that the big sisters were on the warpath, Laura crawled back under the duvet, and James yawned a lot while he hunted for his clothes. When she heard the front door close, Laura went to look through the bathroom window and watched him wander back across the field, his shirt on inside out, and in no particular hurry. He even stopped to light a cigarette.

When she looked around at the bedroom and the shower, it looked like she'd had a wild party. But when Laura went to strip the sheets off the bed, she changed her mind. If she couldn't have him next to her, she could keep the scent of him a bit longer. Laura tried to marshal her thoughts and feelings into some kind of order, but basically her head was mush.

Yes, shell-shocked just about covered it.

*

Maggie unwrapped a huge sandwich, 'I'm really sorry about last night. It must have been all the heat and the alcohol, and I've apologised to James... *again*,' she went on, and rolled her eyes with a smirk. 'He even said I've got great kids and to stop apologising for them. He must be in a hell of a good mood.'

Lunchtime, and it felt like she'd dreamt the previous twelve hours.

'Well then, no harm done,' Laura said, trying to keep her

eyes focused on the chipped mug of tea Maggie had made in the tack room, but her eyes were constantly drawn to the scene outside. James was talking to a small child, carefully brushing grit off her hands. There was a pony cantering riderless around the perimeter of the menage, stirrups flying.

'But,' Maggie was saying, 'I don't know where Jess is, and she won't answer her phone.'

'Jess…?'

'What's the matter with you? You're on another planet.'

'I'm sorry, Maggie,' Laura said, looking back at the cold tea. 'I had a letter from the solicitors yesterday. Simon's declared himself bankrupt and moved to Spain.'

Maggie stopped chewing. 'Oh… I see, so what does that mean?'

It meant she wouldn't get anything. It meant Dragon Designs had been consumed by its own greediness. The next line of enquiry had been the apartment, but she imagined that would sink into the same black hole.

James had said fuck them all, it's only money, even offered to lend her some. Well, quite a lot really, enough to start again. Although she didn't want that, didn't want to be in debt to someone, especially not to a man she had feelings for.

Outside, he'd caught the pony, and was hunkered down in front of the child, still talking.

'Did you do anything last night?' Maggie said.

'No nothing,' she snapped, '*nothing*.'

'All right I'm only asking! No need to bite my bloody head off.'

Maggie stomped back to work, and Laura thought about the mountain of fabric in the cottage waiting to be turned into sixteen pairs of curtains, all with coordinated pelmets and pull ties. It was a mammoth task, but she had to get her head around it, especially in view of the latest financial development.

As she was walking back across the yard, James caught up with her and steered her into the house. 'If I don't eat and drink something I'm going to fall down,' he said.

She watched him cook a mound of sausages, both dogs salivating at his heels. 'James, I don't want anything to eat.'

'Why not? Are you pissed off with me already?'

'I'm just not hungry.'

Someone knocked on the door, and he went down the hall, sandwich in hand, and then it was obvious who the visitors were from all the sentimental greetings. Another occasion where she needed the ground to open up, but Laura was trapped. She couldn't just run out or climb through the kitchen window. She waited to be introduced to Cary's parents, Tom and Stella.

'This is Laura, she's the tenant at the cottage,' James said.

They were polite and enquired how she'd settled in. Laura felt distinctly uncomfortable, certain her sexual exploits with their son-in-law must be etched into her face for them both to read because it was all she could think about, but they weren't really interested in her. Tom barely spoke and had the same dejection in his eyes as James did. Stella was a lot more brisk. 'How many sausages have you got on that sandwich, love?' she said, smiling benevolently and patting his arm. 'I think that shirt's inside out.'

Laura made her excuses and managed to escape. She felt like a spare part, and anyway, she was only the tenant. They probably imagined she was paying her rent.

*

Following ten hours of sleep, Laura's first thought was to make a start on the curtains, but as the day wore on, she recalled the conversation with her sister and took a break from machining hems and cutting out tie backs.

Maggie answered the phone the second it rang, thinking it was Jess.

'Still no word?' Laura said, knowing exactly how she felt.

James hadn't called, although to be fair, she hadn't called him either. She'd seen him from a distance. Just that morning, when Laura was sitting outside on the old bench in front of the cottage, she'd glimpsed him riding Midnight Sky. He cantered around the menage twice, before facing the mare at a coloured pole, but Sky had stopped dead in her tracks. The next time she swerved dramatically around the edge, almost pitching James over her shoulder. They went back to cantering circles and then turned towards the five-bar paddock gate. Laura had jumped to her feet and almost spilt her coffee. What the hell was he doing?

They were going too fast to stop, but Midnight Sky leapt the natural barrier as if it were nothing. They clattered across the yard, and casually skimmed another five-bar gate into the field. At this point, James was struggling to hold the horse, and Laura found herself standing on the bench, shielding her eyes from the sun. She watched them fly over a small hawthorn hedge and plunge into a thunderous gallop. The sound of pounding hooves on the dry ground was like a mantra thudding through Laura's chest. They reached the end of the field in seconds, and Laura thought they must surely stop and turn, but they skewered over the crooked dry stone wall and joined the track onto the open mountain. For a while, she chartered their progress as they flashed in and out of the trees, a black tail streaming out behind.

And then there was nothing, no sight or sound.

*

'No sight or sound of her!' Maggie said. 'I don't like to call the salon, checking to see if she's there. I'm already Mother Witch, swooping about on her magic mop.'

Maggie laughed, but there was no mirth in it, she was too worried, and Laura knew what was coming next. 'Do you want to go down there?'

'Could we?' she said, 'Just to have a, you know, a *discreet* look?'

Laura had a feeling it wouldn't be quite like that, but she did feel compelled to put her sister's mind at rest, and in the cold light of day, felt some responsibility for the situation.

They travelled in separate cars because Laura was meeting the girls for a drink, and Maggie could only spare a couple of hours because they were buying new hens and having a dummy run preparing for guests. Pete was cooking her dinner… a full breakfast with organic eggs. He was on a roll apparently, buying up gallons of Victorian White paint and sanding down the bedroom floorboards. Laura hoped it would work out for them and linked her sister's arm optimistically as they walked through Chester city centre, ignoring the pull to go and look at her old office. That was backwards, and she needed to go forwards like Pete and Maggie, and hopefully like Jess.

When they found In the Pink, Maggie was immediately intimidated by the sophisticated exterior but pressed her nose against the black window and had a good squint inside. Laura pulled her away. 'Maggie, that's not discreet, it's one-way glass. They can see you from inside.'

'Well, you go in,' she said, giving her a little push. 'You don't look out of place.'

Laura pushed open the heavy glass door, and inquired about Jessica Thomas. The icy blonde on reception picked up the phone. 'I'll have to check she's not with a client.'

Minutes after Jess appeared, dazzling in a white tunic and white kitten heels. Her dark hair was pulled back into a sleek ponytail, make-up natural and professional.

'What are you doing here? Has something happened?' she said.

'No, no, we were worried, that's all. After... the pub.'

There was an eye roll, a sigh of contempt. 'I'm sorry about Saturday night.'

'All forgotten,' Laura said, 'but you need to remember your mum.'

When they both looked over to the window, they could see Maggie leaning against the glass in her jogging pants and Pete's old fleece.

'*Oh. My. God,*' Jess said and looked away, but there was something catching in her throat and her eyes. 'Please don't let her come in here.'

'Why not come out for a minute and talk to her?'

They stepped outside, but in the end neither of them could speak because they were both too over-emotional. Jess had the best way of dealing with it when she threw her arms around her mother. After a few moments of standing on the busy pavement, Maggie looked at her daughter levelly. 'You can go now,' she said, wiping her eyes. 'I've got to get back for the egg man. He's bringing us a new cock.'

'The word is cock*erel*.' Jess looked at her with renewed disgust and went back inside.

'Did you see her?' Maggie said, blowing her nose on a sheet of kitchen roll. 'I can't believe that was Jess, all grown up. She's just *beautiful*.'

'I know,' Laura said. 'You're so lucky.'

*

A while later, Trisha told Laura she'd had a lucky escape from Simon and Alice. Pam told her quite firmly that broken hearts were off the agenda as conversation fodder. They were all in Pam's house, slightly mystified as to the location choice, the two bottles of champagne on the coffee table and her slightly giddy mood. 'Right, I've something to announce.'

She waited till she had their attention. 'Steve and I got married!' she shouted, flashing a diamond ring. Laura offered the usual congratulations and admired the jewellery.

'Oh, Pam, when?' Christy said, slightly put out at missing the wedding.

'Bloody John o' Groats over the weekend, can you believe it?'

'No,' Trisha said. 'What brought that on? The menopause?'

'Steve's mid-life crisis?' Pam said, struggling with the champagne cork. 'I don't really know! Look we're having a party July the second at The Roebuck will you all come? Laura, you can bring action man.'

'Love to,' Laura said, accepting a glass of bubbly.

Trisha was confused. 'I thought you were seeing Christy's brother, Mike?'

'No, no, I'm not,' Laura said, checking her phone for the umpteenth time. She looked at Christy apologetically. 'Nice man but no spark.'

'Don't apologise!' she said. 'We can't choose who we fall in love with.'

Pam brought Trisha and Christy up to speed on Laura's landlord, and for a while she put up with their daft banter, but Laura was ready to tell them what they wanted to know. She needed to tell someone how she felt, almost wanted to shout it at them. It had been on the tip of her tongue to tell her sister, but knowing Maggie, she'd go round there and land him one in front of Tom and Stella, and then it would all get in a mess again with Maggie's job on the line.

'So, is he married or not?' Pam said. 'Only you seemed unsure last time.'

'Widower. Only I'm walking in the shadow of perfection. She might be dead, but she's more powerful than any mortal woman,' Laura said. 'I feel like I'm having an affair. He still wears her ring. So go on, tell me I'm running into a dead end.'

'You're running into a dead end,' Trisha said.

Christy rummaged in her bag for Russell Grant's Love Guide. 'Birth date?'

The day of the miscarriage... Laura shot Christy a quick smile and swallowed over her dry throat. 'February nineteenth.'

'So... you've slept with him, and now you don't know where you stand, is that right?' Pam said, topping up their drinks, 'Laura, that's the oldest relationship dilemma in the world.'

'Well, I don't know what her problem is,' Trisha said, popping nuts into her mouth. 'You can get Mike, right, to buy you an expensive dinner, and then the sexy landlord just pops over the field.'

'Oh my *God,* he's on the cusp,' Christy said suddenly, 'with a moon in Pisces. Very deep.'

'I'd just totally ignore him,' Trisha said, 'until he's taken that bloody wedding ring off.'

'And *then* rein him in,' Pam said. 'You know how to play it.'

But Laura had had enough games with Simon and Alice.

*

He called her a couple of days later. Laura was filling the kettle and looking idly through the kitchen window. Two days was a long time to ignore someone, but James wouldn't see it like that, he didn't have much comprehension of time, so she was probably wasting her time being cool.

When her phone rang and she saw it was *James calling*, she made herself count to fifteen. On the point of snatching it up, the ring tone stopped, and she had to call him back. He answered straight away. 'I thought you were ignoring me,' he said. 'Look, I'm sorry I've been preoccupied. Had to deal with the in-laws. I told them about the horse sale.'

'How did they take it?'

'Painfully. I felt a bit out of kilter for a while, that's all. I'm not playing games.'

'I… I've missed you,' she said, and grimaced at the ceiling. She really was pathetic at this.

'Can I pick you up later?'

'What in? I'm not getting in that dirty old Land Rover.'

*

It was almost dusk, and the summer sky was illuminated with a deep strawberry light when James turned up in a dirty old car. He told her it was a 1967 MG Roadster.

Laura climbed into the passenger seat. 'It won't break down, will it?'

James silently drew her attention to a dirty toolbox in the footwell, and started the engine. It sounded noisy, and there was one of those intermittent rattles.

'What was with the James Bond stuff the other day? I saw you on Midnight Sky.'

'Just thought I'd see what she could do before I have to give her back.'

'Why wouldn't she jump the little poles?'

'Well, I reckon she doesn't like anything small or artificial, prefers big and natural.'

'You mean she only respects the real thing?'

He shot her a quick smile. 'Yeah, something like that.'

The car got as far as Gwydir Forest, then ground to a halt. There was nothing but dense fir trees for miles, and there was no signal on her phone. 'It's getting dark,' Laura said.

'Uh-huh.' He didn't seem too concerned, pulled the toolbox out and yanked the bonnet up. He angled a torch inside for ages, then it was a dirty rag and an oil can.

'Well?' she said, impatient when he didn't reply, '*James?*'

'No good, you'll have to give it a push,' he said and dropped the bonnet down. 'Try down the hill. When I give the word you can jump back in.'

'Ha-ha very funny.'

'It's got a bit damp, in the distributor,' he said, showing her an engine part. 'You haven't got a hair drier, have you?'

'No, nor have I got a pair of tights.'

'What do we need tights for?' he said and placed the defective part on the dash. 'Needs to dry out. Come on, let's go for a walk.'

'That's man speak for outdoor sex,' she said, and folded her arms, but she struggled to keep her face straight.

'Well, I never knew that,' he said sagely. 'Have to be careful whom I say it to.'

James took her hand, and they walked down a stone path through the trees. Almost instantly, Laura began to lose her scepticism because it was actually romantic - *he* was romantic. The gentle wind was heavy with the perfume of pine, and he stopped to kiss her against a tree trunk. It was probably a combination of the old car, the unsophisticated nature of their surroundings and the almost reverent way he held her, all transpired to make Laura feel incredibly young. It was like a first date, falling in love for the first time, the anticipation of making love for the first time. She followed him, her hand still in his.

'Can we have outdoor sex anyway?' she said, stumbling over the tree roots.

James turned and smiled at her, but he didn't say anything for a while. When they came to a clearing, he laid her down on a bed of bare dry grass and spent bluebells and pinned her hands to the ground, a willing prisoner. Laura couldn't move an inch, but she knew he could read beyond her eyes. It was unsettling because she couldn't hide anything, but in an odd way, it gave her a sense of security.

'You're not the demure city type you profess to be, are you?' he said.

'I'm not sure who I am,' Laura said. 'I don't recognise myself when I'm with you.'

'I know *exactly* who you are. You're my Midnight Sky.'

*

The car did get them home, but it had no heater, and one of the windows remained jammed down. Back at Mefysen, James lit a fire because Laura was frozen, but it didn't spoil her mood. They'd made love outdoors, made last orders at a virtually derelict pub full of grumpy old farmers, and James had pulled a long bramble out of her hair.

Laura was happy to watch old episodes of Friends, James less so. He read her Gynaecological Guide for about two hours, then fell asleep. When Laura went to take the book out of his hands, he was already on chapter five, and it was incredibly heavy-going text. She folded the page over and knelt on the floor.

'James, it's really late, I'm going to bed.'

'Leave me, I'm all right,' he said, and there was the tiniest sting in his voice.

Laura left him and went to bed, but it felt odd, as if they'd had a row.

In the morning, the sofa was empty.

CHAPTER SIXTEEN

Laura

In June, a letter arrived from her father. Well, Maggie received it and passed it on to Laura because her father didn't have her new address. The writing was old and spidery. He'd printed his address very clearly and explained how much he wanted to see her. There was no love expressed in it, but James said it didn't mean he didn't feel any. He read it twice, understood her reticence to a point, but also pointed out that her father was offering an olive branch and she should do something about it.

'He's swallowed his pride to write that,' James said, handing it back to her.

Laura knew he was right, but six years was a long time and it would take courage to go over there and face him. James read her face as well. 'I'll go with you if you like, when you're ready.'

'Would you?' she said, touched.

Her father would wholeheartedly approve of James because he was a self-made man of the soil with strong principles and ideals. Although James wasn't her partner in the true sense of the word, and she couldn't help wondering if that would be seen as a failure, as well.

Laura wasn't sure what kind of relationship had evolved with James. Was it friendship sprinkled with sex or was she a convenient leaning post for James to indulge in when he felt the need? Physically, Laura could take as much as she wanted, but his mind was like the morning tide. They had an amazing rapport when it was overlapping the breakwater, but at other times it could be far away with a different sun shining on it, and she couldn't reach him.

'Tell me why you get these downers,' Laura said, 'I want to understand it.'

'It's what long-term depression does.'

'Still…?'

'Still, I know what you're saying, but it's been a feature of my brain pattern for two and a half years,' he said, then shot her a mischievous look. 'It's not you, *it's me.*'

No, it's not you, it's *Carys,* Laura thought, but tried not to let it bother her. Trisha would say the dead wife was a bit of a convenient trump card. Pam would say play him at his own game, and Christy would say just give him the space, poor love he's still grieving, two and a half years was *nothing, and* he was born on a cusp. None of them were any help because she concluded they were all right, depending on her mood.

They were in the pub toying with the remains of lunch. They'd been there a long time, having first enjoyed a lazy morning in bed. He'd taken a lot of persuading; it was the longest uninterrupted length of time he'd ever spent with her.

'I'm surprised no one's been on the phone with some argument or problem,' James said and was about to drain his second pint when his phone started ringing. He put the glass down, and they both exchanged a quick smile. His expression quickly changed to one of concern.

'Rhian? Slow down… start again…' he said, flicking his eyes onto Laura. '*Shit.* I'll be there in two minutes.'

'What? What is it… James?'

'Spoke too fucking soon,' he said, grabbing his jacket. 'Midnight's jumped out, cleared everything in her path, including your sister.'

'Maggie…?' Laura said, fumbling to find her bag, her sweater.

James threw some money across the bar and motioned Laura to follow him. They roared back up to the yard in the Land Rover, not speaking, not sure what to expect. As soon as they arrived, Laura could see Maggie sat on the ground, and Ben was trying to lift her, unsuccessfully.

Rhian came trotting across, talking ten to the dozen and very close to tears. Laura had never seen her so upset or animated. 'I don't know how it happened, she just took off!'

'All right, tack up O'Malley,' James said, his face tight.

They both went to Maggie. She looked completely white, but pretended she was all right. 'She just sailed over my head, like Pegasus!' she said, looking from James to Laura. 'You go after her, don't bother about me, I just need a cup of tea with plenty of sugar in it.'

'Maggie don't be ridiculous,' Laura said. 'Look at you. Can you even stand up?'

'It's this ankle, went over a bit funny on it, that's all.'

'Right,' James said. 'We either call an ambulance or Ben and me carry you to the car.'

'I don't need to go to hospital!' she said, but James was already telling Ben how they were going to lift her to minimise the impact on her leg.

'You mean like, half each?' Ben said, 'You can have the end that bites!'

In the middle of the strange procession across the yard, with Laura following behind carrying Maggie's bag and coat, promising faithfully to call Pete and remind him about the delivery of poaching pans and chicken wire; Lucy came charging out of the office.

'Jamie… phone!'

'I haven't got time for that,' he said, carefully lifting Maggie's leg into the foot-well.

'It's that Lord whatshisname,' she said, looking sick. 'Says he's on his way? Says he made arrangements a couple of weeks ago to see Midnight.'

'Well, tell him he fucking well *can't come here*,' James said, throwing his car keys at Ben. 'You drive then you can lift Maggie out the other end.'

Lucy shouted, 'I can't tell 'im he fuckin' *can't come here*, can I? He's like, proper posh.'

'He's not made any arrangements with me,' James said, strapping Maggie into the passenger seat. Maggie made a wailing noise. 'Oh God, this is all my fault,' she said.

'It's not your fault,' Laura said. 'It's not her fault, is it, James?'

'I should have been here.'

'No,' Maggie said miserably. 'I mean, I remember now. It was the day I crashed the computer. I wrote it on a bit of paper, but I was cross with the petrol pumps and everything.'

'I reckon she's proper banged her head,' Ben said, mildly alarmed.

Maggie flapped her hand. 'I'm just useless.'

The vehicle pulled away, Ben making heavy work of the gears and Maggie holding the dashboard with gritted teeth. Rhian was waiting astride Cariad and holding O'Malley.

'What are you doing? You need to stay here,' James said to her.

'No way... I'm helping.'

James shot Laura a perplexed expression. 'I can't really leave Lucy on her own.'

'I'll wait here with Lucy,' she said.

'Right. Thanks.'

He didn't smile, but she didn't really expect him to. He grabbed a spare halter and some binoculars then took O'Malley from a po-faced Rhian. The horse jostled about as he tightened the girth, indignant at all the rough handling and rushing about. They both clattered down the lane at a brisk canter, and Laura and Lucy looked at each other.

'Will you speak to Lord thingy?' Lucy said, texting Jess with the latest news. 'I don't understand his accent, is he, like, foreign?'

Laura called Lord Brixton-Smith and amazed herself with the complicated concoction of excuses of why he couldn't see his multi-million pound steeplechaser, just when he felt like it. She had to save her sister's skin as well, so it took some working out. The man might have royal connections but he was quite rude and intimidating, even had the nerve to tell Laura she didn't know what she was talking about. 'Look, I know a fob off when I hear one. I'm also a very busy man.'

'So is Mr Morgan-Jones, he's trying to juggle a lot of difficult projects at the moment and...'

'Just tell him to call me direct please,' he said abruptly, and left Laura looking at a dead receiver for several seconds.

Lucy said, 'How good a liar are you?'

'He didn't buy it.'

'I thought it sounded well good.'

Laura tried to take that as a compliment.

*

Around teatime, Rhian and Ben both returned, both empty-handed, in time for evening stables, and Laura headed over to Hafod House. Maggie was in the sitting room with a plastered-up ankle propped up on a dining chair.

'Oh Maggie, I thought you'd just sprained it,' she said, sinking onto the sofa.

'Broken in two places,' she said, annoyed. 'I'll have to hand my notice in, can't expect him to wait for this to heal up.' She looked at Laura's miserable face. 'Never mind, we'll have enough on our plate here, should see the size of Pete's breakfasts! So... has he got her back?'

Laura shook her head. James was still out there somewhere.

'I hope she isn't injured,' Maggie said. 'After all that work he's done with her... and I can't take a simple message, just forgot all about it. I feel *awful*.'

'It's not all your fault,' Laura said, getting to her feet. She folded her arms. 'He was with me, all night and all morning. James was with me.'

Maggie looked at her, almost said something but changed her mind.

'Well, are you not going to say anything?' Laura said. 'Go on, tell me I've developed inappropriate feelings or something.'

Pete barged the door open with a large tea tray. 'Well, this is a right to-do,' he said, giving the crutches a wide berth, 'I'll be telling that Morgan-Jones what I think of this bloody fiasco.'

They both jumped down his throat.

*

At Mefysen, Laura poured herself a glass of wine and in-between looking out of the window every five minutes and checking her phone, felt restless. All the drama was happening somewhere else. If Carys were here, she'd be out there with him; maybe she was. Carys still had the controlling share. His house was like a shrine. They'd never made love there, and it wasn't a coincidence. He was immune to Laura when she was on her territory. James took respect to a new level, admirable in one way, defeatist in another.

When she was stuck on the yard with Lucy, Laura had wandered around the rooms, picking up the dusty photographs. She'd stood at the bedroom door for long minutes and surveyed the messy wardrobe spilling its guts.

Was it a shrine, or was it just that he couldn't be bothered to deal with it? When she'd first spent time in his house it had all seemed rather poignant and romantic. Now, it had taken on a totally different meaning for her.

Laura checked her phone again, looked through the window, daylight was fading, and a lone blackbird was calling in the hawthorn. She flipped over the pages of her sketchbook, and it was full of drawings of Midnight Sky.

You're my Midnight Sky.

She'd never been compared to a horse before, but at least she was a thoroughbred. Laura wondered if the early images were directly symbolic. He had a technique where he drew the horse in then turned his back. If she followed that train of thought to its conclusion, it was his fault she'd run away.

But then her emotional seesaw would play the guilt card. When the call came, she was on the point of driving back over to the yard, convinced something horrible had happened, and when Laura saw that it was Jess ringing her, she almost ignored it.

'Just heard from Luce.'

'*And...?* Has he got her?' Laura said, getting out of her car and leaning against the door.

'Yeah, course he has,' Jess said, as if it was a forgone conclusion.

'Where was she?'

'Fucking miles away. Hanging out with the wild ponies on Foel Fras.'

'And... she's okay?'

'Well, yeah... Jamie said she just trotted back to him. Are you, like, *crying?*'

*

On Monday morning, Laura was packing the completed

curtains into her car when James appeared with the dogs. 'I can't believe you've finished all that,' he said, looking at all the pleated, crimped and piped material, all pressed and wrapped in polythene.

'Well, I did. Just got to go and hang it all now.'

'I couldn't do your job.'

'Horses for courses. I couldn't do yours either,' she said, closing the boot of her car. 'Glad you got the horse back, by the way. *Jess* told me.'

It came out with slightly more venom than Laura intended, but it was all boiling around in her head and her guts, and it wasn't just the Midnight Sky incident, it was all of it. It was the dead end coming up to smack her in the face. She was having a Trisha day. 'Excuse me.'

He moved out of her way, followed her into the cottage, closed the door with his foot, and hung his arms over her shoulders so she couldn't escape. 'Is it something I've done?'

'No.'

'Is it something I've said?'

'No.'

'Is it something I've *not* done... not said?'

He was difficult to blank, Laura sighed, 'I hate it when you blank me.'

'I know, and I know I'm not easy,' he said, 'but I am trying.'

She wriggled out of his grasp and folded her arms. 'Yes, *very!*'

He grinned at her. 'Lucy told me what you said to Lord B.'

'What of it? I was trying to save your skin.'

He continued to grin at her. 'You did. Anyway, I've told him he can come and get his racehorse, her Welsh mountain-orienteering training is now complete. She's even got a badge for compass work.'

'You're laughing at me.'

He agreed he was, kissed her down-turned mouth and lifted her onto the edge of the table. When he began to unbutton her top Laura put her hand over his. 'If you're thinking, what I think you're thinking, we can't.'

'Why not?'

'Because... it's only meant to hold two candlesticks and four place settings.'

'I love it when you talk dirty.'

'You can't just walk in here and demand sex on my table.'

'*My* table. Anyway, it's some kind of ancient landlords' visiting rights.'

Laura almost smiled, but pushed him away. 'I'm *busy*. I've got a job to do.'

She could feel his eyes on her as she found her handbag, then went to the mirror in the hall.

'Are you fed up with my criteria already?' he said from the sitting room.

She paused, lipstick in hand. 'What do you mean?'

'You know, all we do is eat, talk and have sex.'

'What's wrong with that?' she said to the mirror.

'Not much from my point of view, but I thought you were a bit of a social butterfly before you got lumbered with me.'

Laura carefully outlined her lips. 'I can live without it mostly,' she said, surprised how true that was, but she still told him about Pam's invitation. It was time to improve the criteria. It was something of a leap from what they had, in that it was something of a public declaration, but Laura had Carys to live with, and she wanted to see how uncomfortable he was prepared to be for her. She went into the sitting room for her jacket. 'It's Friday night, that's July second.'

'All right,' James said, and shrugged.

'Not her birthday or an anniversary or anything?'

He looked up at her broodingly.

Midnight Sky

*

After several tedious hours of hanging curtains, Laura's mood had worked through a Pam outlook to a more Christy point of view. What had she been thinking? It had been a truly disgusting thing to say, she could cut her tongue out. All that smooth sarcasm - where had that come from? By the time she'd driven back and turned in to the yard, she'd executed a complete U-turn in her head.

He was in the kitchen. There was no chance of making up though because Liz, Rhian and Ben were in there as well. Rhian was trying to get a splinter out of James' hand and he was wincing and complaining. She yanked his hand closer to the light by the kitchen window.

'Hold still,' Rhian said. 'Stop being such a baby.'

When he caught sight of her, James said, 'Laura! You've got to be better with needles than she is. I'll never play the violin again.'

'That's not a needle, it's a hat pin,' she said taking a closer look.

Liz and Ben both laughed. Laura found a needle in her bag and Rhian passed his hand over, glad to be relieved of medical duties. There was an awkward moment when Laura had to ask Liz about her holiday, and talk about why Maggie had her ankle in plaster, all while she was holding his hand on the draining board.

'It was my fault. I kept James talking in the pub,' Laura said, meeting his eyes.

Liz scoffed, but with good humour. 'Another one! Maggie says it was *all her fault*, Rhian says it was *all her fault*, James says it was *all his fault*.'

'It wasn't my fault,' Ben said.

'Well, I don't care anymore,' Liz said, pulling her boots back on. 'I'm just glad the bloody horse will be off the premises before the end of the week. It always was a liability.'

They waited till Ben and Liz had gone out of earshot.

'Go on, you can stab me with it if you want to,' James said, indicating the needle.

'Why would I want to do that?' she whispered to his hand. 'I love you.'

*

Hafod House smelt of paint. Pete said he was too busy to chat; he needed to get a second coat of paint on the ceilings, do a weekly shop, collect Ellie from school and make dinner.

'If it's a cooked breakfast again, I'm going to scream,' Maggie said, then poked one of her crutches in the direction of the garden. 'And that bloody new... *bird* keeps us awake half the night.'

'Stop moaning. Pete's a changed man,' Laura said, making space on the table for some tea.

Maggie agreed. 'He's got his mojo back all right.'

'Mojo? Something you're not telling me, Maggie Thomas?'

'It's only because I can no longer run away,' she said, but her sister had a different sort of smile, the slightly self-conscious one she reserved for anything of a mildly sexual nature. 'Actually, I have a renewed respect for permanently disabled people.'

'Like... Annalise?'

'James came to see me,' Maggie said, steadily pouring the tea. 'Brought me a case of wine and my final wages. Oh, and all those yellow roses over there. *And,* he said not to worry about Ellie, he'll carry on teaching her.'

'That was nice of him.'

'Well, he's a very nice man, my ex-boss,' Maggie said, dunking her biscuit.

Laura snapped her eyes onto her sister's. 'You've changed

your tune!'

'Yes well, seen a whole different side to him with Jess out of the way, taking centre stage all the time,' she said. 'Jess has a got a new man by the way, and I think he's only thirty-something, how about that?'

Laura got up and wandered across to the vase of yellow roses and inhaled their perfume.

'Something you want to tell me?' Maggie said.

'We're going to Pam's party on Friday. Am I rushing him? Be honest.'

'Life's too short, that's what I think,' Maggie said, with unaccustomed gravity. 'When I think about Pete, Annalise, Carys... *Mum*.'

Laura continued to stare at the flowers.

'It's only a bloody party,' Maggie said.

*

Friday, 2nd July rolled in with dark skies, and a steady drizzle soaked the heavy summer foliage and churned the ground to mud, but it had a pay off, in that the soft rain released the damp perfume of high summer, and the air was filled with a heady mixture of honeysuckle, roses, and wet grass. Laura walked down the lane with her Burberry umbrella and leant against the tack room wall. There was a smart trailer, and a Rolls Royce in the yard.

Laura didn't announce her presence. It wasn't her moment, and anyway, she was happy to be an observer. She wanted to let the day unfold of its own volition. In a way, she felt she'd already done and said too much. Other than being incredibly thoughtful, James hadn't really reacted yet. He was thoughtful in every sense of the word, careful around her feelings, and doing a lot of thinking.

Presently, Rhian led out Midnight Sky for Lord Brixton-

Smith. Almost instantly, Laura changed her opinion of the man. His eyes filled when he saw his horse, and his hand went to his mouth while he rubbed his chin a lot. Midnight Sky looked like a winner already, a study in controlled, collected energy. Lord B became very animated, and used a lot of hand gestures, but James had his arms folded and looked mostly at the floor, occasionally nodding in agreement. When he gave the sign, the mare was loaded quietly into the trailer, and Lord B pumped his hand for a long time, not letting go until he'd repeated the whole performance again.

When the entourage slowly pulled away, James finally looked across to Laura and gave her one of his serious smiles, a blend of sad satisfaction. But Liz broke the moment of eye contact when she came out of the office and shouted across, 'Why has he made the cheque out to *you*?'

'I did all the work?'

'Oh, so I pocket what I take for pony camp now, is that the new rule?' she said, starting to walk after him. 'James?'

'You know what, I don't give a fuck what you do. I'm sick and tired for all the flack I get for my so-called sidelines,' he said and strode across to the tack room.

Liz saw Laura shaking out her umbrella. 'I hear you're taking him to a social gathering.'

'Yes...'

'Well, make sure he buys all the drinks. He's *seriously* loaded,' she said.

*

Arrangements had been made for the social gathering. Laura had a taxi booked, but James called her very late in the afternoon, to say he'd have to meet her there.

'I'm still at the equine wholesalers,' he said. 'Other side of Chester.'

Midnight Sky

'What are you doing there? Buying something to wear for tonight?'

'Could do. I'm having a muzzle made for Cutie Pie. I'll bring it, shall I?'

'I can think of a few people it would suit,' she said, then chewed her lip. 'James, it's not terribly formal, but...'

'When I'm done here,' he said patiently, 'I'm going in to Chester to buy a shirt and some shoes.'

'Nothing in-between?'

The phone call made Laura feel a whole lot better, lifted her mood considerably. She poured herself a drink as she ran a bath. This time, it was the little black dress with the built in plunge bra and to hell with it. Everyone had twigged they were *almost* a public item. She'd nudged it along a bit that was all.

The Roebuck was fun to start with, until everyone began to ask where James was. Then Laura began to ask where James was. By the time he was a couple of hours late, she went out on to the terrace and tried calling his mobile. Nothing. Pam didn't really notice or she was being unusually diplomatic. Christy kept coming up with a list of excuses, starting with the obvious ones, like accidents or break downs, the suggestions becoming less likely the more inebriated she became.

'Perhaps his sister's been taken ill?' she said, holding on to Laura's arm.

Trisha shot her a withering look. 'Or maybe his hamster's a bit off colour?'

'Has he got a hamster, Laura?'

'She's been stood up!' Trisha said and went to the bar.

By the time he was getting on for four hours late, Laura had to face the humiliating fact that, as usual, Trisha was right. She ran out to her taxi in the rain, gave the address to the driver, and forty minutes later she stood shivering outside his front door. Almost instantly, she wished she'd gone back to the cottage, either let him come grovelling, or not at all… but she wasn't that brave.

The door wasn't locked - it was never locked. She stepped inside, and Lambchop scampered down the stairs to her. Laura scooped her up, not caring about all the white hairs on her black satin dress. She glanced in at the cold empty sitting room, before making her way upstairs. The bedroom door creaked open, and she saw James was sat on the edge of the bed, but he didn't even look up, just stayed staring at the floor.

'No crisis then, no dead animals or accidents?' she said evenly.

When he glanced up at her, Laura's first, irrelevant thought was how gut-wrenchingly handsome he looked. He'd got as far as dark trousers and a dark blue shirt. It was even ironed with no tramlines, and she could detect a slight trace of musky aftershave.

'Just the dead part,' he said, and although it irritated her, his choice of words and the way he said them, sent a chill down her spine.

'So,' she said, 'you've gone to all this effort, just to sit here in a vat of self-pity?'

'You're way off the mark,' he said, his voice still low. 'If it was just self-pity I could do something about it.'

'Do something about it anyway!' she shouted, her heart thudding painfully. The dog leapt from her arms and crawled under the bed. She tried to keep a hold on her emotions, but they'd had all evening to ferment, and she'd had years of backing down with Simon, making excuses and validating everything he did.

'You could start by getting rid of all *this!*' Laura said, snatching open the wardrobe doors, hating what she was doing but the compulsion to get it all out was far stronger. 'You're suffocating yourself with all this *stuff!*' she said, running her hand through the lifeless dresses and jackets.

Several hangers fell down with a clatter. She turned back to face him. 'Keeping all her clothes, wearing her ring. Till death do us part means exactly that! She's *dead!*'

'Don't you think I know that?' he said, and the brooding anger in him took her right back almost to the first time they'd met, as if all the feelings in-between had been wiped out or never existed. 'I was the one who held her in my arms just hours before and then had to carry her down off the moor as a fucking corpse. Have you any idea what that... what it does to you? *Have you?*'

Laura could barely look at him. She had to swallow several times before she could form any words. 'No, course not.'

She perched next to him, wanting to touch him, but he seemed closed off. 'James... I'm the one who's here with you. I'm the flesh and blood. You could be everything to me. I want to be everything to you.'

'I know.'

'Don't you want to feel something *more*, don't you want to feel something *else* other than this... this black nothing Carys drags you into?'

'I do. I'm deeply in love with you.'

He met her eyes, finally. She savoured the words for a moment, then faltered. 'I don't understand...'

She watched him get to his feet, light a cigarette and lean against the dressing table. 'I'm not sure I understand this train of thought, and I know you won't like it...'

'I don't much like this, so try me.'

'When we've been together,' he said slowly, so she could absorb every word, 'when we've been together, afterwards... it feels adulterous.'

'Adulterous? *Why?*'

'I don't know, the strength of feeling, maybe.'

'Do you think about her when we make love?' Laura said, but looked away, not wanting to see his reaction. They were reduced to hurting each other, and there was a horrible familiar ring to it. It was that feeling of being second best.

It had started with Maggie and her father, and then all her relationships had suffered due to a third party somewhere along the way. Maybe Freud was right, the father-daughter relationship had something to do with the men she fell in love with. None of them could fully commit to her, and subconsciously she was locked in, to expecting the same over and over again.

She had to be strong and break the mould before it broke her.

'I thought I could cope with this,' she said, 'but I can't.'

'What are you saying?' James said, his anger gone.

'I'm saying I don't want this... this *weird* relationship any more.'

His answer was to simply close his eyes and take a long drag on his cigarette. So that was that. She'd fallen, and he hadn't caught her. Laura went quickly down the stairs and out through the door, slamming it so hard that it bounced open again.

Outside, it was raining so violently that her dress was soaked through in seconds, but Laura barely noticed, because the bottom had dropped out of her world. When she came to the field gate, she balked at all the mud but climbed over anyway, her evening shoes sinking into the sodden ground.

Ironically, Cariad followed her across the field, snorting and shaking her wet mane.

CHAPTER SEVENTEEN

Laura

At Mefysen, trembling uncontrollably from the cold, the shock of his words, and the finality of hers, Laura realised with a stab of horror she'd left her bag and her keys on his bed. Scratching all her arms and legs, cursing her stupidity, she shoved past the flowering currant bush and the rickety bit of fence down the side of the cottage and climbed in through the slightly open kitchen window.

Once inside, Laura dragged her things off and stood under the shower for as long and as hot as she could stand it. She didn't cry until she saw his packet of razors on her glass shelf, and then she spotted his sweatshirt flung across her Queen Anne chair in the bedroom, the usual pile of loose change, screws and dog biscuits where he'd emptied his pockets. She cried till she was sick, then lay on the bed and stared at the ceiling. Dawn took forever to arrive because it continued to pour with rain, and the sky was impossibly gloomy. She could hear his horses and bleating sheep. No birds.

Everything felt sore, and she wasn't too sure which pain was physical and which was emotional. Eventually, Laura forced her befuddled mind to pack a case. An hour later, she drove to her sister's house.

Maggie answered the door with a towel around her

shoulders, snips of wet hair all over it. She was still limping on crutches but agile enough to swing herself back into the kitchen.

'Have you seen the pub?' she said jauntily. 'Someone's stolen the L out of public house!'

'No, didn't notice.'

'Place is going to the dogs,' she said and hitched herself onto a bar-stool. She introduced Chris, Nathan's *partner,* who was cutting Maggie's hair. He was a hair stylist and played rugby, a combination which confused Pete but gave everyone else endless opportunity for poking fun at his old-fashioned views. On the plus side, Maggie said it had helped to thaw out the situation.

When the three men went to the pub, Maggie said, 'Okay, Laura Brown, out with it. Those Cardin shades look fab on you, but it's as grey as my knickers out there.'

Laura dragged them off, and when her sister saw her swollen red eyes, Maggie poured out the remains of the Christmas sherry and listened patiently while Laura went word by word over the previous evening.

'I think you should let him think about what you've said,' her sister said. 'It's very... all or nothing, now or never. Take it or leave it, black or white.'

'Yes! Exactly,' she said vehemently, 'I'm fed up of all that grey in the middle.'

'He said he loved you, *deeply*. That's not grey.'

'Simon used to say he loved me as well.' Laura sighed and drained her glass. 'I'm going away for a few days, I'm going to see Dad. Have you got the directions?'

'Oh!' Maggie said, 'Well, I didn't see that coming.'

Laura watched her rifle through the miscellaneous kitchen drawer for a moment. 'I need to forgive him over Mum. He did the opposite to James, and I hated him for it, but I can't anymore, *don't* anymore.'

Maggie passed a tattered hotel brochure to her with a

little frown. 'We always stay there. Dad lives just round the corner.'

'Right, I'll give them a ring, book the ferry.'

'What, now?' Maggie said, looking at the kitchen clock. Laura you're exhausted! It's a long drive when you get off the boat the other end you know, and look at the gales! Stay tonight at least.'

*

Laura took one of the new guest rooms, and she did sleep, but her vivid dream sequences were punctuated with snatches of conversation and imagery she'd rather forget. When Laura woke late on Sunday and his body wasn't next to hers, the cruel realisation of why it wasn't next to hers, kickstarted the agony all over again.

Pete got Ellie ready for her riding session.

'Don't say anything, *please,* Pete.'

'I know when to mind my own business,' he said.

But less than an hour later, Pete and Ellie returned to say that James hadn't been there, and Liz was trying to phone round everyone and cancel bookings. She'd taken Ellie for a ride with some other children, but it was so wet and windy that they'd given it up as a bad job. 'It's meant to be bloody June!' Pete said, peeling his waterproof off in the hall, then he looked up at Laura as he untied his boots. 'The ferry won't run in this, love.'

Bored with moping and gaining some courage from the knowledge that James wasn't there, Laura steeled herself to drive over to the yard to get her handbag and keys. It was more like March, with a strong crosswind flattening all the shrubs and rippling the grass. Ben, Lucy, and Carla were muffled up in winter jackets, and gave her a tentative wave from across the paddock. Rhian was feeding the dogs in the kitchen, head down. 'He's not here.'

'I know… I'm just getting my bag.'

Laura glanced in the sitting room and stopped in her tracks. There was an axe through the coffee table. It looked as if he'd swept the entire contents of the wall cabinets onto the floor so that all the books, trophies and photographs lay in a dusty pile, and one of the glass doors had a massive crack in it. Undecided as to what it all meant and slightly unnerved by the destruction, Laura went tentatively up the stairs.

The bedroom was messier than she'd ever seen it, with most of his clothes slung over the unmade bed in untidy piles. The wardrobe doors were wide open, and all the contents had gone, hangers everywhere, as if it had all been grabbed down in anger, a forgotten scarf on the floor, but the journal, the wedding album, and the ring box, were all on the windowsill in a neat pile. She felt slightly heartened by that, as if there was at least some coherent thought there, despite the empty whisky bottle.

With her bag clasped under her arm, Laura retreated to her car, her head down against the wind and rain. Liz saw her and walked briskly across, 'Laura! Have you seen the house?' she shouted, 'Have you seen what he's done? I expect I'll have to clear that up before I can go home.'

'Do you know where's he's gone?'

'No! Smashed everything up in a tantrum and took off,' she said.

Laura looked at the ground. 'We had a horrible row.'

'Guessed that,' she said, and her face softened slightly. 'I'm so sorry, Laura. He's a *bloody* fool. James had another chance with you, and he's blown it.'

*

The following morning, Laura drove across the Menai Straits and onto Anglesey. Puffin Island and the pretty scenery was obliterated by rain and sea mist, but there was no wind, and the water was calm. The ferry was running again, and there was a tiny satisfaction in getting away from the scene of the crime.

However, her sense of freedom was short-lived. No matter how far she went physically, he was still in her head. And as time passed, the pattern of remorse repeated itself. If he'd done something terribly wrong, she could hate him for it, and if Laura really wanted to beat herself up, she was in effect punishing him for respecting truth, honesty and loyalty, and that was pretty repulsive because they were the very qualities she craved.

Laura watched the outline of the Wicklow hills and mountains grow closer until they docked at Dublin. Once through the town, she was out in deep countryside, and it was not a comfortable landscape. It was savage and bleak with peat bogs the colour of dark chocolate, but at least it suited her mood. On the borders of Wicklow, Laura stopped the car and switched off the engine. All she could hear was the wind over the rough grass and the thin trickle of water threading through the valleys, and she willed the peace of it to enter her mind. Now that the time had come it was suddenly a daunting prospect facing her father without the one person who made sense of it all with his simple love and logic, her very best friend.

*

The hotel was easy to find. It was more a large house like Hafod, but not as nicely decorated. Laura showered and dozed in her room and then wandered down to the bar. She hadn't bothered with make-up, only just about managed to drag a brush through her hair. In the bar, she ordered a tall glass of orange juice and found a small table on the veranda overlooking the sweep of garden. It was early evening, and there was still a blush of sun on the grass and the gentle sounds of water running through a fountain. She checked the map Pete had drawn for her and traced the route to her father's house. It was a mere two miles south down an unmarked lane, where the village gave way to the limestone plains and the road to Kildare, horse country.

When her phone bleeped with a text, Laura imagined it would be Maggie checking up on her for the umpteenth time.

MARRY ME.

Her first thought was that it was a joke or a wrong number. She was about to check the sender, but someone called her name, and when she turned around he was there, right in front of her. There followed a strange suspension of time, when all logical thought vanished, and she just kept on looking, trying to work out what was real and what was possibly imagined. Laura was vaguely aware of her chair crashing over backwards and breaking the spell. Within seconds, she was in his arms and holding on to him, and he was holding on to her. He felt one-hundred-per-cent real, her very best friend, her very best lover.

She could have stood there forever, but there were too many questions in her head. 'One question...' Laura said, pulling away slightly so she could look at him. 'How did you know I was coming here?'

'Maggie... I told her I'd break her other foot if she didn't tell what was going on. I told you I'd come with you to see your father,' he said, '...actually I've been here since yesterday.'

'Yesterday... but it was too rough!' she said. 'Please tell me you didn't?'

'Did you *see* the shipping forecast? I did wonder if your

sister had sent me over here on a storm force fifteen just for the hell of it,' he said, then when she almost smiled, added, 'I flew over.'

'Oh… I need a proper drink.'

And she needed a minute to recover. Laura righted the chair at the little wrought-iron table and watched him at the bar. He kept looking back at her, as if she might disappear in an Irish mist. He returned with two glasses and a bottle of Cabernet Sauvignon. There was a band of white skin where his ring used to be. Laura still couldn't think of what to say, so inhaled the familiar aroma and took a tiny sip.

After a while he said. 'I think I was scared.'

Laura placed her glass down. 'Of?'

'Something bad happening to you. I was scared of the whole thing happening again, and I'm still scared I'll eventually drive you insane, trying to keep you in cotton wool.'

She held his hand across the table. 'I like the idea of that.'

'Really?' He frowned at her. 'I'm sorry, I put you through hell, put myself through it as well, but I had to be sure,' he said quietly.

'I yelled at you… all those horrible things.'

'I needed someone to yell at me.'

Laura moistened her lips. 'I saw what you did, to the house.'

He closed his eyes briefly, as if he were back in the darkness. 'I'm selling up, everything.'

'*Why?*'

'I *need* to get away from there, start again,' he said. 'I couldn't ask you to be with me and live there. It would be like living in someone's shadow.'

'You'd do all that for me?'

'No, but I'd do it for us.'

'But where… where would we go?'

'Anywhere! We can do the sorts of jobs we do anywhere.'

'No, we can't,' she said. 'You need big country and I need cities.'

He turned a cigarette end over end. 'So you're going to let that stop us, are you?'

Laura took another sip of wine, not able to think beyond the enormity of his words. She realised then how far he'd come with her, but more importantly it was about how far they could go together.

James was saying something about going to America and his son getting engaged.

'So… he wants the rings. He seems to think Welsh gold would reflect his roots, but I suspect he's just short of cash,' he said with a lopsided smile, and looked at her for some sort of reaction. 'Laura, you've not said anything for a while. I want you to text me yes or no.'

'You want me to *text* you?'

'Yeah, I want it in writing. I know what you city types are like.'

Laura delved into her bag and found her mobile. His phone trilled with her response, but he drained his glass first.

'Okay, is it two or three letters?'

'It might be a tick, or a cross.'

He looked at his phone nervously.

Then he looked at her with his serious smile.

THE END

Jan lives in Snowdonia, North Wales, UK.

This ancient, romantic landscape is a perfect setting for Jan's fiction, or just day-dreaming in the heather. Jan writes contemporary stories about people, with a good smattering of humour and drama, dogs and horses.

For more about Jan Ruth and her books:
visit www.janruth.com

WILD WATER

BY
JAN RUTH

Jack Redman, estate agent to the Cheshire set.
An unlikely hero, or someone to break all the rules?

Wild Water is the story of forty-something estate agent, Jack, who is stressed out not only by work, bills and the approach of Christmas but by the feeling that he and his wife Patsy are growing apart. His misgivings prove founded when he discovers Patsy is having an affair, and is pregnant.

At the same time as his marriage begins to collapse around him, he becomes reacquainted with his childhood sweetheart, Anna, whom he left for Patsy twenty-five years before. His feelings towards Anna reawaken, but will life and family conflicts conspire to keep them apart again?

WHITE HORIZON

BY
JAN RUTH

*Three couples in crisis,
multiple friendships under pressure.*

On-off-on lovers Daniel and Tina return to their childhood town near Snowdonia. After twenty-five years together, they marry in typically chaotic fashion, witnessed by old friends, Victoria and Linda who become entangled in the drama, their own lives changing beyond recognition.

However, as all their marriages begin to splinter, and damaged Victoria begins an affair with Daniel, the secret illness that Tina has been hiding emerges. Victoria's crazed and violent ex-husband attempts to kill Daniel and nearly succeeds, in a fire that devastates the community. On the eve of their first wedding anniversary, Tina returns to face her husband - but is it to say goodbye forever, or to stay?

Made in the USA
Charleston, SC
25 October 2013